Candy finds herself at the heart of a massive plot involving the entire Empire as she is taken into the strange and perverse undersea realm of the Warlord's of Water. As her owner's personal toy, she experiences new pleasures and savage delights, embracing her submission and letting it grow to new and undeniable levels.

Meanwhile, on a secret mission for her master, Lady Uzume finds herself a new plaything in the form of a nubile young girl whom she eagerly introduces to the sadistic delights of the Kami.

Exquisite bondage, sublime discipline, and intense passion rule the sequel to Dragon Candy as more of the strange world of Pangaea is unveiled and new secrets test the loyalty of those enslaved to it.

Dragon Candy Trained
Copyright © 2023 Talia Skye
ISBN: 978-1-4874-3585-1
Cover art by Martine Jardin

Published by eXtasy Books Inc

Look for us online at:
www.eXtasybooks.com

# Dragon Candy Trained Dragon Candy 2

## By

## Talia Skye

# CHAPTER ONE

Corporal Davis continued to stroll down the eerie streets of Kentucket. Although he was in no real rush, he still glared moodily at anyone who blocked his path until they shuffled aside. It was an old salvagers habit and a hard one to break, even in retirement.

The town of Kentucket was a moderately prosperous one. It sat upon a brief range of hills where many small streams meandered through the low grounds, ducking under decorative bridges and squeezing through numerous small dams. The ornate dams created a series of ponds and tiny lakes that supplemented local irrigation, served as rice paddies, or were home to shoals of captive fish.

The numerous streams connected as they fled the hills, forming into one nameless river that rolled down through the Wastelands and fed into the Nias Sea. However, this spectacular water system had nothing to do with delivering the most striking feature of the town.

Large wooden hulks towered above the shops and small homes, and in these ancient pirate junks were housed some of the more prominent businesses of Kentucket. The story of what they were and how they had come to be here was an often told one because they were probably the closest things to a tourist attraction in the Wastelands.

The crews of these vessels had been loyal to the infamous female pirate, Ching Shih and had deserted their vessels not long after the Vortex had ripped them from the seas of Earth and dumped them here. They had quickly made for the oceans, which were more familiar territory and soon afterwards, local settlers had stripped the junks of all available metal before turning them into hardened buildings. It was indicative of the Pangaean mentality. Nothing ever went to waste, and one man's derelict was another man's treasure.

The wooden shells had discarded their threatening pirate insignia and now flaunted inviting signs, bargains, offers, and other enticements to draw people up their gangplanks and drawbridges. Homes had grown on the decks and some of the larger masts bore makeshift windmills.

Sometimes Davis wondered why the existence of the Vortex continued to remain hidden from the nations of Earth. Historical losses such as the pirate ships had been concealed by the passing of countless years and in modern times, wartime casualties were easily attributed to hostile action. Nevertheless, he could not comprehend how anyone could so readily write off those that the rift was taking even today.

The area where the gateway most often opened was a paranoid one with old enmities, covert action, and constant power struggles that could offer a cover, but it still amazed Davis that no action or investigation ever seemed to happen. Still, he was here now and pining about another world was futile. He brushed the thoughts away and surveyed the odd town with fresh enthusiasm.

Davis liked Kentucket. It had a calmer air to it than the more rambunctious settlements of the inner territories. There were some generators offering token power to the more prestigious locations, but the frontier quality of the Wastelands remained and as usual was tempered by the scarcity of any metal.

Davis had been instrumental in offering this town as a destination and had largely done so in the hope of breaking the Captains melancholy attitude. If this did not work, a taste of long-lost home might and so they would follow the river down to the coastal town of Yorktah. This was one of the oldest American settlements, primarily due to the arrival of the USS Cyclops back in 1918. The five hundred- and fifty-foot-long cargo ship now sported oars, catapults, ballista, and trebuchets to guard the town from raiders. It was the only metal-hulled vessel still in operation and was the towns most prized and honoured asset. Cyclops was also unusual in that it had been dragged through from a chance activation of the Vortex near the coast of Bermuda. Most craft were sucked through off Japan, and most of these were dropped in the foreboding depths of the Kami Empire.

Everyone feared the Empire, and it caused great anxiety for Davis when his Captain occasionally looked towards the west where an impenetrable shield wall linked armoured pagodas and sported ranks of artillery to deny access to that strange and decadent land.

Candice had been taken there, and the Captains heart and enthusiasm had gone with her. Davis could entirely sympathise, because even in a land where females were as rare as metal, the woman had been exceptional. Delicate sable locks contrasted blue eyes that sparkled like ice against a midwinter sun. Unblemished pale skin that had clearly never tasted toil or abrasive desert winds contained sublime curves and a toned and alluring physique. There had been something so entrancing about her, a fragility that seemed completely at odds with her brash and rebellious nature. When she was bound, the tight embrace of rope seemed to protect as well as subdue and it had been hard for Davis to refrain from constantly staring at her when she was in this vulnerable state.

Candice had earned more money and prestige for the salvagers than the sale of all the looted material from her yacht, but the slave market that had bought her failed to profit from her purchase.

A sudden brittle crash snatched his attention and Davis

whirled to see a humanoid form fly through a window and tumble onto the street. Shards of broken glass danced upon the wooden sidewalk and the figure briefly pawed at the bare soil of the road before laying still.

Davis drew his sword and instantly broke into a sprint. He burst through the saloon doors and squinted to adjust to the gloom. The doors swung shut in his wake and reduced the amount of light even further.

Two figures drew his attention, largely because everyone else was backing away from them. The barman was hollering for them to stop while fumbling under the bar for a crossbow, but the combatants were paying little heed.

The ragged form of his commanding officer jerked free of a grapple and delivered a stern headbutt that sent his assailant reeling. A nearby table took his legs from under him and he tumbled across the surface before collapsing to the floor.

"Cap!" roared Davis and started to rush over when he saw the barman bring his crossbow to bear.

Davis darted in front of the intended target, dragged free his pistol, and took aim.

"Think again, pal," he warned and cocked the weapon to add emphasis to his warning.

Since they had struck it rich, the squad could now afford firearms. This was a distinct privilege on Pangaea because modern weapons required a lot of valuable alloys and of course, they hurled expensive nuggets of metal. Every bullet was exceptionally precious, and one could sometimes call a gunman's bluff to see if they were either unwilling to waste ammunition or hadn't been able afford to load the weapon in the first place. However, Davis was not lying and was more than willing to prove it in defence of his leader. Without breaking eye contact he sheathed his sword to illustrate his supreme confidence in the capabilities of the firearm.

The bar man stared at the weapon and then lowered the

crossbow back to the counter. He hoisted his hands in surrender and jerked a thumb towards the door.

"Get the hell outta my place and take that drunk with you!"

Only now did the captain become aware of the jeopardy he was in, but it was clear that he hardly cared. He grabbed a nearby bottle and ambled towards the door with a dismissive huff, almost falling over a broken stool as he went.

Davis followed him and kept his back to the door. His aim wove from person to person to dissuade pursuit, but people were already ignoring him and returning to their previous pursuits.

The captain staggered through the door and Davis quickly jumped through and helped hold him up as his legs started to falter beneath him.

Sometimes Davis cursed their good fortune. Finding a stray yacht was an unparalleled opportunity for retirement, but to find a female on board offered even greater riches. The metal they had looted from the boat was a great haul, but it was the sale of its nubile executive owner that had furnished the real riches. Before her auction had finished, a retrieval force from the Kami Empire had taken her, and few people were going to argue with Mitama armed with assault weapons and riding armour plated thirty-foot tall Megalosaurs.

They had assumed that the Imperial warriors had been sent to claim the stray yacht but instead it was Candice who had vanished with the cavalry. The troops had even known her name, and this mystery fuelled more speculation and interest in the beautiful woman. What the Empire wanted with her would never be known, but the Captains regret in selling her was not tempered by their wealth. Something had transpired between them and the veteran officer had been unable to forget her ever since.

"Come on, cap. Let's head south. A change of scenery will do you good."

The officer just took another swig of the bottle, glanced west, and said nothing.

# CHAPTER TWO

Candy gave a jolt and howled as an engorged cock rushed into her attention-starved pussy. Her eyes widened with delight and then focused on the emerging vault of stars that hung over this alien world.

She let her arms relax and they were instantly hoisted back by the brutal mechanism to which Warlord Hachiman had so casually served her.

Candy was currently located amidst the radiant and aromatic gardens of her owner's palace and in a small grove she had been introduced to a most diabolic fate. The device rose from a wooden stage and held her supine with her legs splayed into an acute *V*. Tight straps criss-crossed her entire form and hugged her into the dense and unforgiving struts. Her arms were drawn beneath her and her hands were captured in a fierce single sleeve. When she pulled against the fixture atop this triangular glove, a series of pulleys hauled one of two fates into her proffered loins. One possibility was a whirling dervish of rubber strands that would lock into position and whip her pussy for an agonising duration. The other was a slave girl with a very dextrous tongue and a diligent passion for cunnilingus. However, to Candy's dismay, the girl would only remain for as long as her arms could haul her face between her thighs. Unexpectedly, exhaustion and denied orgasm had become the worst aspects of her bondage rather than excruciatingly tight immobility and flogging.

Numerous times she had almost gained orgasm but her physique had quickly started to fail her. Her arms had become raw and tired, the muscles pulled from the fight to hold the girl in place. Sexual famine was a most effective encouragement and even as her body had succumbed to fatigue she had become better at enduring the anguish to keep the girl where she needed her.

All of these previous frustrations were forgotten as the dark skinned male thrust into her. The two priests had happened upon the site of her torment and decided to help themselves to the penitent flesh that was displayed before them so brazenly.

The brawny and shaven headed warrior closed his hands to her thighs and squeezed to feel her muscles flick and spasm as he dove into her. The full raging length of his manhood filled Candy and made her cry out onto the penis gag that choked her words and pinned her head back against the frame.

The encroaching night was steadily being banished as other priests wandered through the gardens. They lit braziers and torches and caused pools of warm amber light to swell amidst the shadows.

Four braziers were situated around the circular stage that was responsible for supporting her bondage apparatus and when they were lit, the pile of coals swiftly threw up curling flames and cast small clouds of embers into the sky. The chaotic dance of the fires made the shadows shift restlessly and create the momentary illusion of figures lurking in the branches of the trees. An aura of warmth welled around each brazier and quickly started to soak into Candy's bound form. In her nude state it made her feel all the more cosy and languid while she was ravished.

She watched the embers prance overhead and flexed her loins to grip at the solid length that was plunging into her. The priest gave a licentious moan when he felt her tighten and accentuate his pleasure.

The slender companion to her current lover noticed the new arrival after he had momentarily paused in his duties so he might enjoy the show. He hallooed him and brief words were exchanged as the slap of hips to her thighs offered steady applause.

"Toshiu? What are you up to?" he growled, his attention suddenly wavering from the trussed female before him. Candy gritted her jaws and bit harder to the gag while praying that he not stop.

"Nothing," came the covert reply.

The male paused and withdrew, causing Candy to fear that he had given up. Instead, he grabbed his shaft and traced his tip around her pussy. He tickled her clit with a few brief swirls, making the ring that transfixed the intimate morsel dance and bring fits of bliss. He then continued to draw it up and down the length of her sodden and ravenous sex.

"No, seriously, what is it?" he asked, and slowly sheathed himself into her again. Candy ground her teeth on the gag and shuddered as she savoured the slide of his tumescent shaft back into her depths.

"I said it's nothing!"

Her lover gave an irked sigh and his burly hands reached up and started to caress her breasts. The priest continued to thrust into her, and his fingers traced her contours before offering some whimsical pinches that only made her pleasure rise to new levels. His irritation with his friend inspired sadism, so he started to pinch and pull at her nipples with added strength. He slipped his little fingers through her rings and started to conduct some pulls and minor turns so that the metal hoops dragged against the fleshy tunnels.

Candy groaned against the gag and flexed within the confines of the numerous straps. A pull to the sleeve yielded no results and it seemed that the mechanism had been switched off for now. She could only imagine the frustration of the slave girl who would be listening to the actions of her lover as he dove into a spread-eagled submissive, mounting the very region she had been lapping at just a short time ago.

"Well, I said it was nothing, and I think that *nothing* is precisely what should be said," commented the other priest. His voice was close now, near to Candy's head.

"Ah, now I see."

Candy tried to turn around and gain a glimpse of what was being intended so she might prepare herself. The tightness of the strap and the moulded phallus parting her jaws prevented her.

"So, do you mind if I assist, Ushi?" asked Toshiu and Candy heard a subtle wooden clicking noise.

"Feel free. I'm sure she won't protest. Well, at least she won't once you've finished."

The slender and pale countenance of Toshiu appeared above her. His braided brown hair appeared black in the dull light and the many barbed decorations transfixing it glittered cautiously. A fierce grin ruled his acute features and he started to unfasten the strap that was keeping Candy silent and subdued.

Ushi slowed his rate, and his hands began to wander across the captive fields of Candy's skin. His digits traced the straps and assessed the power they held over her body before he continued to grope at will.

The gag slid from her maw and was dropped aside. Candy looked up into Toshiu's features with an imploring expression that caused him to laugh and act with sudden celerity.

He grabbed her lip and suddenly snapped a peg to it. The compression caused a sudden blast of mayhem in the tender flesh and Candy winced. A startled croak emerged, and this sound became a mewl when another peg was applied. She could now see that he was drawing them from a bag, one acquired from the priest that had since vacated the area.

Candy tried to shift her head away but the strap across her forehead greatly limited her efforts. Toshiu chuckled as her face turned into a tight grimace and her lips trembled as another peg was added. The trio were spaced along her bottom lip, and she could not get the infernal things off.

Toshiu let go and Candy tried to suck her lips in and push the implements off, but the gag had dried out her mouth and there was no saliva to help her shed the baleful decorations.

"Oh, so you want more do you?" accused Toshiu, and grabbed the central implement.

"No, please, don't," she tried to say, but the words were garbled as he drew on the peg, stretched her lip, and made her shudder.

Candy gave a long whimper when he pulled down on the vicious anchor. She immediately stopped fighting him, knowing all too well that it would only enhance her travail. However, she was sorely tempted to resist when she saw more pegs rising up toward her features.

"Still a little room here," he commented.

The cruel priest added a final peg on either side of the central one to create a solid queue of wooden pincers that left her lower lip coursing with thumping vituperative rigour.

"Don't forget her upper lip," hissed Ushi.

Candy felt his cock twitch within her. The arousal at her abuse was bringing quivers of fresh delight.

"Of course not," purred Toshiu. "Such negligence would be unworthy of this fine specimen."

Candy began to offer a corrupted plea that was completely distorted when he snatched her upper lip between his fingers and lifted it to accept its first adornment.

The distress in her lips was starting to dilute the ecstasy of being ravished. The discomfort was making it harder to focus on the pleasure and was stalling the possibility of orgasm. Ushi's diminished rate was not helping either and Candy feared whether she would be able to acquire climax if Toshiu continued to torment her.

Candy clasped her hands together within the tight apex of the leather sleeve and fought to endure Toshiu's harsh attention. Every peg he added contributed another swell of anguish that made her spasm and offer renewed mews. Ushi was clearly enjoying the reaction to each application, because he made sure that he was buried within her when it came so he might revel in the clench of her channel to his cock.

Finally, all five of the intended items were applied and Toshiu released his toys. Candy's quaking jaws made the pegs sway and skip. They clicked on one another and added to her ordeal as they flopped back and forth, hauling at the skin that they held captive.

"More, Toshiu! More!" huffed Ushi.

His delight in seeing her suffer and the feel of her reactions to it were driving him into a libidinous frenzy. His eyes were locked to Candy's face and his hands strayed all over her legs and torso. His hips swayed and he dove deep and paused to relish her woe before continuing with his lethargic ravishment.

Candy sobbed as she felt another peg snatch her earlobe. The flesh pulsated with an icy beat, and more were soon established along the length. Candy just burbled incoherently and struggled against her bonds.

This spiteful pain was hard to withstand. She had taken the cane, had taken savage chastisement from the most profligate lovers, but now she was having distinct trouble in weathering this trivial abuse.

Candy's body was drained from her fight against the predicament of her bondage. She needed rest, a time to recuperate, but more than that she needed to come. Candy had been striving for that reward for hours and it had taken her exhaustion to impossibly severe levels. If Toshiu would just stop abusing her then she could focus on ignoring the pain in her arms and the enervation of her body and dowse herself in well-earned and much needed ecstasy.

Candy scowled as more pegs were applied to the other earlobe. Closing her eyes, she threw herself into her slave mindset and grabbed the stamping angst that was ruling her lips and ears. She focused on the slow diligent thrust of Ushi's manhood into her and the pressure of the straps that hauled her into the wooden frame. She also made sure to drench herself in her times with Warlord Hachiman and dreamed that she was ruthlessly cinched not before these priests but under the implacable glower of her true owner.

Almost immediately she felt her body react and a dark and sinister pleasure swirled around her pain and started to elevate her rapture. Candy's chest rose and fell on great lustful gasps that inspired Ushi to grab her breasts and knead them with renewed callousness.

The two men misinterpreted her overt reactions as those of pain and so they marvelled at what they had conjured. Inspired by her suffering, Toshiu started to thread a length of cord through the springs of each peg. He then made sure to loop it around once and then proceeded to the next.

"Oh yes! This is going to be most pleasing!" snapped Ushi and clapped hands to her hips as he held tight and hastened his rate.

"Curb yourself," he suggested. "This will take a moment more to prepare, and you won't want to miss this."

Ushi slowed and let his hands trek across her belly and ribs. His partner continued to weave the cord around the pegs, licking his lips with anticipation as he did so.

Candy could see what was coming and was now aching for it. The eerie charm of her masochistic nature had been awoken and when this ravenous creature was at large, Candy was helpless against it.

Ushi's rhythm began to accelerate as his own pleasure rose to levels that he could no longer easily deny. The sight of her splayed and tormented was a titillation of no small effect and in readiness, she felt his hands again clap to her hips and take firm hold.

Candy's breathing hastened as his cock rushed in and out. Her face throbbed, her pussy burned, her mind was saturated with a deviant ecstasy that gathered new power when she felt Ushi's manhood starting to swell within her. He was getting harder, his rate was becoming faster, and in just a few seconds she knew that she would join him in release.

"Now, Toshiu! Now!" he roared.

His potent grip crushed her flanks and his body convulsed. His head arched back, and he filled the air with a roar of exquisite rhapsody.

The venomous henchmen hauled at the string with a steady and unwavering motion. Candy screeched as a sudden flood of sensations pounded her and her body flew to stark attention. This caused Ushi's animal bray of passion to rise higher as his cock found itself being squeezed most ferociously and while the pegs were being removed, Candy could not relax and deprive him of this delight.

The pegs on her ears were being drawn on one at a time in quick succession. They clutched desperately to their charge and the pain they inflicted leapt to a ghastly zenith before they finally slid away. The worst moment was when they pinched to a final tiny sliver of skin just before they dropped away and clicked shut. Meanwhile, her loins erupted with delight when she felt Ushi's length spasm and liquid heat washed through her channel.

The pegs fled her ears and started to haul at and then flee her lips as orgasm ruled her and the agony of removal conjured a plateau of unbridled sensation. Her body had been thrown to complete rigidity by pain and pleasure and as the last peg came away and Ushi's lust began to wane, Candy dropped against the reassuring arms of her bondage.

Her holler tapered away into brief sobs and moans. Her senses were reeling. Her mind was washing from side to side as the world seemed to turn over. Sporadic convulsions caused Ushi to gasp as his sheathed cock was subjected to rolling internal ripples that revived hints of her joy.

"Thank you, master," she managed to hoarsely whimper as tears rolled down her cheeks and dripped from her smarting ears.

The feeling of relief was beyond intense, and she was lost to a euphoric stupor that made every moment of her restraint and abuse an absolute treasure.

Lips touched hers and without pause she reciprocated. The area that Toshiu had so merrily abused was now treated to a delicate kiss and his tongue traced the perimeter of her aching maw before it curled against Candy's tongue. His hand stroked her hair and the other reached up to embrace a breast and tease a nipple.

His lips clamped harder to hers and then Ushi fled her body. Candy jerked and the mouth of her tormentor smothered her squeal. The eruption of feeling made her shudder and fight to stay calm as a secondary barrage of bliss echoed through her deserted sex. The feeling of Ushi still lurked within her, and she renewed her impassioned kiss with his partner.

"That was quite the show."

The voice was feminine and sibilant. It echoed through the small grove like fingernails down a blackboard and caused Toshiu to jump back and look around to find the source.

Candy's eyes flicked open. She panned around with her limited ability and tried to find out what was going on.

Shadows moved within the upper reaches of the trees and several figures launched out from within the cover of the

15

leaves. The sultry female figures landed almost without sound, sinking into crouches just out of Candy's sight. The long prehensile tails that had trailed from their silhouettes left Candy with no doubt that these were the half human, half Wani daughters of Toyotama-hiko, the Dragon Warlord.

"What brings you to the gardens, honoured guests," announced Ushi.

"We are just out for an evening climb," said one of the women.

"Taking in the sights . . ." said another.

"And the tastes . . ." announced a third, and Candy felt a long serpentine tongue take a libertine lap of her inner thigh. The voices of the women were so similar that she was having trouble telling them apart. It sounded as though the same being was addressing the priests from multiple sources. The effect was highly confusing and helped make this strange encounter seem even more dream-like and unreal.

" . . . of your master's hospitality."

"Well, if there is anything we can do t-" began Toshiu, but his words were cut short by a sudden and stark order.

"You can leave. We want to experience this creature."

"Well, when w-" said Toshiu, his tone being both humble but resolute in its intent to stay and finish the enjoyment of the bound slave.

"Is that disrespect that taints my ears?" hissed one of the women.

"I think so."

"It was positively insulting."

"Perhaps Warlord Hachiman should hear of this churlish behaviour," chided another.

There was a capricious spitefulness in their words, one that exposed their desire to cause mischief should their intentions be interrupted. Candy knew that the Wani were fanatic warriors and wondered if their female counterparts were just as resolute, but rather in their lust for the carnal rather than for carnage.

Toshiu paused and then spoke with meek reverence. He obviously wanted to continue to indulge himself with Candy but now that the guests of the palace were here his own wishes were subordinate to their desires. The two officers had made mention of Candy's time with the daughters, and she detected an envy there because such interaction was no small privilege. Nevertheless, they were currently enamoured with the toy of the Warlord, and it was plain that the daughters wanted Candy, and nothing to do with Ushi and Toshiu.

"My most heartfelt apologies, honoured guests. We shall leave you immediately. Enjoy this offering of our House as you will," he stated with practised obeisance.

"That still leaves the matter of the insult," purred one of the women.

They were not going to let Toshiu escape so easily, and Candy considered if it might be because of what he had done to her. The women were not taking revenge for his lack of respect, rather Toshiu's sadism had trodden upon their favoured territory and they were motivated by irritation at his trespass.

"What wh-" he began, and again the women cut off his words.

Candy could guess that they were probably trying to rile him further. Perhaps to a level that would allow them to punish him for his impudence should his civility falter.

"Kiss," she said firmly.

Candy saw the tip of a tail rise into view and Toshiu knelt down. He held it reverently in both hands before placing several adoring pecks to it.

"Both of you."

Ushi had been silent until now, suggesting that his partner were the more senior officer of the two. Candy wondered if that difference in rank was also exposed by his penchant for sex. Had Toshiu grown bored of such mundane lust through overindulgence, or was he seeking to emulate the depraved Kami with his acts and thus earn promotion? Anyone could ravish a slave, but to bind, torment, and train them with expert skill was a trait to admire. Perhaps that was another aspect of his desire to torment her because then he would be punishing a slave that had been subjected to the callous delights of the Kami themselves.

The burly male stepped forth and wilted to one knee before offering the same show of servility to the guests. The tail fled from between his fingers and patted him on the head.

"Good boy. Now off you go."

The rugged priest bowed deeply and retreated backwards. The sound of the pair marching from the grove faded and left a hesitant quiet in its wake.

Candy had already felt the passion of the daughters and was concerned about encountering it again in her current flimsy state.

A lithe and elegant female form arose beside her and lifted a curvaceous leg high into the air before she pivoted and then straddled Candy's chest. The woman glowered at Candy with slitted pupils that lurked beneath a heavy brow. Her lips were drawn tight upon a wicked smile, which was more than a little unnerving because of its rabid malice. The hints of her scales could be glimpsed in the light, as could the purple patterns that rolled down her neck and onto her back.

Their appearance was too uniform for her to distinguish if this were one of the daughters she had encountered in the playroom. That specific dalliance had been cut short by the arrival of Warlord Hachiman, and it seemed that they were not so willing to leave the palace without having had their chance to play with Candy's body.

Candy gave a soft moan as she felt the long alien tongue of

a daughter continue to bestow laps around her inner thighs. The energetic organ rolled and curled upon her skin, offering the tantalising possibility of plunging into her but not delivering on this glorious act.

"Well, if it isn't our little visitor from Earth. Enjoying your time in the garden, slave?" she asked and cupped Candy's chin in one hand.

"Yes, mistress," she replied honestly. "I'm here to serve and I'll do all I can to please you."

"I'm sure you will, and this time, we'll take you further and bathe you in the pleasures of the Wani. Perhaps even drown you in them if you are not up to the task."

The laps at her skin stopped and the female addressed her compeer.

"So you've already tasted this one, sister?"

"In the playroom. I've been deep inside this creature, and she is quite delicious," murmured the woman atop her and then leaned over to let her tongue trail around Candy's throat. The organ was cool and slick, and could reach all the way around her neck like a fleshy collar. Candy mewed as the tip slithered up her cheek and traced the perimeter of her lips.

"Praise of her attributes hangs on the lips of Lady Uzume herself," said the third daughter, who had wandered over to the previously ignored slave girl and could now be heard fondling the contained form. The sound of her sheer catsuit rustling was met with the groan of her straps as she tested them. Subtle pips of fright and exasperation then began to sound when she was more thoroughly teased and manhandled.

"Yet she does not seem that impressive," came the voice between her legs and the licking recommenced.

"She was a ruler in her home. She was Mikado—a being responsible for running a great house, save that truthfully, it was she who was the true power behind the throne."

The hips of the Wani started to shift back and forth as her

licentious desires began to take over. Her taloned hands began to move up and down Candy's bound arms and clasp her shoulders as she pecked and nibbled at the neck and collar of her prisoner.

"A devious tyrant then?"

"All bound and captive."

"Trained."

"Available."

"And all ours."

"Someone must want her very badly."

"Is there a nice stiff cock somewhere, just aching to finally claim her?"

"Perhaps we should ferry her off to Yomi, where she'll never be found again. No more Warlord Hachiman. No more Lady Uzume. Just another Hafuri-tsu-mono."

The last words snapped Candy from the strange trance that their voices wove. The similarity in their vocal patterns as they issued from all around her—from her feet, into her ear, it was like being lost in a cloud of these creatures, and all around her were their words and their tongues. But the vile threat shattered this tranquillity.

"No, pleeeease, mistress, don't," blurted Candy.

The thought of being taken away from her master was terrifying. Her time with him and his agent had been the most wondrous experience in her life and there was so much more she could experience and learn from them. Also, their words had revealed hints of other possibilities. Had her capture been orchestrated? Did someone want to own a powerful figure from Earth? Candice had been a wealthy and highly influential corporate magnate, and to own what could be regarded as Mikado or even a Kami from Earth had to be an alluring one, especially for the debauched desires of the Empire's elite castes. Candy knew that Hachiman had bid for her against others and had purchased her from the Moon God. Had this agency been acting on behalf of another power and Hachiman had managed to outbid or outmanoeuvre them for ownership of her? If this were the case, surely other intrigue would begin to unfurl as this enigmatic power sought her acquisition. The mystery was tantalising, and she desperately wanted to find out the truth. It made their threat even more horrible because Yomi would not only steal away those she loved, but also rob her of any hope of discovering that truth.

Of course, the Wani could merely be taunting her, even though the threat of being sent to Yomi was a very real outcome. Candy had briefly been educated about it and had even seen a glimpse of one of the entrances to the underworld. She knew that it was a terrible purgatory from which there was no escape and she had no desire to call the daughters bluff. Even Hachiman would not be able to free her should she be thrown into the depths on some cruel whim of these hybrid dominatrices.

"Then you had best please us, slave," warned the female sitting atop her.

The figure curled her legs up and this placed a lot more weight on Candy's chest. The wind was pushed from her lungs and the daughter stretched the limbs forward and hooked them over Candy's bound shoulders. With a methodical haul, she drew herself along and squashed Candy's breasts beneath her firm rear. Hands promptly unfastened the strap at her forehead and the female snatched the sides of her head before hauling it up into her sex. Straddled across Candy's face, the woman pulled her in and gave a hissing moan when she felt her prisoners tongue eagerly launch up into her body.

"Yeeeessss. That's it, slave," murmured the female, and there was a distinct purr in her voice.

Candy clamped her lips to the woman's clit and offered several brief sucks and light nips before she again started to hurl her tongue deep and then swirl it against the stiffening nugget. The powerful thighs of the Wani hybrid trembled as Candy devoted herself to gratifying her. The quicker she could sate them, the sooner they would leave her alone so she might rest and recover. Her entire frame was battered and bruised and the night was still far from over. Indulgence with the daughters might well be an honour, but not when she was too enfeebled to properly appreciate it.

Candy was pulled deeper into the woman's pussy and her breath was stalled. The reason for this sexual gagging became apparent when a dextrous tail rose and suddenly encircled one of Candy's breasts. The strong appendage tightened in waves and formed a brutal garrotte around the root of the soft mound. Even as the base of her breast was crushed and the flesh filled with a struggling ache, the tip of the tail began to tickle the presented nipple. Even as her breast was being assaulted it was also being teased and this perplexed Candy as to how to react.

Closing her eyes, she renewed her oral efforts and in response the Wani just chuckled and tightened the hold bequeathed by her tail. This made Candy try even harder and her tongue thrashed against the woman in order to sate her and hopefully, get rid of her.

The woman levied weight to her loins and pushed Candy's head back to the frame. One hand then closed into her hair and pinned it down before she moved back, removing herself from her slave's tongue.

Candy's roots flashed with distress and after a moment to savour her pained expression the free hand of the daughter started to slap her about the cheeks. Candy jerked and offered shocked pips of fright.

"Bad, slave. Bad! What's your hurry? If you don't settle down, I'll take my pleasures from you in other ways!" she hissed while continuing to lambaste Candy's cheeks.

"Ow! Sorry mistress! Ow! Ouch! Oh! Please! I'll do better!" she stammered with her eyes clenched shut to defend them should the hand miss its target.

"You will!" snarled the woman and briefly ceased her attack.

Candy quailed beneath her as the female lifted her hand outward and readied to offer even harsher slaps. The muscles of her arm tensed, and the threat of another stern spank made Candy quiver under her.

"Ready?" asked the woman.

Candy's response was deemed too slow, and the woman slapped her across the cheek again.

"Answer me, slave!"

"Yes! Yes, mistress! I am! I am!" she barked when the woman leant weight to the hold in her hair and made her scalp thunder with additional woe.

"Open your mouth!" she said with a snarl.

Candy threw her jaws apart and received another light slap a moment later.

"Wider."

She stretched harder and the corners of her mouth lit up from the strain.

"Wider!" demanded the Wani and some more slaps made Candy stretch until she feared she might dislocate her own jaw.

"Tongue. Up. Now!"

Candy fired her organ into the air as the fist into her hair clenched more ferociously to keep her under control. The tail suddenly let go of her breast and returning circulation roared through the released flesh. Her nipple pounded with an awful beat that made her tongue lower and her jaws close a little as she set free a croaking shout of anguish.

"I said open! And up!" snapped the daughter and again began to smack Candy's cheeks.

The skin was becoming hot from the abuse and prickly riots of sensation lurked in the abused regions. As the spanks continued, Candy fought to restore her former pose even as the tail enclosed her other breast and treated it to a repeat of the crushing and tickling assault.

"Now don't you dare move!" growled the angered sadist.

Candy was rapidly becoming aquatinted with the fact that her own gender, regardless of species, were often the more cruel to her. It made her long to return to the care of Warlord Hachiman. The only exception she could think of was Yakami, her roommate, but now that the Warlord had returned and had taken charge of his Earth born possession, she doubted she would ever see that delicate sultry concubine ever again.

The woman lowered herself until the tip of Candy's tongue met her pussy. She shifted until her sex grazed the extended tip and then she started to rock her hindquarters, tickling herself with the slave's organ.

Her tongue was burning with strain and tears gathered in her eyes as she fought to hold the position. The Wani gave a long and self-indulgent hum of ecstasy while she masturbated herself on her captive tip. The pain of the position grew worse with every passing second.

"Don't you dare wilt, slave!" snarled the Wani and the tail tightened its hold. Candy gave a brief cry and applied more effort to retaining the pose.

The Wani started to gasp and groan as she stole her delight from Candy's face, and Candy prayed that she either come or just get bored.

The woman shifted back a little and hoisted Candy's face back between her thighs. The extended tongue shot into her wet pussy and spread the taste of the Wani's stark arousal across her entire palate. The woman settled down and her tail and hand eased their rigour.

"You may continue as before," commented the woman and leaned back to take hold of Candy's shoulders. A long murmur of satisfaction echoed when Candy again began to pour her burning organ onto the roused clit of her oppressor.

"She seems to be lagging in her dedication, sisters. Inspire her," announced the impious female. She had detected Candy's acute enfeeblement and even the slightest failing was not to be tolerated by this alien tyrant. Candy was powerless to resist but too exhausted to serve adequately.

Her eyes widened and she stared up along the lithe torso towering above her before she met the amused glare of the Wani. Lips had embraced her toes and had begun sucking upon them. Candy shivered as the women continued to tease her extremities and she watched as the female ensconced atop her released her shoulders and instead scooped up her own breasts, flaunting her freedom to the trussed captive between her thighs. The Wani caressed the alluring flesh and her head lolled back so she might fire heady gasps into the air.

"Now, sisters. Inspire the slave as only we Wani can," she groaned.

Candy's yelp rushed against the woman's pussy when teeth grabbed hold of the root of her big toes and drew up to bend them back. A scream followed when each woman's tail flicked like a bullwhip and stung the revealed and naked soles. The tender skin detonated with effulgent wrath and Candy fought to curl her toes in and protect the targeted area. The women giggled, held tight with their maws, and easily stopped her.

The tails of the daughters continued to snap against her feet as Candy squealed and fought to service the woman atop her. Those who were craned over her legs and holding her feet started to draw their claws over her thighs and abdomen. The scratches were vexing but did not pierce, rather they just offered a minor distress that made her shake and fight to escape her bonds with renewed dedication.

With the savagery of the session ruling her, Candy found new strength. She cast her tongue to the clit of the woman and attacked it with swift and fluttering laps.

"Oh yessssss. Like that, slave. That's soooo much better. You see? All you needed was the proper motivation."

A pair of simultaneous tail whips caught her instep and Candy's squall ended as she locked lips to the stiff clit and hauled at it with waves of potent suction. The Wani squealed with delight and her tail tightened involuntarily to bring even more pernicious force to Candy's captive breast.

A flashing tongue returned to continue and Candy ferried the wicked creature into orgasm. The woman's hands lanced straight out, and her muscles rippled as her fingers clawed at the open air. The limbs then jerked back to lock around her own torso. Her legs shook and her wail of rapture filled the night air. Her partners instantly tightened their teeth and offered a swift deluge of whip cracks that made it even harder for Candy to maintain her rhythm. Clearly they had enjoyed their sister's abuse of her body and were secretly trying to encourage more.

Candy fought against the pain and dedicated all her willpower into pleasuring the woman that was riding her face while her siblings unceasingly tormented her.

Unfortunately for her, the Wani was as insatiable for pleasure as she was willing to cause pain in order to get it, and Candy had to fight long and hard to quench her appetites. The woman yelped and squealed with glee as she continued to feast upon her orgasm until eventually she could take no more. She jumped forward off of Candy's trapped face, whirled, and sank down onto the ground where she embraced herself and shook with lingering rapture.

"Ooh, that was delightful. With the proper incentives she can be quite an impressive oral servant."

The maws of the other Wani released Candy's feet and she gasped for breath. Her soles were resonating from the eldritch whipping but she was powerless to soothe them or shield them in any way.

"Perhaps I should take the next turn," commented one of the others.

Candy closed her eyes and prayed for deliverance. She could barely move her tongue and her body had been pushed beyond all tolerances. She knew that she would be tormented greatly if her performance did not measure up to the one displayed by their sister, but there was no chance she could accommodate them.

"Unlikely. She is required by others this night," came a stern male voice.

The women turned to the intruder with an angered hiss. They had been aroused to a savage state and were anxious to take brutal delights from Candy as well as to punish and torture her for their amusement. Candy knew that the Wani were a servile caste in the Empire and no doubt this lingering resentment was to be eased by the brutalising of an Earth elite.

The enraged hisses instantly turned to gasps and muttered apologies.

"Sorry, Warlord Hachiman, we mistook you for . . ."

"A mere priest? Would that have mattered? You are still guests, and although my priests are dedicated to serving you, they are still my officers and are to be treated with the correct respect. Do the daughters of Toyotama-hiko have so little reverence for my house and its servants?"

"Of course not, Warlord, we merely-"

"And you compound your folly by using such a tone in front of my personal possession."

A pause followed as the women cowed before her owner.

"How can we make amends, Supreme Warlord?"

"Show that you respect my House, even down to the

lowest Kami-tsu-ko. One serving as a garden ornament for instance."

There was a sudden flurry of energetic movement and Candy gave a shocked gasp when hands gently took hold of her inner thighs and then her sides. A long spry tongue eased into her pussy and others rolled along the same areas that had been tortured by the tails of the women, except this time, the appendages were far more licentious and approving.

Terrified of irking the Warlord, the three Wani applied every subtle and pleasurable oral technique their long and prehensile organs were capable of. Candy's delirious response to the bliss tested the restraints in full as the trio heaped pleasure on her to a degree that far eclipsed the pain they had engineered.

Candy screamed aloud as a tongue encircled her clit and continued on into her depths. Others rippled her breasts and surged around her erect teats. The abuse had been a known commodity, one that she could understand and process. This level of inhuman embrace was like nothing she had ever experienced or even conceived possible.

The slick organs warped her mind with orgasm after orgasm, each one growing in potency as their tails and hands caressed and groped her body, working in ululating waves to enhance her absolute joy. Candy screamed and howled into the night with each episode, her long sexual famine being broken by a gorging.

"Your apology is accepted. Now be off with you before my generosity fades," announced the Warlord after Candy endured another excruciating climax.

The tongues, hands, and tails fled like a morning mist, leaving Candy quaking in her bonds and lost to the aftermath of the affair. She was so giddy that she was glad that she was so methodically bound. Had she been free, she was sure that she would be tumbling crazily about the floor.

Her master appeared above her and she regarded him with utter adoration. Slender and lean, his muscles were well defined in the light and his smooth skin shone like silk. Only the discreet scars that crossed his arms and chest broke the unblemished view.

His features were calm and his short black hair had been slicked back. His dark eyes regarded her with his usual regal and uncompromising power and Candy found that she could not speak, so she merely wept softly as he soothed her cheek.

"I was not aware of the daughters being in the palace until now. They are spiteful are they not? But they do have other attributes that compensate for their penchant for villainy."

"Yes, master," she hoarsely whispered. Her elated screams had left her voice just as fractured as her vitality.

Hachiman brushed a few strands of sweat sodden hair from Candy's brow and leaned in to kiss her cheek.

"I think you have been out here long enough. Let's get you back into the palace. Uzume is becoming quite impatient."

Candy stared up at the stars as she felt the strong hands of her owner unfastening the many straps that had for so long contained her and left her served to the whims of others. Like an accommodating lover, Hachiman took her hand and helped her from the wooden device and through a mixture of weariness and subservience she sank down onto her knees. Candy glanced to the other slave. She did not even know her name or even what she looked like beneath her blindfold and the plexus of straps that kept her folded and pinned to the vertical pole. She was just another trained toy, another anonymous bauble that served the House.

Her steel collar accepted a leash and Hachiman curled the chain around his fist and used it to draw her back onto her shaking feet and towards the palace. Candy was scarcely aware of her journey until a trio of priests rounded the corner at a swift jog. They immediately froze and bowed deeply when they saw the Warlord.

"What urgency prompts this haste?" asked Hachiman.

"We were on our way to the gardens, Warlord. We . . ."

The words of the priest stammered and trailed off. The true answer was betrayed when he gave a surreptitious glance towards the leashed slave.

"Off with you," chuckled Hachiman, and the priests now continued their run to slip away rather than head for Candy as was obviously their original intent.

Candy now realised just how briskly word could spread in the palace. Those who had used her had spoken or bragged to others. Slaves or priests had overheard. Slaves would quickly tell those they served should that person have expressed interest in her and by doing so, garner their owners gratitude. News that Hachiman's personal and most prized property was available to all comers had rushed through the palace like a wildfire, but after only a few hours he had chosen to liberate her and leave them frustrated. Such a notion made Candy smile to herself as she imagined countless libidos now thwarted and the concubines who would have to endure the consequences. She wondered how many other slaves would be cursing her name as they were whipped to ease the frustration of their appointed priest, or how many others blessed her name as the furiously aroused manhood that had dreamed of Candy now thrust into them instead.

Together, they proceeded up into the higher floors of the palace and reached a large antechamber. A set of paper doors had been painted with images of fierce dragons that curled amongst pillars of roaring fire and this large portal occupied much of the far wall. Kneeling humbly on either side of the two massive panels was a female form. Sealed within a comprehensive second skin of leather, their waists were crushed by ferocious corsets and their heads were lost within equally tight hoods.

Candy glanced to the numerous statues that were lurking in the shadows along the wall and then gave a shocked gasp as she realised now why the doors were so flimsy. Stationed along the walls were massive eight-foot-tall Wani. The armour that so resembled that of the Samurai was comprised of elegant ceramic plates that were decorated with the emblems of fire and many detailed ideograms of allegiance. They cradled a variety of heavy machine guns, and the huge drum fed weapons were worn just as casually as the monstrously dense armour. Paired katana were worn on their backs and their inhuman eyes peeked out from beneath ornate helms that followed their elongated snouts and added to their ferocious image with spikes, horns, and wicked fangs. The ranks of deadly warriors were poised in endless patience, never tiring, and fanatic to their duty. At the first instance of peril they would strike without pause and although this level of security was reassuring, the beasts still frightened her.

The women by the doors heard the approaching footsteps and reached up with hands that were sealed within mittens. They pressed them to the gossamer doors and slid them aside. Hachiman paid no attention to either the slaves or the guards and just continued in with Candy in tow.

The corridors of this wing were much wider and like the rest of the palace they bore numerous impeccable works of art, most of them depicting Kami at play and committing the most deranged acts of sexual excess on a plethora of adoring slaves. The couplings were depicted in such detail and were so lifelike that Candy shivered lecherously as she observed them. Elsewhere in the castle there were alcoves or displays that bore constrained females but here there were none. Also, the traffic in the corridors diminished sharply, indicating that this was some sort of personal wing for the Warlord.

Hachiman turned and wandered into a wide chamber whose centre was dominated by a spacious bed. A low perimeter of dark wood ran in a circle and created a bowl that was filled with large and inviting pillows. Eight ornate posts were spaced around the edge and each rose up to embrace a round lantern. The shades were delicately tinted with red and this filled the room with a soft, pink hue that greatly influenced the silvery beams pouring in through several large skylights.

As sumptuous as the room appeared, Candy's eyes immediately locked on the covert rings of black metal that adorned both the perimeter of the bowl and the columns, offering anchors to restrain a struggling subject. She also noticed the covert panels along the top that suggested cabinets and other storage located within. Although the exact nature of the contents was unknown to her, she could guess as to their general purpose.

A few pillows were flung aside and Lady Uzume lifted herself out from beneath them. The lithe beauty was naked save for her stockings. Her long black hair was wild and dishevelled and little makeup remained on her aloof features.

Hachiman approached the bed, removed the leash, and pushed Candy onwards. She lifted a knee onto the wooden sides and then flopped into the interior. The soft satin and silk of the pillows was a delight to her skin, and she slid her arms out under them to feel the fabric slither against her skin. The sound of her master joining them reached her ears and Candy curled up and let her eyes close as she readied to grab some much-needed sleep.

The hand of Lady Uzume knocked a pillow aside and then ran along Candy's thigh.

"What happened?" she asked before dropping back onto a small mound of cushions.

"It seems that word spreads quickly when my slave is made available. The daughters were having their way with her, and I suspect some of my priests were doing the same before them."

"You were not intending this?" she asked lazily.

"I anticipated some token encounters, but it seems your affinity for her has made her name more known through the palace than I thought."

"I was making sure she was ready for you," coyly uttered Uzume, and rolled onto her front to regard the Warlord.

"Well, now that I am aware of her fame, I will ensure that I keep her close by at all times. I did not expend so much time, effort, and wealth to have her open to all. This trinket is for special occasions and my own private enjoyment."

Candy gave a brief sigh of relief. The time in the grove had been exhausting and brutal, but it had brought a definite and positive result. Now she would be at Hachiman's side, and because Lady Uzume was always nearby, the two of them would now exclusively rule her life. Uzume's hand again brushed Candy's body.

"Well, such a treasure should be kept on display then," she offered.

Hachiman looked up and caught the mischievous expression of his agent.

"By all means go ahead."

With a sudden enthusiastic shuffle, Lady Uzume slithered away and moved to the edge of the bed. She opened one of the subtle cabinets and grabbed a pair of leather shackles. They had a padded interior, and the exterior had several sturdy buckles and a pair of dense *D* rings. The two rings were situated on opposite sides and already had a chain attached to them. This reached up to fasten on either side of a padded handgrip before they continued onward and culminated in a thick ring.

"Here, slave," ordered Uzume.

Hachiman propped himself up and watched as Candy crawled over and settled onto her knees. She lifted her hands and took hold of each grip so that Uzume could buckle the cuffs into place. The level of padding on the inside did not indicate easy or simple restraint and Candy could already surmise what Uzume might be intending. She wanted to say something, to complain that she needed rest, but her need to remain compliant was a far graver concern and so she allowed her installation to unfold without protest.

Two coils of rope were acquired and Uzume tied each to the ring. This kept the knot well out of Candy's reach because even when she stretched her fingers as far as she could from the handgrip, she was still a few inches short.

The coils were then hoisted up and slipped through rings situated half way up a pair of posts. A knot left two feet of rope stretched between the two rings and despite her fatigue, Candy could not help but stare with lust at the smooth majestic female form twirling and shifting before her eyes.

Lady Uzume seemed to notice her lecherous stare and glanced over her shoulder to see Candy staring at her stocking-clad legs. She cocked one leg out toward the kneeling submissive.

"Kiss. And if I feel skin, I'll tan yours," she warned.

Candy shifted forward and laid her lips to the smooth dark band at the top of her thighs. The soft warm scent of Uzume's skin roused her hunger, but the woman was just teasing her.

She slipped away and once again delved into the cabinets to produce a matching pair of fetters. The cone shaped affairs swiftly cradled Candy's feet. Two sturdy straps were riveted at her ankles, and they stretched out and then offered a large *D* ring. These also accepted a coil of rope that abruptly reached up and slipped through a corresponding ring on the other side of the bed.

Once more, Lady Uzume proved that her slim physique was in no way weak and with a steady series of hauls she caused Candy's left leg to slither back. She dropped onto the covers and gave a long mewl as the limb was hoisted up into the air. The woman continued until Candy was stretched taut, and then grabbed the other rope before repeating the act and leaving Candy spread-eagled in the air above the bed.

The pillows beneath her wobbled as Uzume danced back onto the bed and stepped beside the suspended concubine. Gentle fingers rushed up and down her back.

"Mmmm, much better," she commented.

Candy held tighter to the handgrips as her joints continued to curdle with strain. She couldn't possibly be expected to endure this pose all night. Additionally, to have the image of Uzume and Hachiman entwined beneath her would make it a torture beyond endurance.

Uzume revisited the surreptitious cabinets and acquired a head harness. The item was comprised of a rigid leather plate which bore a metal rimmed aperture at the front, much like a static O ring gag. Thick belts were riveted around the edges of the plate and after Uzume put it to Candy's face she started applying them with testy wrenches.

First, she hauled a strap around the back of her head before tightening it until the plate was pushing to her lips. With the plate established, the straps on either side of her nose were drawn up. These connected at the bridge and then continued up over her crown before they connected to a fixture on the belt that was traversing the base of her skull. This strap also bore a dense ring at the summit. A final pair of straps emerged from the lower reaches of the gag plate and in Uzume's hands they reached down to fasten under her chin.

Another trip to the containers acquired rope and what appeared to be some sort of phallic meat hook. The rigid polished steel item was smooth and quickly acquired a fleeting measure of lubricant from a tube that was then frivolously tossed aside. Candy instantly saw what was coming.

"Please, mistress, no! I . . . I . . ."

The words became a startled gasp as Uzume began threading it into her rear. Candy bucked and strained against her bonds but this only heightened the stress that lurked in her limbs and joints.

"Oh! No! Stop! It's too much. I can't take any more, mistress!"

"Stop whinging, slave! By the Sun Goddess, you'd think this was the first time you'd ever been bound and penetrated!"

A spiteful tug to the butt hook made Candy cry out. She bit her lip to stop anymore of her words inspiring chastisement or even worse, an escalation in her bondage. Lady Uzume was a sadistic vixen and repeated complaints could well annoy her to a degree that would have her greatly magnify her intended torments.

Candy turned her head around and looked to Hachiman. Her master was reclining and watching the scene with obvious relish. His cock jutted into the air as an indication of his delight, and his eyes glittered to see the misery on his slave's face as well as the glee on that of his agent. Candy knew that no mercy could be gained from her owner.

The hook that invaded her rear accepted rope that was swiftly applied to the ring atop her head.

Candy gave a startled mew of concern and then offered a squeal when the rope was drawn tighter to hoist her head and cause the hook to take firm rein on her sphincter.

"Is that enough?" asked Lady Uzume.

"Oh I think she would appreciate a little more," said the Warlord with a wry chuckle.

Candy's gurgled sobs were given more volume as the woman stole more of the rope and caused her head to arch back even more. Her neck coursed with mayhem and she gasped for breath to help her endure this malicious abuse.

"There, that should do," commented Uzume after taking

another infernal measure of rope away. She patted Candy's juddering rear and then continued to caress the length of her back.

Candy's head was craned painfully back and her whole body was shivering from the ferocity of her ordeal.

"But do something about her noises. I want to get a decent night's sleep," said Hachiman.

Candy's eyes widened in horror as she realised that she was to be left like this all night. Her body was drained and felt moribund, and to be surrendered to this horrible fate until dawn would be a monstrous trial.

The sadistic female appeared before Candy's hoisted eyes and lifted a rubber orb into view.

"Although, she has been through a lot. Perhaps we should be gentle with her. Is that what you want slave?" she asked staidly.

"Yes, oh please, mistress. Just let me sleep. Do anything you want to me afterwards, but please, pleeease, just let me rest."

"Pleasure me, and I might consider it," purred Lady Uzume.

Candy was suspended at the perfect height to pander to this wish, and Lady Uzume shuffled forward to slot her pussy against the gag plate. Candy's tongue flashed into activity. Every movement of the exhausted organ was painful but the suspension and the prospect of it being an all-night affair easily eclipsed this.

"Mmm, so dedicated. You must be anxious to evade this," crooned the woman.

Uzume's torso shivered and her hands took hold of Candy's stretched arms to steady herself while enjoying the attention. It was an awkward pose, but Candy could still work from it, especially if it were to gain her a reprieve.

"But, I like to have the stars, or a slave, above me when I

sleep."

Uzume stepped back suddenly and crammed the deflated rubber bag into the gag hole. It rushed over Candy's teeth and left a slim pipe emerging from the aperture. The tube dangled an inflator bulb from the tip and as soon as Lady Uzume closed the small valve between bulb and pipe to ensure air only went in, she swiftly began to crush the egg-shaped device in her fist.

Candy gurgled for mercy but already the rubber balloon was growing within her mouth. The taste of the material poured across her palate and eclipsed the taste of her mistress, and then it began to lean force to her tongue. In just three squeezes the balloon had become too big to force through the opening of the gag and Lady Uzume was still inflating it. The rubber barged against her jaws and sought to spread them even as the plexus of straps tried to keep them pressed together. Snorting for air, she felt her mouth reverberate with new degrees of havoc as she looked into the callous glare of the beautiful woman.

"More? Or are you inflated enough to ensure you keep quiet, slave?" she asked, and traced her fingers down the side of Candy's flushed cheek. A prod to the flesh revealed the tautness that the balloon was creating.

Candy burbled her assent.

"I see we need more then," stated the woman and added another vindictive squeeze.

The pressure in her mouth elevated further and she squeezed her eyes shut as tears trickled onto her cheeks.

Another squeeze made them jerk open and regard her tormentor with utter imploring.

"There, that's what I wanted to see."

The woman leaned over and placed a single kiss to Candy's forehead before she straightened and held the captive chin.

"Goodnight, slave."

Lady Uzume dropped down onto the covers and Candy burned with resentment and envy as the sound of her and her master embracing reached her ears.

"Is this sadism due of the Wani daughters?" wondered Hachiman.

"What do you mean?"

"Afraid they showed Candy that they were fiercer than the dreaded Lady Uzume?"

"Of course not. I just wanted to make sure we had a nice decoration for the night. And should the whim take you, then your cock could still vicariously taste her mouth, despite its being choked with rubber right now."

Candy heard the obvious signal of Uzume turning over and offering her saliva lubricated sex to her master. It was an invite he readily accepted, and Candy was left hanging in the air, bound and in misery as the two made heated and passionate love beneath her. The slap of skin to skin, the groans and murmurs, the brays of ecstasy, all were as maddening to her as the bondage, and as they settled down and slid into a contended sleep, Candy was left snorting in apathy as she continued to suffer for their impish amusement.

# CHAPTER THREE

Candy's recent trials had been exceedingly demanding and even against the horror of her current pose, she managed to steal a few moments of fitful snoozing. These periods of semi-sleep were constantly corrupted with dark images that abruptly forced her back into awareness and each minute became an eternity that she swore she could not withstand, and yet somehow she still managed to keep her cries in check. Every part of her was distinct because of the pain possessing it and any attempt to lessen a particularly testy area only increased it somewhere else. If she sought to ease her throbbing neck, her rear suffered. To offer solace to her legs, brought more woe to her racked arms.

Hints of light started to appear as the sun inched up towards the horizon and Candy wept with joy that her torment was finally going to end. Every hesitant measure of new ambient light made her pray for her owners to wake up and release her, but their frenzied lovemaking had left them in a deep and satisfied slumber.

Golden beams started to streak across the room and bath the entire hall in brilliance, but still they slept on. Candy sobbed in apathy, unable to tolerate her punishment but equally unable to do anything about it.

Her heart leapt with joy when she heard footsteps. A messenger might mean that there were duties requiring her owner's attention, and then she would be released so she could accompany the pair. However, the footsteps simply stopped at the edge of the bed and no other sounds followed.

A soft moan emerged and the sound of someone stretching reached Candy's hoisted ears.

"Ah, breakfast," commented Hachiman. "You may set it down and leave us, slave."

A soft metallic clatter revealed the tray being deserted on the perimeter and the footsteps vanished into the rest of the wing.

"Is that it?" criticised Lady Uzume.

"We have a busy day ahead of us. A quick snack is all we can afford."

"Mmmm, then I'm glad I had a nice hot feast last night," she mused, and Candy felt a stocking-clad toe stretch up and stroke her stomach.

The sound of bowls moving and of rapid munching wafted up beneath her. The smell of food touched her nose and immediately made her belly grumble as she realised now just how hungry she was. Her miserable position had been one that left her famine unrecognised because there was no way for her hunger to compete with the effects of brutal suspension and terrible contortion.

"And what business could place such a demand on Warlord Hachiman?"

"All will be revealed soon enough," he replied after swallowing and taking a sip of tea.

"Ah, so it's not yet official, and you're waiting for confirmation?"

He finished another mouthful and took another sip.

"As always — scheming and plotting."

"Just as my master taught me," retorted Uzume.

"True enough."

The Warlord finished his meagre meal and then climbed off the bed.

"Make sure you feed, Candy. And let her get some rest."

"As you wish," said Uzume with a sigh. She was clearly

disappointed that she would not be able to indulge her more spiteful inclinations towards the hovering pain-wracked slave.

The sound of Hachiman striding from the room faded and Uzume broke into activity. A twist to the valve on the dangling tube caused the air to rush from the balloon. Candy gave a wail when her cheeks seemed to expand around a storm of fresh anguish. The skin had become accustomed to being stretched and her jaws to being forced against the straps. The sudden change in this long endured pose made her holler and bounce against her bonds.

"Still some life in you then," muttered Uzume and drew out the emptied gag.

"Is my slave hungry?" she asked.

Candy declined to speak and tried to nod, the action attacked her sphincter and made her murmur.

"Maybe this hole is not the only one that's hungry."

Uzume traced a finger around the gag plate and lifted the sodden balloon close to Candy's features.

"Perhaps I should stuff this in your rear and pump you up while I feed you. Would you like that, slave?"

Candy fixed her chagrin stare to the bulb.

"Just like this," stated Uzume, and started to slowly squeeze the inflator. The thick rubber bladder grew immediately.

"Pump . . . pump . . . pump."

The thought of it entering her body and stretching her channel as it swelled within her with every squeeze was not a welcome one. Uzume continued to intimidate her with a display of what might well end up occurring inside her body.

"Pump . . . pump . . . pump," she continued, her eyes savouring Candy's mortified study of the bloated orb.

The sphere grew quickly, and Candy realised that if she could not regurgitate it because of acute inflation then she would be stuck with it. A giant latex bubble would be paining her innards, unable to escape because her opening was too small. Candy remained mesmerised by the frightening image of Uzume pumping up the ball. Every time it swelled, she winced in sympathetic horror as she imagined the added grief the increase would bring to her rear.

Uzume laughed aloud at the chagrin expression and simply dropped the toy.

"Another time perhaps. Our master has said that today is a busy day, and we can't have you distracted by distending that cute bottom with all this luscious pain."

Lady Uzume vanished momentarily and then arose before her, this time with a bowl of rice and a pair of chopsticks. She proceeded to gather small measures and slot it into the gag. It was hard to swallow, but Candy did not know when next they would bother to attend such a trivial chore.

Candy could see the iniquitous crook to Uzume's impassive features and knew that she was trying to goad Candy into begging or pleading for her release. Uzume would obey her master without question, but if Candy were to misbehave, then she would be justified in punishing her. Candy held back her words and continued to eat what the woman gave her until finally the bowl was cleared.

"Very well, I guess I shall let you down," she announced with a minor huff of annoyance. "But it's such a shame. You look so delicious up here. Soaked with sweat. Your body trembling with such exquisite agony."

Bare hands traced along her back and assessed her oppressed form. Another sigh followed before the rope was freed from her butt hook. Candy's head flopped down and her neck coursed with mordant pangs after its long containment. The extraction of the hook was another measure of distress and she just clenched her teeth as tightly as she could. She had survived the night. Now she had survive being released.

The knots that had been used to hold her were expert ones that could be set free with a mere tug. So, with a simple pull her legs dropped to the soft cushions. Candy suddenly curled them in and quaked with pain as they thundered with powerful waves of discomfort.

Her arms were released and she hauled all her long stretched limbs in to her, cuddled them, and waited for the trenchant might running through them to fade. As she recovered from her suspension, Lady Uzume unfastened her harness and her bonds, then set them aside.

"You suffer so beautifully, slave," she said, and shuffled in closer to hug Candy from behind. She slithered up against her and soothed her with gentle strokes. This was the Lady Uzume that Candy remembered from their time beneath Hachiman's throne — the sensual creature rather than the vicious dominatrix.

"I must admit, I was rather angry that you got to service my master while I continued to suffer. But when I saw you being taken to the gardens, I knew you would pay for it. The trouble is, when you later appeared in this bedroom, well, that same jealousy returned and I just *had* to see you pay for your previous good fortune."

"I couldn't refuse him, mistress," mumbled Candy.

"Of course not, and I would not expect you to. Disappoint our master or disobey him in any way, and I'll bend you into backbreaking bondage poses that will have you screaming for an entire week, slave. But then I am blessed with Kami status. You are a slave. It is my prerogative if I spitefully want to punish you for enjoying the Warlord's attention instead of I. Is that not so?"

"Yes, mistress."

Lady Uzume's foot reached up and over so she could rub up and down Candy's own legs. The nylon offered soft murmurs against her skin as she was caressed.

"The sound of you suffering all night long. It was a delicious lullaby. I slept most soundly because of it, even if you did not. But that is why you are here—for our benefit. No doubt the Wani daughters taught you that."

The woman began to comb her slender fingers through Candy's hair and the feel of her stiffening nipples was distinct against her back. The points drew small swirls against her skin as the woman recalled the noises in all their arousing glory. The thought of what the daughters must have done to her had Uzume's mind thundering with possibilities, and this was obviously exciting her.

"They did, mistress," whispered Candy.

"Then imagine if you were theirs to do with as they please, at any time, and in any way."

Uzume gave a laugh as she felt Candy cringe at the prospect. As heinous as her night had been, the thought of being given to such vicious beasts made her realise just how fortunate she was to be under the strict care of Uzume and Hachiman.

"So many of the concubines are just abandoned to their lot in life. They savour every experience, every chance to bask in our presence, whether they are screeching in agony, wailing in ecstasy, or doomed to numbing containment as a bondage ornament."

"Yes, mistress," she whispered, and a faint nod against Uzume's soothing hands caused the woman to lower her grasp and trace delicate touches down Candy's neck. She craned her head back and offered the flesh to her in full.

"You have seen this?" asked Uzume and her hand started to stray down onto Candy's collar where it brushed the steel band before continuing on towards her cleavage.

"Yes, mistress. I saw it my former roommate. She would have done anything to take my place."

"What was her name?"

Fingers brushed Candy's nipples and strayed from one to the other as Uzume casually examined the concubine nestled in her arms.

"Yakami."

"Ah, my Mikado has her as his new plaything. I suspected that you might have had something to do with that."

"She was kind to me, mistress. I wanted to make her happy and she had somewhat of a crush on your Mikado. He asked if I required anything, and I asked him to . . . well . . ."

"Such a benevolent creature. If she were not receiving such attention from my Mikado, I'm sure she would be missing you very much. But now you are with us, and the Warlord does not want you used by others unless it benefits him."

"I won't be going back to my room?" asked Candy, seeking to verify that Yakami was indeed lost to her.

"No. Your time in the rest of the palace is over. A larger scheme is at hand, and you are an important piece. Perhaps this is why I have been so hard on you, slave."

"I've only ever wanted to please you, mistress," was Candy's honest reply.

"As you should, but I want you to fear me as well."

Uzume suddenly grabbed Candy's hair and pulled back to pin her head down and hoist up her face so she could stare down at it. Squirming beneath the domineering form, Candy winced and grabbed hold of some pillows for strength.

"Do you fear me, slave?" growled Uzume.

"I . . . I do, mistress," was her genuine answer. Uzume was an unpredictable creature, especially now. When the Warlord was absent, she was a relentless and implacable noble sadist. When Hachiman was present, she could either be the most humble and adoring submissive or become a vicious rival for his affections, one that wanted Candy to suffer terribly for even the slightest regard from her master.

"You know that if you disobey or do not live up to your part in what is to come, I'll make you pay a terrible price?"

"Y . . . yes, mistress," said Candy, unsure of where this conversation, or indeed this scenario was heading. It was one of the things that enamoured her with Uzume. She could not foresee her actions or motives and everything came as a surprise.

"And if even if you do, you'll still suffer for me should the mood take me."

"Of course, mistress."

"Kiss," she said, and moved her torso forward to offer her breasts to Candy's lips.

Still pinned down by her hair, Candy parted her mouth and began to take each nipple as it was given to her. She lapped lethargically at the engorged points while Uzume let her head loll back and her eyelids flutter. She moaned and savoured the adoration, keeping her hold firm and making sure Candy could not move. She teased Candy's mouth, tracing the tips around her lips before placing them back for her attentive tongue to fawn upon.

With a casual and almost disdainful shove to enforce what she had said, Uzume threw Candy away and reached over to the perimeter. The chastity belt that Candy had worn when first being presented to the Warlord appeared, save that now, the cushioning interior plugs that absorbed vibration had been replaced with two phallic steel rods. A solid box also existed on the side of the garment, but there were no clues as to its purpose.

"Up onto your knees, slave. Hands on your head."

Candy clenched her teeth, rolled, and shoved into the bed. In the few minutes of relaxation it felt as though her body had become petrified. Every muscle was stiffening and was most testy at being coerced into use. With a series of awkward motions, Candy managed to rise up. She swayed when she lifted her arms because her balance was now a highly precarious thing.

"Spread those thighs," said Uzume as she opened the waistband and encompassed Candy's midsection just above her hips. The steel belt was established and then the semicircle that would deny her access to her own intimate regions was taken up.

"Suck them, slave," ordered Uzume and presented the rubber-coated interior to Candy.

Her mouth dropped open and she allowed the woman to slide the toys into her. She curled her tongue around the devices and imparted a layer of saliva that would ease their voyage into her body. Her pussy had responded to Uzume's groping attention, but her rear was another matter and so she made sure she surged her tongue and tried to coax forth as much natural lubricant as possible for this particular intruder.

The crotch band fled her lips and the cold steel rods began to slide into her body. Candy clenched her fingers to her crown as she felt her anus being opened by a chill metal rod. A soft croak of discomfort spilled from her lips as Uzume rocked the rounded head against her sphincter and then started to slither the probe into her. The pussy probe went in with greater ease and the upper ends of the band slipped into the locking slots that were waiting in the waistband.

Uzume shuffled around and cocked a leg beneath the kneeling slave. Her knee pressed to the underside of the crotch band and her hands reached forward and around before they grabbed Candy's thighs. A sudden tug outward parted Candy's thighs and she dropped onto the poised band. With Uzume supporting it from below, the plugs rushed deeper and the locks sank into the waistband and clicked into undeniable place.

Candy arched back with a gasp and then curled forward as she was invaded. Her breath rushed in and out as she sought to get used to the device and slowly, her channel grew more tolerant of being filled and the chill of the metal started to fade.

"Rest, slave. I will be back for you later," decreed the woman and spryly clambered from the bed.

Candy watched the sultry form sidle out of the room and then turned her attention to the belt. It was skin-tight and she couldn't even get a finger under the bands. The box at the side of the device was as enigmatic as it was devoid of seam or lock. Her examination was halted by a long wide yawn that revealed the ache that was still loitering in her jaws.

She winced and rubbed the corners to try and soothe them. Her eyelids briefly lowered and she felt herself sway unsteadily. The silence that had descended after the departure of her owners was a most powerful soporific and when she acquiesced to its power, no sooner had she laid her head down to the pillows than she was asleep.

# CHAPTER FOUR

Her sleep had been exceedingly deep, and Candy was having trouble clawing her way back out of it. Her body was still raw, but had recovered enough that she felt ready for whatever else her owners desired of her. There was also a tingling sense of excitement and expectation that helped energise her. New and great things were coming and it seemed that she was to have a ringside seat.

Uzume had mentioned this greater scheme and although it thrilled her, it also puzzled and troubled her. Candy had managed to give up her old life. She had become a slave and dedicated herself to that goal to gain power and influence with her skills, restoring that which she had lost. However, the Kami were far more insidious tutors than she would have thought and they had awoken and nurtured an abiding lust to be abandoned to the command of others. It seemed that the act of becoming a true slave was the easy part and that staying one would be more difficult. There was condemnation to Yomi if she truly erred, and there were others who wanted to steal her away, and this included someone who had genuinely desired her and been thwarted. She inspired jealousy, she inspired plotting, and in many ways she wished that she were just another anonymous creature like Yakami. As a standard concubine she would only have to concern herself with pleasuring the priests and partners she was sent to, and would not have to fear the ramifications of being the possession of a high profile ruler of the Empire such as Hachiman. It had reassured her to encounter the daughters because now she would be kept closer to her master and this made abduction less likely.

Thoughts of Hachiman ruled the coy warmth of her mind. Her trials had been forgotten and her fatigue was gone. The aches in her body were medals earned through her submission to her ruler. Just a mental picture of him made Candy squirm and curse the existence of the chastity belt, and the fact that she was denied only cultivated a higher state of arousal. Her hands clasped the warm steel and stroked the control he had established on her through his agent. Each clench revealed the metal struts that were locked within her.

Candy had encountered a number of dominant men since she had been hauled through the rift between worlds, but none of them was a nine hundred-year-old supreme ruler of elite armies. Thousands, perhaps millions considered him a God, and she was his plaything. How many other concubines lay weeping with jealousy as they thought of her being subjected to his rule? It was a strange throwback to a forgotten life, where the multitudes dreamed and envied the wealth and luxury she enjoyed and took for granted, salivating at it from afar and knowing they would never acquire even the most fleeting taste of it save through the most outlandish good fortune. Instead they were left to drool over glimpses of it in the media, or to stare longingly at the mansion, penthouse, or passing limousine that Candice regarded as so commonplace.

Candy decided to stretch her limbs, to loosen the flesh and make it easier to move. She rolled onto her front, shoved herself upright, and strolled towards the perimeter.

She jumped from the edge and landed on the cool marble tiles. She immediately gave a startled scream and her hands slapped to the chastity belt. Her abdomen bucked and she dropped to her knees before collapsing onto her side. Her legs kicked and she cried out as a stern blast of power caused her anus and pussy to crush themselves to the probes. The devices were coursing with a brutal charge that tricked her nerves and made them flash to excruciating attention.

Candy instantly surmised what had happened. The belt bore the same technology that was used in shock training collars for animals. A perimeter had been established and if she breached it the device activated.

Clawing at the ground, she tried to get up and back onto the bed but her legs were locked together and were difficult to use. She cried out in anguish and managed to clasp the side of the bed and drag herself up as her body was disciplined for its escape attempt. Every inch was a hellish feat to acquire while her hindquarters were continually being ravaged by the intense shocks.

With a final shriek she lurched around and collapsed onto the pillows. The shock ended immediately.

She gasped for breath and wiped the tears from her eyes. She tried to steady her racing heart, but her loins were throbbing from having been forced to remain at such brutal rigidity for so long. Candy instantly committed herself to remaining on the bed.

Held prisoner by technological shackles, she crawled back into the middle of the bed, slid under some pillows and decided to just go back to sleep.

Barely a few minutes had passed before the sound of footsteps caught her attention. Candy pulled the pillow off her head and jerked up, expecting to see her master. Instead, she saw one of the female servants.

The maid was greatly hampered by a most oppressive uniform. A layer of fishnet smothered her tall and athletic physique but this was by no means the end of her containment. A longline bra held her upper body and the leather garment had apertures that allowed her breasts to emerge through circular elasticised bands. These caused the pert flesh to swell, bulge, and remain on constant offer.

A tight hood of the same black polished hide entombed her head and the buckles that reached across the item had small locks set in place to prevent any removal, not that she could accomplish this by herself because her arms had been folded up behind her back. A sheath of leather had then been used to capture them there and with her wrists near the top of her spine, a slim chain could be seen attaching them to her tall and uncompromising posture collar.

A cluster of tiny holes existed before her eyes, granting her limited vision. The holes were small enough that they eluded a first glance and this made it seem as though she was kept blinded by the hood and that she operated solely by training, experience, or sound.

A pair of tall ballet boots poured up her legs to her upper thighs and kept her tottering on a ridiculously lofty heel. A set of buckled straps at the summit and at her ankles bore another set of locks as well as *D* rings. These anchors allowed a slim and rather abrupt length of chain to stretch between her legs and each hobble chain passed through a length of polished metal. The bar ran from her ankles, between her legs, and vanished into her pussy, curtailing her steps and stopping her from sitting down or even bending over.

Near blind, monstrously bound, and tottering on wicked heels, the front of her collar unleashed a pair of chains that stretched down to grasp the ends of a serving tray. Her waist was set into an indentation and a strap across the back stopped it escaping her. Upon this serving tray was a selection of bowls that poured curling lines of steam around the shuffling maid.

The captive creature moved to the edge of the bed and simply stopped.

"For me?" asked Candy, and realised that because of the uncompromising posture collar, the servant could not even nod.

"Never mind," she chuckled, and crawled over towards the statuesque form.

With complete impunity, Candy reached up and ignored the food so she could stroke and play with the woman's breasts. The slave gave some meek whimpers when Candy pinched the tips but she did not move. Candy's hands wandered for a moment across the leather and mesh that contained the girl. It was strange to have such freedom to indulge. Ordinarily it was she who was the captive, and the chance to help herself to another was a most agreeable one.

Candy grabbed the pole and jiggled it. The slave gave some gagged whimpers of protest and swayed as the inserted portion of the shaft shifted and rocked within her.

She offered a satisfied laugh, let go, and took the bowls of food. The strange plants and meats of this world again introduced her palate to an eerie variety of previously unknown flavours and the intense tastes greatly revitalised her.

Candy finished the last of the minor banquet, put the bowls back, and sat back to admire the stringently trussed woman. The maid instantly turned and started to scamper away. Candy dove forward to catch her before she escaped but made sure to leave her hips on the cushions lest she set off her chastity belt. Her fingertips grazed the backs of the frantically pumping thighs but fell away.

Wearing a fanciful smile, she lay on the edge of the bed, her thwarted arm hanging down the side. With her head on the wooden surface, she watched as the maid swiftly ambled off into the rest of the palace, and when she was gone, she turned and sprawled out again, only to hear another set of footsteps. These were heavier and she again wondered if her master had returned to her.

When she turned, she gave a gasp and involuntarily shuffled back in fright as a monstrous form appeared from around the corner. The Wani was identical to the ones she had spied before entering this wing, save that his armour was a striking red hue with black flame emblems rolling around it.

The warrior stomped forward on three clawed toes and his relentless march made Candy quail. The beast stopped at the perimeter and jolted to attention. Candy's fear of him was almost causing her to flee and the recall of what would happen should she leave the bed was the only thing that stopped her.

"The Warlord has asked me to collect you and bring you to the Chamber of Blossom," he growled.

Candy paused and regarded the towering beast. She garnered new resolve and began to crawl forward towards the static form, all the while fighting to stay calm. Candy told herself again and again that she had been used by the hybrid females of this race, had been ravished by their ruler, and was slave to their absolute master. The residual fear of them gained from her first encounter with their primitive tribal brethren had to be defeated.

"What is your name?" she asked as confidentially as she could.

"Iha, miss."

"Miss? Not *slave.*" Why did you use that term?"

"The Wani are pledged to the service of the Kami, the Empire, the House. The breath of every Wani belongs to the House they serve, miss," he stated with indoctrinated conviction.

"But I am Kami-tsu-ko."

"Of House Hachiman, miss."

"So I outrank you?"

"I am pledged to your will, miss."

"That's very interesting," she uttered.

It had not occurred to her that the hierarchy of the military could be so precise. It seemed that the Wani were the lowest caste, the human Mitama were the higher-grade warriors, and the priesthood of the House were the officers. Even as a slave to a House, she was still considered a member of the priest class.

"The Warlord has asked me to collect you and bring you to the Chamber of Blossom, miss. The Warlord is to be obeyed."

"Did Warlord Hachiman tell you to bring me this very instant?" she asked, seeking to test a theory.

"No, miss."

"Then stand still, Wani," said Candy with all the conviction she had within her.

Ensuring that she kept her hindquarters on the bed, Candy prowled forward to the creature she feared above all else. Toyotama-hiko was a hybrid, while this was a pure-blooded Wani, of the race that had almost killed her upon her arrival in Pangaea. Candy was determined to quickly exploit this hiccup in the chain of command and rid herself of a lingering phobia.

Employing hesitant but determined movements, she took hold of the dense ceramic slat hanging from the front of his breastplate. The diamond shaped slab weighed a great deal, and she realised then just how strong these beasts were. They were sheathed in a material of which even a single piece would greatly encumber a normal human. The Wani had to be virtually bullet proof in such a shell.

"Lift this," she stated.

The Wani moved instantly and caused her to jerk from shock. She calmed when he simply snatched the section of armour and hoisted it without effort to reveal a skirt of chain mail.

"And this," she said.

Again, the warrior complied with fanatic celerity to expose his naked groin. It seemed that the Wani were still very humanoid despite their reptilian origins, and their great size extended to all aspects of physiology. Suddenly, Candy was very irritated by the existence of her chastity belt.

"You are elevated amongst your own?" she asked while reaching forward to close a hand around his cock. The flesh was cool and slick.

"Elder second grade. Honoured with service directly to the Warlord. Defender of the fire-sanctum," snapped Iha.

Candy started to move her fist back and forth.

"And everything in it?" she asked.

"Without mercy or hesitation, the House must be defended."

"So loyal," crooned Candy as she felt him begin to stiffen against her efforts.

"Have you ever been with a human?"

"Kami-tsu-ko belong to the House. The Wani defend the House so the Kami may enjoy their property."

"That does not answer my question. Have *you* been with a human?"

"It does not happen, miss."

"An oversight to be corrected," she said, and stretched forward to enclose his shaft with her mouth.

The Wani did not move, but she could feel him shudder as she started to curl her tongue against him and lower her mouth as far as she could before retreating. Each dive of her maw caused him to shiver, and she started to hear soft grumbles from his throat. Finally, her fear was fading. She was controlling this warrior, taking pleasure in pleasuring him as he stood to attention and obeyed. These creatures would do anything for her, and her fright was now groundless.

It was difficult for her mouth to attend him so she moved back, grabbed him in both hands, and steered him between her breasts. She had done this for Hachiman, and this time she delighted in the feel of the Wani's phallus rushing through her breasts as she crushed them to his manhood.

The Wani convulsed as she brought him to climax and his

massive arrays of muscles rippled and caused his armour to clank and chime as he spattered her throat with his seed.

Candy flopped back, purged and feeling a hint of what it must be like to be Kami, to be so utterly surrounded by the deadliest and most fanatically loyal of beasts.

"The Warlord has asked me to collect you and bring you to the Chamber of Blossom, miss. The Warlord is to be obeyed," he repeated.

"Of course he is, Iha. Take me to him," she purred wantonly while cleaning herself with a pillow.

Hands dropped his armour and then grabbed her. Suddenly she was hauled into the air and dropped to her feet. She gave a gasp as she expected the belt to activate but the perimeter had been shut down and the probes did not react.

The Wani produced a leash from within his armour, snapped it to her collar, and was then striding away. A yank to the chain caused her to stumble and jog to catch up. The Wani moved rapidly and Candy had to adopt a swift pace to keep up as he stormed into the passages.

Another open area beckoned and the scent of flowers preceded her entry into a large solarium. The chamber was located on a corner of the palace and so two adjoining walls were comprised of towering glass panels that reached up to a domed glass roof. A smooth marble path trickled around the interior garden where small cultivated streams burbled and sparkled in the late afternoon light. Lush beds of flowers allowed tall trees to rise and each was bedecked in a glorious display of red or white blossoms. Loosed petals drifted gently to the ground and formed patches of silken colour as a series of wooden wind chimes played a delicate and soothing song. It was a spectacular display of radiant pulchritude.

Iha led her deeper into the large interior garden and to a clearing at its very heart. Sitting naked in a column of light was Warlord Hachiman. Locked in a rigid stance, a sheathed katana was held at his side. His eyes were closed, and his breathing was barely visible. The only disruption to the serenity was the glockenspiel accompaniment of the wind chimes.

Candy looked to the instruments and saw how it was that they could be played when no wind graced this halcyon locale.

Lady Uzume's hands and feet had been tied together by an intricate and methodical weave of rope that reached out to embrace shoulder, torso, and hips. The compiled bonds at wrist and ankle had then been fastened to trees to stretch her almost horizontally between two trunks at a height of about three feet.

A series of cords had been tightened to her limbs and around her breasts, and from these dangled the wind chimes whose weight caused the slender lengths to haul fiercely at her flesh. Her head was tucked down so that her bound arms remained overhead. Her mouth was open and her tongue had also been wrapped in a tight plexus of cord before being drawn out and left exposed by the burden of a set of weighty chimes. A simple cloth blindfold had been applied to deprive her of sight and the woman's body glittered with many gems of perspiration. Candy licked her lips as she studied her duress.

Lurking a short way into the trees were two other women. Both were petite and of indeterminate heritage. They had slender and highly alluring faces that had been given some accentuating shades of makeup and a bright red lipstick to match the flame-like hue of their long hair. Red vinyl opera gloves and dagger heeled thigh boots cruised up their limbs and even their pubic hair had been dyed the same ferocious colour. The only contrasting colour was that of their pale skin and the silver rings that transfixed nipple and clitoris and the steel collar that encompassed their throats. Movement was clearly forbidden them because from their rings and the *D* ring at the front of their collars hung a few inches of chain that each bore a brief cluster of tiny bells. Even a deep breath would bring chimes whose metallic chirp was sure to differentiate their disobedience from those tunes being created by Lady Uzume's suffering.

Each of the slaves held a wonderfully carved wooden box and kept their eyes unfocused and aimed forward with absolute obedience.

On the other side of this eerie grove were six more naked slaves. The diminutive females were all kneeling upright and five of them had their heads lowered and cocked to one side so that they nuzzled against the hilt of a sword. The sixth woman merely stared at the ground because Hachiman currently bore her charge.

Each katana was held along the front of their body and the scabbard was pressed to them by a very intricate pattern of rope. The diamond pattern weaves contained their entire torso with their arms held behind them so that a trio of strands could connect their wrists to their ankles.

The Wani removed her lead and pushed down on her shoulders. Candy sank onto her knees whereupon the warrior nudged the back of her head and made sure she kept her gaze subdued. Without another word he marched off to leave them in a tentative quiet.

Candy peeked out from the corner of her eyes and continued to study as Lady Uzume shuddered and strove to endure her bondage. Her fingers pawed at the ropes and her legs quaked as every movement made the chimes swing. Petals drifted down and sometimes stuck to her damp skin.

A sudden explosion of movement snapped her attention back around, and in that instant, the act was already over. Warlord Hachiman was now kneeling and holding up the sheathed blade. At a near imperceptible speed he had drawn the weapon, sliced at the air, performed another manoeuvre, and sheathed the sword. Candy had seen this in a previous life when her business in Japan had brought her into the presence of the most powerful, some of whom still revered the old ways. Iaido was the art of mental presence and immediate reaction, where the practitioner sought to draw, perform a fatal strike, remove the blood, and return the weapon to its scabbard in one move, from any position, at any time. The capability to react from any pose was once considered an essential skill for Samurai and her business rivals had taken her to displays of Iaido being performed in order to impress her. Of course, they also sought to give the impression that they too had considered every aspect of the coming financial battle and were ready to react to any eventuality she might present. Implied power was a very useful tool, especially when presented through association at a seemingly innocent social event.

Hachiman lifted the weapon horizontally and then slowly placed it to the ground. He bowed most deeply to the weapon, lifted it vertically, and then stood up.

The Warlord returned the sword to the slave, threading the scabbard down through the harness of rope, through her cleavage, and down until it reached her thighs. The girl instantly leaned her cheek to the weapon and snuggled against it. Candy saw her sniff at the hilt, catching hints of Hachiman's scent on the woven grip.

The Warlord turned and regarded Candy as though he had not even been aware of her arrival. He wandered towards her and began to circle her. She kept her eyes lowered and watched his legs pass her while he spoke.

"What do you think of the Chamber of Blossoms, slave?" he asked.

"Beautiful, master. And most tranquil."

"Indeed," he said softly. "Kamube!"

The two women moved around the trees that were

supporting Lady Uzume. Their bells played a brief tune that was compiled of sharp tones, and they summarily approached before holding out the boxes for their ruler.

"Rise, slave."

As Candy climbed back onto her feet, Hachiman opened a chest and removed a set of leather shackles that he quickly applied to her wrists. The suede interior was soft and luxurious, but the density of the hide suggested that they were capable of containing even the most virulent struggles.

The sight of Uzume's travail was causing her to seek a similar state. Her brief moment of self-indulgence while cathartic, had left her feeling hollow. Candy did not want to be in control, she wanted to be used. Even orgasm seemed to be a forbidden thing unless it was truly earned. Only once she had suffered for her owners, screamed and howled, danced under a lash or been left quaking from bondage did she feel worthy of being given climax. The prospect of being arbitrarily disciplined and then ravished had her tingling with excitement and she had to endeavour to keep her breath steady.

A bright red length of slender rope was removed and one end fastened to the rings on Candy's cuffs. The rest was then cast over an overhanging branch so that it dropped and dangled beside her. The opposite end was taken and hauled in to bring Candy's arms high over her head and leave her stretched upright. The end was then tied to the ropes that crossed at the base of Lady Uzume's back.

The Warlord strolled to the other Kamube and flipped open the lid of her chest. A key was acquired and the item was slipped into the locks of her chastity belt to part them. The crotch band slid from her body and she shook from the feel of the warm steel probes fleeing her. The waistband was also opened and both items were set back in containers as his hands again delved into the rest of the mysterious contents.

Candy gave a licentious mew when she saw him draw free

a jewel decorated stave from which spilled three long and slender straps of leather.

Hachiman walked back towards Candy and combed his fingers through the strands. As though this was a completely mundane event, he cast the whip back and then swung around to lay it across her rear. The length of the strands made the impact loud and also quite painful. A bilious shock rushed through her cheeks and Candy jerked to tiptoe and cried out.

The rope hauled at Lady Uzume and as Candy dropped back down, the stretched form of the woman bounced to have the chimes sway and haul at the cords responsible for carrying them.

No sooner had Candy's shout passed than she yelled out again as another swipe laid leather tendrils to the small of her back. She danced forward and clutched her thighs together as her fingers groped at the rope.

Another swipe caught the backs of her thighs and her legs jumped up into the air. She held them up to her body and the resulting yank to Uzume made her squawk as Candy's body-weight stretched her upward.

The pain faded and her feet dropped back to the ground. She sagged to hang from the rope and her legs trembling beneath her. Uzume was also lowered slightly and gasped for breath after the sudden racking of her physique.

"Stand still, slave!" demanded Hachiman, and hurled another swing at her back that caused the straps to reach around and lick at her breasts.

Candy jolted to attention and gave a holler as ardent woe stung her chest. She clenched her body and tried to suppress her movements but as Hachiman continued his assault it became harder and harder. Her jaw started to throb from grinding her teeth and fighting back her cries. Her body jiggled as she stood and squeezed her head between her elevated arms for endurance against this barbarous treatment.

She filled her mind with reassuring litanies of submission, dedicating herself to obedience and the service of her master but the whip was a mordant foe and was hard to withstand in silence.

Hachiman continued to pace around her and lay the weapon to her thighs, beneath her breasts, to her back and her rear, and the power of the abuse began to possess her.

The beast that dwelt within her started to awaken and reach out through her mind and body. The scorching impacts began to send ripples of debauched gratification through her skin, like echoes that started to gather, reinforce each other, and create a masochistic haze. The disparagement of her abuse began to evaporate, her breathing hastened, and her heart stamped in her chest. Tears rolled down her cheeks and sweat trickled down her body while she shuddered and began to lose herself to an intoxicating and corrupted trance.

"Legs apart, slave," ordered Hachiman upon seeing her sink into this depraved state. He knew what he wanted from her and was determined to acquire it.

Candy spread her thighs and a full-throated wail echoed in the hall as the whip began to seek out her untouched inner regions. The first few strokes challenged her obedience, but then the intensity of the trial stole this new source of pain and warped it. The corresponding increase in endorphins briskly took her giddy bliss to a new and potent plateau of ecstasy.

Candy cried out freely, ignorant now of how she was bouncing Lady Uzume up and down when she danced and whirled against each stroke. Her power to obey was lost. The whip and her master's use of it controlled her. She whirled and cringed, jerked, jumped, and shrieked while the deluge of strokes continued to come from every angle and seek out every vulnerable spot she presented. No matter what she tried, she could not defend herself and her abandonment to the abuse grew immeasurably.

When the flogging stopped, it took her a few moments to realise it, and even then it was only because she started to descend from the rapture of her algolagnic stupor. Words formed in her mouth to try and beg him to continue but her throat was hoarse, and her lips just trembled.

She felt someone touch her breasts and she managed to open a bleary eye and see the Warlord opening the end of the rope. He had set it free of Lady Uzume and was breaking the twin strands apart so that each could be tied to a nipple ring.

Candy gave a dismayed glance at her rings and was mortified to see him stepping back and once more readying the whip.

Her words to seek clemency were cut off when the weapon caught her flank. Candy jolted, and this tugged at her rings to make her shriek and throw her hands up as far as they would go. The whipping commenced with all its previous intensity and rekindled Candy's delight in it. After just a few lashes, she was starting to tug deliberately at the rope. The whip would land and impart brutal rhapsody to her burning hide, and in the split second that followed, she would haul at her bonds and make the rings punish her nipples. The tips seemed to swell from within with a tornado of sensation that poured out into her breast when she then released them from this self-engineered purgatory. The result took her even higher and had her aching for the next stroke.

There was a brief pause, one that she failed to register and suddenly in the wake of a stroke, something cool and wet slapped against her abdomen. A moment later she flew to a rigid stance and squealed as volcanic heat sank into the skin that had been covered. The whip then landed on her rear to have her swirl and cavort anew.

Her vision was a shifting veil because of her tears, yet she could see the glow of a large red candle in Hachiman's hand.

In the other was the whip that now continued to streak out and lick her body. He stepped aside and jerked the candle forward, unleashing the molten reservoir. The small measure of wax splashed the front of her right thigh and stray droplets landed on the inner region of the other.

Candy arched her head back and threw her scream into the air. The agony melted into ecstasy and the whip lapped at her back with a trio of oscillating swipes before the accumulated wax was hurled onto that punished region.

Hachiman prowled around her like some sadistic ghost, laying down insubstantial splashes that manifested as searing regions before the whip cracked and made her sing aloud again. As the wax dried, he would then assail it, cracking it and stripping it away so he might flog that region and then apply more searing punishment.

The most grievous applications occurred when he would spatter the issue of the candle into her cleavage or across her breasts because she feared he might whip them afterwards. In token consideration to his slave, he removed this wax with his hand and applied spanks that made her assets ripple and reverberate with additional mayhem.

While he swatted the encrusted layer away, Candy kept her rear thrown out and her breasts thrust forward to ensure he had a decent target due to fear of a miss and consequently an accidental strike of her rings. But no sooner had his chastising hand removed the layer on her breasts than he simply poured the candle into the cleft of her rear.

The duration of the spanking had created a significant stash of molten fluid and Candy's wail was hearty and long as she launched her hindquarters forward. Burning trails had reached her sphincter and trundled down her inner thighs. She swung her hips from side to side, instinctively trying to get away from the scorching liquid that was already drying on her.

A swift deluge of strokes crossed the fronts of her thighs and threw her back the other way before he again turned his attention to her rear and began to lay the whip to it. Candy thrust it out for him, delighting in the vicious wrath that now ruled her hindquarters.

Candy was not the only one finding the most intense arousal in this play and finally the Warlord could take no more provocation. He grabbed the strands of the whip at root and tip, flung them over her head, and hauled back. The amassed strands slipped into her parted maw and dug into the corners of her mouth. Hachiman reined her in and thrust with consummate accuracy. His cock charged into her sodden pudenda and Candy flew to a degree of rigidity that even the whip had failed to create. Her scream reverberated through the solarium and then halted suddenly as Hachiman jolted free and sank himself into her rear. After having stolen a full layer of her lubricant he exploited it so as to invade her bottom.

Candy's world turned over and her eyesight rolled. She stared straight forward and was left speechless. Her body jiggled at a frenzied rate and her thighs remained stretched and fixed as she felt her master thrusting deep into her rear. The slap of his hips to her welt covered cheeks revived and reminded her of every stroke, and as he pulled back and hoisted her gaze up towards the ceiling, she immediately climaxed. The orgasm had little physical reaction because she was already too buried under intense sensations and could acknowledge nothing further.

As Warlord Hachiman held her makeshift reins and continued to fire himself into her, orgasm after orgasm surged through her. Her breath stopped as the relentless tidal wave of ecstasy continued and against all reason, she felt it built higher when she noticed his shaft flick within her and sow warmth deep in her anus.

There was a flash of movement and the support of the rope was gone. Her legs gave out, she collapsed forward, and when she fell, his shaft simply poured from her rear. Candy arched and screamed from the sudden brutal application of pleasure this brought.

Her body slapped to the floor and she curled her limbs in. She placed palms to the cool stone and prayed for strength. Everything was tumbling around her. Her senses were reeling. She felt as though she was about to have a seizure, so fast was her pulse and so agitated was her anatomy.

"Oh God, oh God, oh God," she mumbled, unable to comprehend how mortal physiology could endure such monstrous sensory input and still remain functional.

A hand stroked her hair and she felt her master kneel down and start to soothe her addled form. She immediately devolved into a sobbing fit while she crawled forward and clutched to him for support. The exhilarating sensation of purging once again wafted in as the ferocity of the masochistic frenzy passed. Her gratitude, her adoration, her delight in being his had never been more potent. She wished that she could articulate it, but her awareness of reality was strained to breaking point and she was lost in a realm of sensual excess, one that had almost devoured her whole.

At a most tardy rate, her internal processes began to step back from the precipice and ease her down towards a state resembling normality. She started to become aware of the chamber, of her body, her master, and the lengthening shadows that were stretching through the hall. A few blinks shed the droplets that were clustered on her eyelashes and she saw the two Kamube staring at her. Their eyes were wide and glittering, their jaws were agape and they were literally shivering with excitement and astonishment. Candy closed her eyes and clasped tighter to her master. The awe of other slaves did not even matter. All she needed was her owner.

The scent of his sweat and her own arousal easily swamped the smell of the trees and this perfume continued to keep Candy in a luxurious state.

Warlord Hachiman just continued to caress her and assuage her quaking hide after he had treated it to such harsh attention. No words were needed, she was his, and he knew that her commitment to him was absolute. Words could not capture this bond, and in fact it seemed that they would only sully its purity.

The sound of awkward footsteps and the staccato click of high heels interrupted them. Candy turned and through tear filled eyes saw the maid coming towards them. Her tray was gone and instead, slender cord had been employed to bind her breasts. Both inviting orbs had been bound and then tied together so that they embraced and held a roll of paper that bore a waxen seal on the front.

The woman shuffled over and arched her chest upward in indication. The Warlord set Candy aside, stood up, grabbed the message, and drew it from the tight bondage tunnel. He broke the seal, unrolled it, and quickly took in the contents.

"So it is now official. Excellent."

Hachiman re-rolled the item and slotted it back into place. The woman turned and started to totter away, and Hachiman swung outward to lay the weapon across her cheeks. She gave a muted howl and swayed unsteadily before she regained her stance and continued away at a much swifter rate.

The Warlord grabbed her chin and gazed into her eyes. Candy stared back with utter awe.

"Events are starting to hasten, slave. I will have some Imbe come and prepare you. It will give you a chance to mitigate Lady Uzume's resentment."

She momentarily considered that it was odd that beings that were essentially immortal could still be affected by the constraints of time.

The Warlord smiled and deserted her. Candy curled up and closed her eyes. She focused on easing her mind and soothing her battered body. A few flecks of wax were the last lingering residue of their encounter and she slowly let her fingertips pick them from her skin.

The heavy booted tread of several men started to come from the corridor and she managed to lift her weary head to greet the new arrivals.

The four priests wore dense leather waist cinchers that had sections of steel riveted to them, and this metal had been engraved with various ideograms and spiralling patterns. Matching bracers covered their forearms and a flowing silken skirt draped to the floor to hide their weighty footwear. Each was shaved bald, and intricate and colourful tattoos covered their shoulders and upper chest.

Two of the men walked over to Lady Uzume and began to set her free of the ropes while the other two came to Candy and started to remove her cuffs and then bring her to her feet. Supporting her by the arms, they led her out of the Chamber of Blossoms and down a series of corridors that left the Warlord's private wing and restored her to the rest of the palace. Still a little delirious, she keenly anticipated her next encounter with what the Empire had to offer, especially because her master had suggested that Uzume would be party to it.

# CHAPTER FIVE

Candy was escorted towards the ground floor and delivered to room where a set of steel manacles hung from a chain in the centre of the ceiling and another weighty door existed on the other side of the chamber. Several lamps that were shaped like curling dragons adorned the walls. A tear of blue flame erupted from their spread jaws and together they filled the small room with a sapphire glow.

In the middle of the room was a sunken bath that was surrounded by candles, a series of elegant glass vials, an array of brushes, and several towels. Standing in the warm water were two naked slaves who were immersed to their upper thighs. Their hair was fastened up into a high ponytail and each was equipped with a sponge. The steam rising from the bath had coated them in a glaze of dew and the pale tendrils created a faintly obscuring veil that made the nude women even more teasingly alluring by hiding them from full view.

The perfume in the waters immediately caught Candy's nose and it was an aromatic and enticing scent.

The Imbe marched her forward and a brief set of steps carried her down into the soothing bath. The slaves scooped up her wrists and delivered them into the manacles to leave her stretched up and served to their intentions. The Imbe marched past and took up position on either side of the second door.

The whole process was performed without a word as though it was a mechanical event or a pious ritual, she could not tell which. An event of great importance was imminent so she assumed that this was an almost religious preparation to ensure she was fit to appear at it. Such reverence suggested Kami, and probably more than one. Candy may have been at risk from the plotting and subterfuge of others who sought to possess her because of her former higher birth, but she also got to see and be used by some of the greatest powers in this world. There were ancient and wicked entities that few had ever even seen and they were using her as their pleasure toy.

The women began to sponge water up and over her body with rhythmic motions. Viscous coloured fluids were poured onto her and rubbed into a lather that made the pain in her weals fade and her skin tingle with a superb odorous freshness. She was methodically shaved, and then other gels were worked into her hair before she was rinsed with several jugs that they gathered from the bottom of the bath.

The cuffs were opened and the women led her up the steps on the other side. They stood beside her and embraced within towels so they might dry every inch of her. Once they had finished, they pushed her down onto her knees and began to attend her hair. Combs removed knots and then brushes were poured through the locks to make them fall in silken sheets.

Warm from the bath and pampered so that she felt almost regal, Candy was then offered to the Imbe.

The door was opened and she was shown down a long corridor where six Wani guards cradled combat shotguns and stood to attention against the wall. The warriors were apparently defending a dense reinforced door with iron bands running its edges.

The Imbe pushed open the vault-like door and revealed a large circular hall with a low ceiling. Stone buttresses reached up at the walls and a circle of pillars supported the central area. Situated between each pillar was a dense wooden pole that emerged from the floor and bore a horizontal and padded strut that aimed out towards the wall. Laid before each pole was a pile of dense straps and some other items whose intent was clear because she could see them already installed on other slaves.

Most of the poles bore a gorgeous female whose head was sealed within a tight rubber hood. The gleaming black material had Imperial writing set on the forehead and this proclaimed the identity of a high-ranking officer. She could see names for Warlord Hachiman as well as for the other Fire Kami.

Their fronts were pressed to the pole that ended at their collarbones. The straps hauled them against the wood and their folded legs were also bound to it.

Each woman wore a set of knee high boots of a strange construction. The details were lost in the sedate gloom of this underground cell and also because their heels were buried into their buttocks but there was something definitely strange about the way the heels vanished between their cheeks.

Supported by the padded strut between their legs, each woman hovered in the air with their arms folded back and contained in a single leather sleeve.

Candy's ability to gauge what her fate was to be vanished when she was rapidly escorted towards a vacant pole. The Imbe parted her thighs and she settled down onto the cool leather cushion.

Three thick belts were taken up. One slipped around under her arms, another ran at the base of her shoulder blades, and the third was set into her waist. Small ratchets were applied and the Imbe pumped the levers to steal the slack and slowly create a crushing influence.

Candy felt the stern straps hauling her into the wood and the pressure of the pole into her ribs grew to ferocious levels before the Imbe stopped and turned to the rest of her containment.

She had felt the pole move a little as she was being

attached, which meant that it was not static. The floor was too solid to permit a descent, so she stole a look upward as they acquired the rest of her bondage attire. There was a domed indentation in the ceiling immediately above her and there was also a small hole, one just big enough for her throat. Candy gained insight as to what was coming and was suddenly charged with exaltation. She inhaled as deeply as she could to make the straps bite at her skin and clenched her thighs to the supporting pole.

The triangular sheath of hide was hauled up her arms to contain her fingers at the apex and it was tightened to make her shoulders ache from the severe contortion. Another pair of bands was set over the sleeve to pull her arms into her back and elevate the crimp on her chest.

Another pair of bands was applied to her thighs. The belts pinned them to the post with main force before the priests took up her footwear. The boots were odd indeed because once they had finished applying them, although she found that they both laced up to her knees and held her feet in separate shoes, the heels joined and formed a single strut, the purpose of which was then graphically introduced to her. The slick and rounded stiletto heel was hauled up without warning and Candy whimpered as they bent it inward and tried to locate her orifice.

Her knees and ankles swelled with pain as they bent them around and levied their brawn to make her comply. She flexed her arms and desperately tried to get free and escape, but the Imbe were much stronger than she was.

Candy cried out from the terrible influence and swore that she could not cope with this maltreatment. Nevertheless, the other slaves all wore the same fixture so clearly, despite the fear that her joints would dislocate, she knew it could be done, just so long as no one cared for the effect on the bound prisoner.

The single heel slid into the cleft of her rear, and they snatched this upright length before applying their strength to bend it and take aim. With one of them holding the heel in place, and the other contorting her legs to make her wail, they offered a final haul and then shoved. Candy's legs straightened as much as they could, and the heel breached her sphincter and charged deep into her anus. She launched against the straps and gasped for breath as her bottom throbbed and any movement of her acutely folded shins now caused the inserted heel to pull at her. With her feet held captive by her own tracts, Candy was offered the final part of her uniform.

One Imbe gathered up the rubber hood and the other quickly wove her hair into a brief plait. She saw the words to proclaim her as the slave for Lady Uzume written upon the forehead of the hood a moment before the smooth cool folds were drawn down onto her features. The strong smell of the material floated through her nostrils as she snorted through the two small vents while waiting for the mouth slit to be set in place and permit her unrestricted breath. There were no eye slits so she was left in darkness to await whatever fate had been prescribed for her.

Crushed against the pole and left blind, she listened as three more women were brought in and the sound of ratchets, leather, and latex being deployed drifted through the quiet as well as the groans and cries of the anal heel being installed with customary indifference.

A lengthy pause followed the departure of the Imbe and suddenly the room reverberated with mechanical sounds. Cranking grinding noises rose from below and a similar tune came from above. Candy felt herself being hoisted upward as the pole was pushed towards the roof. The top of the beam struck the ceiling and stopped, telling her that the domed area had opened to let her head emerge through the floor of whatever chamber lay above. A moment later the two slats closed in and touched the base of her neck to create a close seal. She could move her head a little and the room smelled fresh and warm, but she had no other clues as to what was going on.

Bare footsteps entered the room as a small crowd wandered around and then settled in to the rustle of soft cloth and the covert sounds of immediate oral attention. Silk brushed against Candy's hooded head and legs folded around her. The scent of Lady Uzume was unmistakable and with a brief shuffle the woman moved forward to bury Candy's mouth between her legs. The formal cross-legged pose adopted by each occupant now clutched to a diligent female head.

Candy reached forth with her tongue and took a long lick of the succulent pussy of the dominatrix before she began to slowly and carefully pour the flat of her organ against her. Uzume had suffered in the Chamber of Blossoms and her benevolent master had given Candy this chance to ease Uzume's choler. The devotion that she showed the woman was as committed as she could muster and Candy felt herself drowning in submissive ecstasy. She pushed with her feet to churn the heel in her rear and surged against her straps as her hindquarters sought to rock and play herself against the supporting strut. The motion was a hesitant pleasure, one that only helped inspire her to greater oral efforts. Her servile lust was raging and because of it, Candy only managed to place a token attention to the actual events of the meeting.

"Izanagi and Izanami watch over us. The blessing of Sun-Goddess and favour of Moon-God be upon the Great Houses of Fire," stated Warlord Hachiman, and a unified collection of voices repeated the prayer before he continued to address them.

"No doubt you have heard the rumours concerning a move against the other side," said Warlord Hachiman. Just the sound of his voice made Candy shiver and she locked her lips to Uzume's clit to offer it some gentle but adoring sucks.

"For many years, the plain of Izanagi has been subjected to intense research and experimentation. Recently however, the House of Tsuki-yomi has declared that it has enough information to plot the path of Izanami on the other side and permit return voyages for sufficiently large forces."

"I thought only small units could be sent through, like the House Amatsu mika hoshi agents?" asked a jovial male voice.

Candy returned to tickling her mistress with the tip of her tongue as she wondered if this were Ame-waka-hiko, the Mikado of her master. Despite his high rank, she had never even seen this man.

"It seems the obstacle responsible for defeating our endeavours was one that was too obvious for the keen minds of the Moon Gods wise men to grasp," answered Hachiman and the patronising edge in his words gained chuckles of agreement from the other dignitaries.

"Izanami travels within a certain region off that land called Japan, save for occasional fluke openings in a larger area on the other side of the globe. Should Izanami and Izanagi be in conjunction, an interdimensional gateway may form and any material within the area will be drawn through to our world. Izanami is made more energetic and therefore more likely to open a rift should there be quantities of metal present at the time of conjunction. As we know, this allowed the Moon God to plot the paths of both forces on both worlds and send Earth craft into the confluence at the right time to promote the desired rift. By reversing the process, we can reverse the direction of the rift."

"I'm still not sure I grasp what you mean," came the deep hissing voice of Toyotama-hiko. Candy recalled the feel of him ravishing her as Lady Uzume watched, and the recall of his daughters tails within her body caused her to again push and twist her shins so that the sheathed rod teased her rear.

"When Izanami encounters metal, if Izanagi is in the

correct location, the magnetic fields attain a strength sufficient to haul that material and anything else in the area through to the other side. The less metal present, the more closely the alignment must be in order to generate a rift. The more metal that is present, the more inaccurate the confluence required to open one. Now, if enough metal is in the correct location on the plain of Izanagi when this conjunction is plotted in reverse, it is Izanagi that acts as the catalyst whereupon the doorway between worlds will open the other way and the material will be sent across."

"What material will they send? How do they intend to inspire the creators to take us through?" asked Lady Uzume. Her voice was cool and precise, and one would never have thought that an adoring bound female slave was servicing her or indeed anyone else in the room.

"Warships are being created even as we speak. The Houses of Earth and Water are toiling to forge great vessels, each armed and armoured to an intense degree. These battle barges will carry legions of Wani and Mitama through and begin the conquering of Earth. The areas where the rift opens are both mostly composed of water, and so an arrival upon it is likely. But if they arrive on land, the craft can easily be used as static forts from which to send forth our troops, offering them a secure base of operations and a place to retreat to."

"Can the creators be inspired to be so active," asked a male voice that she recognised as that of Warlord Ashua, the guardian of the courtyards and inner lands.

"There is a tunnel between our world and Earth. It seems that the molten iron cores of our respective worlds and the electromagnetic fields they create keep each end of the tunnel in existence and do so above an area where some sort of potent spatial disruption occurred during the initial forming of our planets. These areas on the core lie directly beneath the plain of Izanagi, and also beneath a triangular area of ocean on Earth. Apparently, occasional random fluctuations in the magnetic fields cause the Vortex to invert and this is what creates openings on the other side of the Earth, or deposits them as Strays on our side. Because these forces are generated by and funded by magnetic power, metallic elements play a significant role in their functioning. Therefore, powerful electromagnets are being arranged on these warships. Tuned correctly, they will generate a potent field that will effectively make them seem hundreds of times larger to Izanagi. With such a vast metallic goad, even a slight alignment will be enough to generate a rift and this will also work to bring them back. Effectively House Tsuki-yomi has created a limited but nevertheless highly efficient means of two way inter-dimensional travel for the Kami Empire."

"The powers of the Earth nations will simply launch nuclear weapons and vaporise our armada the moment it appears," snarled a potent male voice, one that resonated with a hint of jealousy and a greater degree of resentment towards the power and threat of atomic weaponry. Candy could guess that this was Take-mika-dzuchi because only the Warlord of the artillery regiments would be so vexed by being outmatched in this specific field of warfare.

"Agents of House Amatsu mika hoshi are already working on global destabilisation. Old feuds are being re-ignited and lingering hatreds fanned. Whole regions are being pushed towards civil war, open conflict, invasion, or to dangerous experimentation so as to cause outrage. Acts of sabotage and destruction are being used to keep the rancour of the various factions vibrant and when the time comes, the Houses of Fire will manifest and expand across their oceans. Before anyone has determined a course of action we will be on their lands and those ships that arrived on the ground will be inside other nations, stalling any nuclear reprisal against them out of fear of contaminating their own, hurting an ally, or irking an enemy. The Houses of Water are massing their own armies and will be instrumental in securing the oceans. Domination of the skies has been instrumental for nations to prosper on Earth but now, we of the Empire shall hold rule of the depths where they are powerless save for a few lurching submarines. With this exclusive lair we can take dry land with ease."

"It seems that much rests on the Houses of Water in this endeavour," offered Lady Uzume.

"A correct observation," offered Hachiman.

"If our House is to rely on them to ferry us to the foe, I would appreciate some faith in their tactics and forces," she continued.

"Which is why we are going to visit them. The Kami of Water are being called to the palace of Toyo-tama-hiko to discuss the recent news. We will be travelling in howdah with a cavalry escort."

"I thought it was a celebration because his Mikado was just given the honour of another sip of Lingzhi."

"A useful coincidence to cover their congregation. The Sun-Goddess informed only I and the Supreme Warlord of Water about the plan in order to give us time to arrange our affairs. If we proceed correctly, when the news is revealed properly and officially to all the Great Houses, our armies will be ready, and confidence will be inspired in all because of our apparent meticulous foresight."

"What do you wish of us in the meantime, Warlord?" asked Toyotama-hiko.

"Ready to visit the undersea palace and make the usual gifts and offerings. Enjoy yourselves, be gracious guests, but remember that we have an ulterior motive. Use your best agents, keep your enquiries subtle, and find out as much as possible about the readiness of the Houses of Water. In particular, any hints as to experimental forces and weapons, or new and unannounced tactics or changes in leadership. Who is in favour? Who is not? These are the trinkets of data that will prove a most valuable coin. No doubt the Warlords will reciprocate and seek the same from us but reply honestly and without exaggeration. I am confident in our forces and the truth is the sharpest of swords. Lies shall only dull that blade," he stated, and then paused to let these final words attain appropriate gravity.

"You have the day to ready yourselves."

The assembled guests began to rise but as Lady Uzume shifted, the Warlord addressed her.

"Lady Uzume. I wish you to remain."

"Yes, Warlord," she answered with a small hint of satisfaction. She quickly settled back down and continued to relish Candy's attentions.

The other Kami bowed, offered their gratitude to Hachiman, and filed out. Once the room was cleared of all save Lady Uzume and her owner, they continued their conversation.

"Is Candy pleasing you, my most trusted agent?"

"Yes, Warlord. A most gratifying servile. Not too fast and not too slow. Dedicated and precise, as I desire."

"Excellent," he announced, and then their secret meeting began in earnest as Candy's heart swelled with pride and she continued to offer her tongue and the techniques she had learned to her mistress.

"It regards the approaches of Toyotama-hiko," said Hachiman.

"I am loyal only to you, Warlord," she replied with stern conviction.

"Of course, but we are rapidly approaching the greatest day of the Kami Empire, and I intend to leave as little to chance as possible."

"What do you wish of me, Warlord."

"My Mikado will handle the Mitama adequately, but I will

require you to undertake a mission to cover other eventualities," said Hachiman with soft tones that hinted at a nefarious duty.

"I am yours to command," was Uzume's unequivocal response.

"News of a stray arrival will soon reach the Houses. A cargo vessel, one filled with illegal arms that were purchased and shipped out by the Imperial agents on Earth. Supposedly these arms are for some civil conflict abroad and while they are smuggled across the ocean they are being sent on the correct heading to have them sail straight into a suitably intense congregation of Izanagi and Izanami. Unfortunately, the cargo vessel did not appear on the plain and was deposited in the Eastern Provinces."

"A most valuable prize. You wish me to mount an expedition for it?"

"Yes, but you will find nothing. You will fail and earn my displeasure."

Candy felt Lady Uzume's thighs clench and a stunned silence followed. Candy accelerated her attention to try and help ease the woman's obvious dejection.

"I . . . Warlord, I would never . . ."

"The news is false. I have already arranged this fake report with the Moon-God, along with other considerations for our future," announced Hachiman. Candy could feel Uzume trembling.

"Why am I . . . have I . . ." she stuttered, but the Warlord merely continued to enlighten her as Candy thrashed her tongue to the woman's pussy to try and commiserate her.

"When you fail, Toyotama-hiko will again approach you. Your recent failure will make you receptive to his words of dissent. You will accept joint responsibility for the Wani and this matter will be taken to the Moon-God, whose agreement I have already arranged. News of your failure will arrive while I attend the gathering of the Water Houses as a guest, and my reaction to your failure will cement their unity in backing your appointment as co-ruler of an independent House of Wani. This formidable power base will assure the blessing of the Sun-Goddess and you will be made co-ruler of House Wani."

"Warlord, you wish me sent away. Why?" she asked with an almost sorrowful tone.

"The people of Earth will be fleeing in terror when legions of armoured Wani begin pouring across their soil. Our cavalry is likely to have a similar effect. However, in the aftermath of victory comes a harder duty—that of holding what we have conquered. It will be easy to sway rulers and elite, and the Mitama are more than capable of policing the cities. However, the rural lands and areas where the stalwart shall retreat to will have to be tackled by the Wani. Failures will occur unless a more level head is there to temper Toyotama-hiko's more *unruly* decisions."

"He is indeed a ferocious warrior and will attack without mercy," she offered calmly, but her thighs were still holding tightly to Candy's head. Uzume's fright was clear. "So I assume that guerrilla forces in hiding will exploit his rashness and use it to their advantage to generate sympathy and help prolong rebellion."

"Defeats will reflect poorly on the Houses of Fire, and House Hachiman in particular. I have heard the whispers that I have too much power, especially from the Water Houses. If I am the Supreme Warlord in the assault on Earth, these whispers will become less indistinct and will inspire plotting against me. If the Wani regiments are taken from me, in addition to my own most vaulted agent, these voices will be quietened while also helping distance our House from any failings the Wani may endure. If I were to continue to hold the Wani, all of their failures will be mine, and those who think I am too powerful will have all the justification they need to take *everything* from me."

"So you want to arrange this situation so that he accepts me as an equal without fear that I am still your agent?" she asked.

"You will always be mine, Lady Uzume. This subterfuge is being orchestrated to solidify the power of our House and leave us ruling a stable Earth. The Wani will be instrumental in the coming war. They are a berserker force, while the Mitama are a more cogent weapon to be used with more discretion and with more effective results. When Wani are inevitably slain in large numbers, I have no intention of being held accountable for it."

"But I will be. Especially if I am sharing their rule equally."

"And just as Toyotama-hiko will accept you as his compeer to escape my displeasure and the consequences of failure, I will accept you back into my House for the very same reason."

"But who will be blamed for making off with the shipment of arms? If I am accused, I will be shamed and stripped of all title. Even Toyotami-hiko will not dare approach such an outcast."

"Rumours of disloyalty will only make your change of allegiance seem more genuine, but there will be a more immediate result in fears that the Eastern Provinces have taken it. I will encourage these rumours to mitigate the ones of your involvement. The powers are more likely to fear an enemy country than persecute an individual scapegoat."

Uzume calmed and settled down as it started to become clear that her master was relating a massive plan, one that would change the fate of the Empire and also completely rework the destiny of Earth. The invasion and subjugation of her entire home planet was being discussed at this table and Candy felt it strange that she bore no other opinion or feeling on the matter save how she could tickle her mistress" pussy with her tongue and fulfil her own desires.

"If they were so effectively armed with Earth weapons people might believe they could be inspired to attack the Empire," she considered.

"Especially when we draw in such a large portion of our forces to send across to Earth. A weakened Kami Empire might make them bold enough to try and breach the shield wall and invade."

"But how could they possibly know what we are doing?"

"The possibility of spies cannot be discounted. It would be a simple feat to let a dedicated agent be taken as a slave and once in our palaces they could learn much."

"I see," uttered Uzume as she mulled over the possibilities and like Candy, wondered if any slave she had seen, whipped, bound, or ravished, might have been such an agent.

"The invasion of Earth is risky and by no means guaranteed. It would be wise to ensure we have a secure home to retreat to in the event of catastrophe."

"Earth has no clue that the Vortex even exists. They allocate losses to supernatural forces, the wrath of the sea, covert operations, and other simplicities. Without the ability to track Izanami, even if they finally detect Izanagi, they cannot find a way across to pursue us in the event of retreat," said Uzume.

"A strong argument, but I would not like to find out otherwise if our affairs on Earth take a dire turn. Should they find a means to pursue us across, then our position would be uncomfortable. Hostile beings could be in the heart of the Empire and if stray travellers land elsewhere on Pangaea they might decide to unite with the Provinces in a bid to do away with us."

"The Eastern Provinces are to be crushed?" asked Uzume.

"A tactical warm up before the main battle and a precaution for the future. We have tolerated their existence long enough," said Hachiman with a vague snarl. Candy could assume that the Eastern Provinces were populated by the other nations of the orient and because of the Empire's Japanese heritage some hint of the old hatreds was likely to have remained, creating enmity between the displaced descendants of those lands.

"What of the Wastelands?"

"Ignore them. Bandits, panhandlers, ranchers, farmers, and cutthroats. Disorganised self-absorbed rabble that we can easily brush aside on our way to make the Provinces pay for their supposed theft of Imperial property."

"Pangaea will be ours," she purred and Candy felt her twitch as she neared climax.

"And then so too will Earth," growled Hachiman when he too was spurned on towards orgasm.

"Oh the Empire will endure forever," panted Uzume and Candy thrashed her tip to the woman's clitoris as she groaned with delight. Uzume had been reassured that she was Hachiman's, that she was to be offered a duty of absolute importance and that afterwards she could once again be returned to the loving ownership of her master. The thought of conquest, intrigue, and ownership brought her abruptly to ecstatic fulfilment.

"And House Hachiman will be standing at its forefront with Lady Uzume restored to its ranks in the long and reassuring peace that will follow," he announced as Uzume cried out and clutched to Candy's head to endure her frenzied attentions.

Lady Uzume pushed Candy's head back, signalling an end to her efforts. The woman compiled her breath.

"I will prepare the expedition immediately, Warlord. Should I allow our forces to come under attack?"

"Your reasoning?" asked Hachiman and he spoke through clenched teeth while savouring the rhapsody wrought by his own oral slave.

"I can send scout forces towards Suju, on Calaloom Lake. It is a vital source of imported bamboo for the region and will most likely attack, fearing Imperial invasion. A small retaliation force could sustain heavy losses against the town, and this could further cause the Houses to suspect the Provinces of malice towards us."

"Do not endanger yourself in this mission. You are too valuable," he panted.

"I will remain with the primary force, Warlord."

"Your idea meets with my approval," said Hachiman and then growled with bliss before bringing the toil of his servant to a halt. "The slaying of Mitama and Wani, especially by those who stole from us will have every House bellowing for radical action. I will miss you at my side during the coming fray."

"As will I being at it, Warlord," murmured Uzume, and pushed herself back onto her feet. With her mistress gone, Candy licked her lips and quivered with lecherous happiness at having performed so well.

The two leaders stood up and strode from the room, leaving a collection of rubber sheathed heads surrounding an empty table, each coursing with inflamed libidos but unable to do anything about it save churn the heel that was thrust into their bottoms.

# CHAPTER SIX

Even though the meeting had ended, the priests and slaves of the Great House were still intent on drawing Candy through the same revered ritual of preparation. Once released from the pole, she was again bathed, and fresh cosmetic shades were applied. They were far more blatant with her makeup this time and after powdering her face until it was an unblemished white, they darkened her eyes and surrounded this heavy shading with elegant black swirls. The colours they added around and within the patterns rose from a dark crimson and faded out to create vibrant red and yellow tips. Her lips were painted the same violent red with a yellow vertical line placed in the middle of her bottom lip.

Once her features had been painted to an extent that it made it hard for her to even recognise her own reflection, an ornate headdress was established. It locked into her hair and the extravagant item had numerous curling silver limbs that bore many fine jewels and other detailed ornaments. The gems swayed with her movements and sparkled against the light, making her feel like a regal monarch. As wealthy as she had once been, even she would never have been able to acquire such an item, but the material was no longer the measure with which she judged her success. The vaulted taste of Uzume on her tongue, and the exquisite possibility of her master's attention trivialised the value of even this jewel-soaked treasure.

Fine stockings and a suspender belt was the only consideration to an undergarment before she was slipped into a pair of ankle boots. The red patent affairs had a towering heel and a buckled band that ran over the top of the white laces.

Finally, she was eased into a voluminous but gossamer kimono. The delicate fabrics tickled her skin with every movement and once it was fastened about her waist with a wide band of folded material, she was escorted towards the main entrance of the palace.

The diligent processing of her body and application of her attire had left Candy in a daze. Her head was already swimming from acute arousal at having serviced Lady Uzume while bound so tightly, and she could still feel a vague ache in her rear from the anal stiletto. Often during her passage she clenched just to intensify the discomfort and this immediately inflamed her libido.

The halls and corridors passed by and she felt as though she was floating through them, lost in a wonderful and perverse dream. However, what awaited her in the courtyard immediately snapped her from this listless state.

Six monstrous Brontosaurs dominated the view. The huge quadrupeds were over a hundred feet from the tip of their long tails to the snout that was supported on a long and serpentine neck. Their massive bodies had been painted with convoluted patterns and dazzling colours that made them seem even more unreal, and upon their backs had been set a glorious three storey miniature palace.

The ornate pagodas had fluted roofs and considerable superfluous decoration. Gemstones were set on golden lattices and there were sufficient quantities on just one side to have purchased a small country. The mobile palaces glowed in the sunlight and were dazzling displays of absolute scrupulous opulence.

Protecting these lofty domains were ranks of Tyrannosaurs. The monstrous fifty-foot-tall predators were clad in a dense layer of armour, as were the Mitama warriors resting in the saddle, each with a variety of firearms sheathed around them. Banners bore the emblems of the Houses of Fire and the great monsters stood still and obedient to the command of their rider.

One of the palaces extended a pair of elegant arms from its side. Winches paid out a length of chain and a small wooden platform was delivered to the ground. Candy was shown onto this lift and abandoned there.

Without warning her ascent began. She immediately grabbed one of the support chains and watched nervously as the land dropped away. Beset with a little hint acrophobia, she held tighter and was hoisted up the side of the great beast before reaching the doors of the great howdah.

The dark wooden portal bore the emblem of House Hachiman and it had been engraved and filled with what looked like titanium. She pushed the portal open and revealed the sumptuous lounge of the lowest floor of the dwelling. It appeared much like the room she had been brought to the Empire in, with wooden pillars to help support the upper storeys and pillows and drapes established everywhere. In addition to the considerations for comfort she could see dense rings and other locations that would be ideal to anchor a captive and to one side, upon a series of racks were hung meticulously woven bundles of brightly coloured rope.

Candy closed the door behind her and settled down onto her knees to await her master.

A few minutes passed as the convoy finished its preparations and then a mighty note sounded on a horn. The howdah started to rock gently and it was borne away from the palace and off into the rest of the Empire.

The spiral staircase in the rear of the chamber echoed with footfalls and Hachiman marched down into view. Dressed in the regal and functional armour of his rank, his face was hidden by a ceramic mask that depicted a snarling demonic face.

The eyepieces were opaque and she could see hints of technological apparatus about them.

The Warlord marched past her, whirled, and stood to attention beside a wooden frame. Candy realised what he wanted from her and she summarily shuffled over to begin stripping off his armour.

Starting at the shoulder guards she begin to unfasten straps and untie laces before setting the pieces onto the frame whose hooks and slots greatly helped her figure out the correct location for each part.

"I do so enjoy a good long howdah ride. A few days separated from all the duties of the House and nothing but indulgence and rest," he said lightly.

Candy continued to remove the armour, paying extreme care as it started to reassemble next to her. Some of the plates were very heavy and she could see that as with Iha, they were highly decorated sections of ceramic composite, some of which had hidden blades and other items located covertly upon or inside them. It occurred to her that although he was a powerful and wealthy leader, he was also a masterful warrior and could lead by example as well as with an undeniable order.

Finally, beneath the shell she found a second layer of defence. It almost looked like a normal bullet-proof vest but it seemed to be made of woven discs, all forged from the same advanced substance. The final effect made it look as though he wore scales and Candy surmised that because each disc had its own separate integrity, it would be even harder to puncture this final layer of armour and reach her masters flesh. It seemed that the immortality of the Kami extended to immunity to age and disease but not violence, and so they made sure to defend themselves from this eventuality with their consummate level of perfection.

"You have ridden in a howdah before, slave?"

"No, Warlord. Lady Uzume collected me in a vast coach."

"Well, let us ensure your first experience is a memorable one," he said. The libidinous snarl in his voice made Candy tremble with anticipation and without further discussion he collected rope and began to bind her.

# Chapter Seven

Lady Uzume accepted her daisho from Ammalia and fixed the blades into place on her belt. Armed with sheathed katana and wakizashi, she turned to the more advanced defences that her Mikado was currently offering her.

"Travelling a little heavy this voyage aren't we, Lady Uzume?" asked Warlord Ashua. The warrior looked about the courtyard as Wani rushed around, forming into tightly organised ranks while Mitama clambered up the sides of armoured dinosaurs and slipped into saddles.

Uzume took the assault rifle and slapped a fresh drum magazine into place before cocking the potent weapon. The ground gave a shudder when the monstrous clawed foot of her mount landed a few yards away. The Tyrannosaur gave a hissing murmur as it pulled on its reins. It could smell the open plains and was eager to run amok.

"Hardly," she replied while shouldering the rifle. "I'll be leaving my Mikado, my Nakatomi, and all my pets behind this time."

"So what will you do to entertain yourself during this mission?" Ashua asked casually.

A priest scrambled down the flank of her mount, bowed deeply after delivering his charge, and then jogged away.

"This is no paltry foray into the Wastelands for some trivial toy. A shipment of firearms was lost and may have appeared either near, or actually in the Provinces," she grumbled.

Uzume reached up and fondly stroked the chin of her Mikado. She would miss her servants on this trip but she had no wish to endanger them or tangle them in the plot that was being orchestrated. Her deliberate failures abroad might attach disgrace to them and she loved them too much to do that.

"You think they are advanced enough to actually use them?"

"I'm not taking any chances. Whether they have the cache or not, I am charged with its recovery."

"A perilous mission then," said Ashua.

"Very."

"Well, Masuda is an excellent warrior and an experienced Tyrannosaur rider. He will be a most efficient second in command and will serve you well."

"We shall see. Now, if you will excuse me Warlord, I must depart."

"Sun-Goddess and Moon-God bring fortune and victory, and may they clear your path of danger," he offered.

Her Mikado and two Nakatomi bowed deeply and remained where they were. Their farewells had been made in private and Uzume's head was cool and collected after such a passionate coupling.

"For the Empire," she replied, and started to climb up the side of her mount and then enter the massive saddle. She settled into place and began to apply the harness that would stop her being tossed free when the monstrous beast commenced its run.

"Open the gates," roared Ashua and the great portal started to crank open and expose the dry and barren plains beyond.

Uzume took the reins and pulled to turn the great carnivore around. Immediately behind her were several dozen mounted Mitama and while the elite cavalry all rode Tyrannosaur, three times their number each rode a Megalosaur. Behind these ranks were two battalions of Wani who would march at the flanks of the expeditions supplies which were borne by trio of Diplodocus. Each massive quadruped bore a hardened three-storey howdah with battlements atop it and machine gun nests situated on turrets at each corner. Spikes jutted from the small forts to dissuade boarding and arrow slits with dense bamboo shutters flecked every level.

The centre howdah was her private abode, but Uzume had decided she wanted to take her steed for a run while they were still near the safety of the great wall. The denizens of Pangaea rarely came close to the Empire's primary line of defence. However, hateful locals would not be able to resist a chance to sniper a Kami so once they had travelled deeper into the Wastelands she would have to ensconce herself in the armoured howdah and conduct the mission from its impregnable chambers. Another consideration was that her mount was chomping at the bit to enjoy a sprint, and a Tyrannosaur bred for war had quite a chomp so it would be wise to calm it down.

Uzume drew her sword and hoisted it high into the air. A turn of the blade caught the sun and made it flash against the eyes of her troops.

"I conquer!" she bellowed.

The Mitama repeated their motto with gusto and the Wani screeched with frenzied fealty. The ground then shuddered as it was pounded by hundreds of tons of armoured reptilian feet. The force started to march through the gates and Uzume found her mount agitated and a little unresponsive, it could see open land and wanted to bound across it.

One of the first perils she might encounter this close to the wall would be the Saur. The tribes in this region were fragmented and weak but still not to be ignored, so she kept her mount reined in until the entire advance unit were through the gates. As part of a group, she could then let the great beast gallop.

Uzume knew a lot about Saur and had studied these

matters at length in preparation for any missions involving the species. The mountain range that started at Saseho — where her master was heading — stretched south for hundreds of miles down the middle of a great peninsula. On the east, the Wastelands finally gave way to dense jungle where amiable tribal primates dwelt, but the western side of the range held great plains of grassland in which roamed massive herds of untamed dinosaurs as well as many tribes of their evolved kin. It was here, in these Wild Lands, was where the first clutches of eggs had been stolen to breed the Wani. Uzume herself had made several trips into this realm to acquire fresh batches to replenish the genetic stock.

The Saur tribes dwelt in the mountains or in places that occupied an elevated position such as a rocky outcrop or small plateau on which they basked during the day, gathering the heat and energy to fund their activities at night.

These locations were easily identifiable because they were covered in etchings that detailed the history and actions of the tribe. The locations also kept them up and out of the way of passing carnivores but not safe from Imperial retrieval units.

Uzume had been surprised to find that the Saur made no distinction between male and female. In their society, the most skilled members of the tribe hunted, while the less competent gathered firewood, and the hardy but slow guarded their tribal ground.

The Wani worshipped the Kami, but their uncivilised brethren still worshiped the sun because it was a provider of heat, a creator of growth, and a hatcher of their young. Fire was seen as a sacred avatar of their god and was used on the most pious of occasions, especially when making an offering to their deity. This residual belief was maintained in the Wani and assisted the Houses of Fire in cementing their loyalty.

Those outside the Empire often assumed that the Lizards, as they called them, were cooking their food, but Saur could only ingest meat in its raw form. In truth, they were making an offering to their deity and serving it up through its avatar.

The Saur believed that strength and other skills were an innate property of the flesh, and so, by devouring the bearer of these desired qualities, they acquired them. This resulted in Saur often wearing talismans. These feathers, teeth, and bone fragments from prized kills were worn as spiritually evocative jewellery that ensured the consumed traits remained strong through the connection to this relic of the flesh. This belief also caused them to burn certain highly prized offerings because it transferred such qualities to their deity, the sun.

There was a single pass that breached the mountain range in the extreme northern range a few hundred miles south east of Saseho. Here the Empire came in force to gather the most powerful specimens to raise as Wani. To Wastelander eyes, the area was one to avoid because wild Saur preyed on each other and due to the lack of dinosaurs in such inhospitable terrain, they had become cannibals. In truth, the pass was considered a testing ground for the strongest of the Saur and those seeking to become the most accomplished of warriors often migrated there to try to join a tribe and learn from it in this unique feudal setting.

Saur who could survive and flourish there returned home to their tribe and became the most valued of members because of their extensive combat experience. With a psyche and anatomy forged against intense warfare, such Saur were the most sought after of mates and their story often ended up carved on the tribal territory.

However, those who could not withstand the psychological and physical demands of this eternal battleground were shamed and dared not return home lest the negative traits in their anatomy be carried back to weaken their tribes. These Saur headed deeper into the Wastelands where they eked a new life and competed with the indigenous humans for territory and food. Their shame and desperation made them unpredictable and a constant hazard even to an Imperial task force. The chance for redemption by attacking Wani would be too great to resist, especially because they regarded the Empire as a sort of devil entity, one that stole their young and then corrupted or possessed them.

Uzume's mount gave another growl and pulled impetuously at its reins. Uzume felt confident that the plains would be safe for a time. Saur rarely came within artillery range of the wall and humans would be too afraid to approach. She decided to let her steed get some exercise and calm it down. With a mild flick of her reins the great monster obeyed with alacrity. The lurch of acceleration would have torn her from the saddle had it not been for her safety harness, and suddenly she was rocketing across the open land at an exhilarating pace.

The wind pulled at Uzume's armour as the great steed rushed onward. With a howl of elation she tightened her hold on the reins and brought the beast to a full run. Having been cooped up in the stables for the last few weeks the creature was anxious to comply.

Uzume was concerned about the unknown hazards that awaited her in this savage realm, but a long gallop would help clear her thoughts and let her focus. She could not be distracted by fantasies about Candy's delicious tongue between her thighs or her master's manhood between her lips. She had a duty to attend and there was no time for play.

# CHAPTER EIGHT

For a week, the great conveyance continued to march along through the lands of the Empire, heading always south. Candy found the time most tranquil. She waited on and served her owner in any way he wanted, be it the bringing of food from the uppermost level of the howdah, being bound and used beside him in his sumptuous bed in the centre storey, or being tied up and ravished in the lower level.

Hachiman exclusively used the store of rope and this simple medium created a seemingly endless encyclopaedia of positions and effects. Hachiman wove the strands upon her with the dedication of an artisan and as she was lost within knot and pattern, he would contort and twist her until she was sobbing for him to take her. Sometimes he assented, and sometimes he merely studied her travail and frustrations as her body glittered with sweat and strained against the cocoon that embraced it. Hog-ties, suspension, inversion, she never knew what he would do with her next. The nights spent bound and helpless beside him were amongst her most treasured because often in the night as each breath fought whatever fierce bondage encompassed her, his hand would stray onto her and appraise his possession.

Candy had never felt so abandoned to another as she now did with Hachiman. Her sense of self was almost gone. She was more an extension of his whim, part of him that he could use to amuse as the mood took him while the days rushed by. The level of peace and gratification she felt could not have been more absolute and for a time, all plotting, mystery, and scheming was forgotten as the howdah became her whole world.

# CHAPTER NINE

L ady Uzume continued to bounce against her harness as her
  steed trotted along the edge of the forest. They had been
travelling east for many days and she had grown frustrated
with the inactivity in her transport. Uzume was tingling with
need. She had not anticipated just how vexing it would be to
deprive herself of pets, priests, and slaves. She yearned to
bind and punish a struggling form, or to subject herself to Hachiman's devious attention.

Uzume's savage desires had been further inflamed when
she found a store of toys and restraints. The chests had been
looked over when the carriage was being readied for travel,
and to have these items at her disposal without a body to use
them on was quite maddening.

She had played with some self-bondage and often pleasured herself as she remained alone, bored, and idle within the
rooms. She could not take a lover from her force because she
was Kami and had to remain the pure deified military leader
so she could properly inspire and motivate them.

Joining the scout force had been a means to clear her head
of this lustful frenzy but already she was succumbing to the
temptation of some sly pleasure.

Taking hold of the lower belts, she gave them a truculent
haul. They tightened another couple of notches and pulled
her against the saddle. Uzume gave a soft moan as the steady
lurching sway of her steed continued to jostle her and grind
her into the seat with rhythmic motions.

Her hands clenched tighter to the reins as her eyes rolled

and deep sighs made the harness distinct against her chest. The pleasure between her legs started to heighten as every sway dragged her loins back and forth. Uzume licked her lips and dreamed of a bound and contorted Candy, her supple body fighting its bondage as she pulled down and brutally tightened a nice leather hood onto her head. Uzume mentally replaced the saddle with Candy's smothered nose and glorified in the thought of her slave's angst as her mistress used her face like a sex toy. She pictured teasing her with dialogue, revelling in her usage of her property, taunting her with how she would have to make do with just the scent of her mistress because she wasn't going to get the chance to taste of her. Uzume then imagined the mortified mews and shivers of her concubine.

It was a nefarious masturbation, and Uzume fought to keep up the façade that she was still attentive to her duty and not stealing orgasm. The small squad did not notice her shivering within her armour and grinding her teeth as she struggled to hold back her hollers. The climax was long and ferocious, especially because of its hidden nature. Such iniquity made it all the more succulent and when she could take no more without screaming she gave a strained bellow to call the force to a halt.

She hauled at the reins and her steed slowed. The last few steps still made her shift and Uzume shook with profligate strain from enduring the last few sumptuous rubs of the saddle against her sex.

To offer a reason for the delay, she drew a telescope from her saddlebag and lifted it to her eye. Panting softly, she smiled within her helmet and hid her recovery with some faked scanning of what lay ahead.

The forest to the north was a dense and foreboding place, quite unlike the lush and scrupulously tended woods of the Empire. They were still travelling in the Wastelands and because this land was largely the preserve of western civilisations, the forest had been named after an assassinated president of old. The exact name eluded her because she had not studied the reports on Earth history for some time.

In the distant east she could see a brief range of mountains. These peaks would be her point of access into the Provinces and they formed a hub that divided this continent. Several rivers poured from the mountains and merged to wander north until they reached the sea. This formed the western boundary of the Provinces. A great lake on the other side of the mountain range fed a river that rolled south to the ocean, and this separated the Wastelands from the Savage Lands. The lake also sent several waterways east to give the Provinces a natural border to the realm to their south. These Savage Lands were filled with dense tropical jungle and dark reports suggested that some sort of advanced intelligence lurked there. Vague reports from various expeditions told of the walking dead and of strange lights in the sky, but nothing could be confirmed.

Uzume put away her telescope and loosened her harness a little. The mountains were getting close and they had left the main force quite a way behind. The Wani could run all day to keep up with the supply column, but the cavalry could cover considerably more ground and make sure the path ahead was clear. Uzume had got a little carried away with her jaunt but she needed to stay out of her howdah or she would go mad with frustration.

Deciding to risk travelling further, she kicked her steed into a run and continued towards the peaks.

# CHAPTER TEN

Warlord Hachiman was resting upon a small hill of pillows and observing Candy as she suffered. It was a torturous pose, and she was trying to cope with its demands as best she could but its unpredictable nature made this hard. Only the image of her owner kept her quiet save for the odd mewl and whimper. She bore no resentment to her master, rather she cursed the dinosaur bearing them because every misstep or tiny distortion in its measured tread made her suffer.

She was laid supine and was willingly arched up into a ferocious bow that made her spine throb. The position was so acute that she almost rested on the top of her head and this was how she acquired her inverted view of her owner and thereby the inspiration to continue to show courage.

A large pliant ball gag had been forced over her lips and it spread her jaws wide and swelled her cheeks. She could not regurgitate this choking orb because a slim wooden strut, much like a chopstick, had been slipped into each nostril and then brought down over the exposed bulbous front of the gag before the other end was captured by cord. The strand held both bases and went around her head. The result was that any attempt to push the gag out stretched and pained her nostrils.

Her chest had been encased in both cross sections and horizontal lines of rope. They squeezed her breasts together and held a tall red candle that jutted straight upward from her cleavage. Her arms were crossed behind her and they had been pulled fiercely to her back. Meanwhile, her legs had been splayed wide before her calves had been drawn to the backs of her thighs and the limbs melded together within an intricate plexus. Lines of rope reached from her knees and connected to her arms, ensuring that she could refuse the lewd split.

A crotch rope gnawed at her hindquarters and another large candle was pressed between the lips of her pussy. Both candles had been burning for a lengthy duration and any movement on her behalf made them wiggle and dribble wax down their sides and onto her most sensitive areas. Only by keeping to her agonising pose and by suppressing every tremble could she stop the candles from tormenting her with molten wax.

As time continued to pass and the candles ate away at their length, the degree of movement that would bring pain grew less. Soon, even the most minor twitch send a sudden line of liquid fire down the waxen towers and she would squeak and mew when it reached breasts and crotch to impart burning torment.

The candles were at a level where she could feel the warmth of the flame on her skin, and any misstep by the dinosaur caused another trickle of wax to streak down the sides from the large well. Frozen lines had already reached down her breasts and had extended onto her neck and chest as well as to form frozen stalactites from her shivering buttocks.

Candy had been concentrating on absorbing every wobble, but the candles now held a great reservoir behind flimsy walls and she knew that these dams would soon crumble and the whole pool would spill upon her. She wished she had moved more often and gradually released the amount before they built up to this degree, but the scorching touches had made her fearful enough to hope that her master would let her out before the candles reached her. It seemed that he was in one of his more spiteful mood this day and wanted to see her truly squirm.

Hachiman stretched his naked body and then lifted himself back onto his feet. Candy gave a whimper of elation to see him rise and choose to end her gloom but when he arrived at her side he did not extinguish the candles.

The desire to ask for mercy was strong, yet the need to remain obedient still kept her silent. The gag helped a little because if she started throwing her pleas against it, then the sticks would again dig into and push at her nostrils.

A series of droplets from a new candle landed on her thigh and Candy gave a shocked gasp before she scowled with endurance. More drops landed on the other thigh and she shuddered a little. A brief dribble escaped her pussy candle and ran down between her legs to reach her sphincter. This made her chest sag from its pose and some drops landed near her nipple. Candy groaned and strained herself back into the arch that kept the candles erect.

Hachiman used the new candle and added some more drops to her exposed stomach, and then another few drips to her shoulders. Targeting regions that had not been touched thus far brought flares of fresh travail and made it even harder to remain where she was.

A slow methodical deluge began to spatter her, each spot unleashing a jolt of lucent misery before it cooled. The rhythmic landings were driving her mad and her body screamed for her to just hurl herself aside and escape them. This defiant movement would only pour all of the fiery candles stash of wax onto her intimate regions and what was of greater concern would be the pain of her owner's discipline for such disobedience. Candy knew that her present distress would be minor compared to such an eventuality.

Drops began to avoid her metal collar and land on her stretched throat and Candy cried out as they slid down the exposed skin and reached to the back of her head. She bared her teeth and snorted for breath while Hachiman continued to apply drip after drip across her body and throat.

A horn sounded and reached out even over the deep background noise of gigantic reptilian stomps.

"Ah, Saseho. It seems our ride is almost over," announced Hachiman.

Candy heard him blow out all three candles and then her sigh of relief became a scream as he nudged those that were bound to her. The pair spilled their entire searing contents and her torso jerked up in response, only to be stopped by her bondage. The ropes twanged taut and she dropped back down and convulsed while the heat gouged into her tormented body.

The pain started to dwindle and she shook and sobbed freely as her owner started to unfasten the ropes. While he worked, Candy lowered her body back down onto her arms. Her neck was resounding with lingering pangs from the time she had spent hoisting herself up by it but her delight at having made it through the session left her feeling satisfied and accomplished.

Candy was slowly extracted from her bondage and her shivering body caused the solidified wax to crack and fall away. When all had been removed and the gag was taken out, he enclosed her within his arms and she wept tears of utmost euphoria.

Once she had calmed down, Hachiman arose and snapped a leash to her collar. He drew her onto her feet and Candy walked awkwardly after him as he headed upstairs and to one of the forward facing windows. With a grand gesture he threw open the shutters and revealed their destination to her.

The lush lands of the Empire stretched forth in all directions with farms, fields of crops, and corrals of small dinosaur herds. The convoy was heading south and crossing a great stone bridge. The river it vaulted quickly widened and spread out into a small bay before entering a body of water that stretched out over the horizon.

Sitting on the headwaters was a sprawling elegant settlement. Larger than a town but not quite a city, there was a significant port with many huge junks flocked before it.

As the river spread ever outwards, the land to the right became a rocky delta while the land to the to the left hoisted great ragged cliffs. They jumped from the waters and turned into a sky piercing mountain range that reached onwards into the distance. It was plain that the cliffs were formed from broken peaks because smaller fangs of rock peeked from the waters before these cliffs. The eroded towers of rock created a series of tiny islands and vicious reefs upon which could be seen flocks of flying reptiles.

Candy was taken away from the window and after diligently restoring her owner's armour she dressed herself and reapplied her regal robes and head-dress. A chastity belt that was mercifully free of the vituperative probes appeared and she accepted it without complaint. Together, they proceeded to a balcony on the upper floor of the howdah.

Relocated outside, she settled onto her knees and Hachiman stood boldly to display his presence to the populace.

As the procession entered the Saseho, the people uniformly bowed until their foreheads touched the ground and there they remained until the convoy was no longer within sight.

Candy could see that the citizens of the Empire had emulated their deities and everywhere she could see servile creatures in bondage. The Kami were gods and their desires and predilections were regarded as equally divine, so the citizens dedicated themselves to these revered pastimes with an obsessive fanaticism. Many shops sold items of restraint, bondage furniture, toys, weapons, and many of the more expensive locations focused on one aspect of depravity, becoming in effect an elite sadistic boutique.

It was clear that the status of a citizen could be measured in the state of their slaves, and the quality and skill in which they had been attired, subjugated, trained, and bound. Everywhere human beings could be seen as pets, as servants, or condemned to immobility as a sign, a display, a decoration, or an object of furniture.

When they reached the docks they were delivered back to the ground by the lift and with armoured Mitama forming a protective wall behind them, they marched towards their conveyance.

It looked like a normal carriage, one made of glass and metal before being decorated with coral and emblems of the deep. It hung low in the water and the rear of the craft yawned wide to offer a set of steps that led in.

Traces stretched out from the front of the carriage and an interconnected series of harnesses captured a herd of huge dinosaurs. They looked a little like dolphins but they were over thirty feet in length, and each held ranks of pointed teeth on their long jaws and had large bulbous eyes. Sitting upon the lead creature was an armoured diver with reins that would allow his mount to steer the entire shoal.

Candy followed Hachiman into the sumptuous interior of the carriage and knelt down at his side as he merely stood proudly in the middle with arms folded across his chest. Candy looked out through the transparent walls and regarded the aquatic world in which she now found herself. The town sitting on the headwaters was by no means all of the location named Saseho, in fact most of it lay beneath the waves.

The waters were crystal clear and allowed her to see all the way out into the nearby ocean. Everywhere there were signs of life. Underwater cabins had been carved from the rock, and their dense windows permitted light to pour out across the coral and stone. She could see people inside, conducting their daily routine, independent of life on the surface.

Farmers in diving suits tended fields of kelp, sponge, and seaweed. Other divers harvested clams, oysters, and other shellfish by hand, straight from the floor. Some herded shoals of fish from the back of beasts like those about to tow their carriage or they rode on the backs of giant turtles that were almost fifteen feet long. Other divers towed strings of pots for crab, shrimp, and lobster, prowling the seabed and visually scanning for the best place to deposit their traps and capture the migrant biomasses.

Candy's eyes widened in horror and she moved a little closer to her owner when four monstrous abominations emerged from the hazy middle distance and quickly began to close in. They continued to grow larger, and Candy's fear continued to mount as the scale of the terrors endlessly swelled.

They looked like a cross between some sort of gigantic pike and a crocodile. Each had a smooth hide and instead of limbs they had great flippers that steered them with a consummate grace. Their vast tails thrashed against the sea and sent them hurtling forward until they turned and arched around to fall in about the carriage.

Easily sixty feet in length, the beasts had a discreet rider who was settled in behind the their heads. The saddles were elegant and streamlined and they themselves were clad in armoured diving suits with large harpoon weapons at their side.

Hachiman was completely at ease with the appearance of these sea demons that made Great White Sharks look about as intimidating as goldfish but because of the fright they generated, Candy dared not stare too closely at them.

One of them cruised in and Candy shuddered. The vast leviathan swam up beside the carriage, and thirteen feet of flesh rending head flowed past. When the massive fang filled maw dominated her view and the huge fixed eye of the beast passed them, Candy gave a scream and grabbed hold of her master's leg. She gripped tight and closed her eyes, but the image of that reptilian glare still hung on her mind's eye and refused to leave.

Hachiman's hand reached down and petted her head as she quailed in terror and just prayed for the monsters to leave.

"They scare you, slave?"

"Oh God! They're hideous! I . . . I can't bear to look at them!" she barked.

"They are Kronosaurs — one of the most potent weapons in the arsenal of the Houses of Water. I can assure you that their fearsome visage is most definitely matched by their capabilities in battle, and your fear is justified. But they are here as escort only," attested Hachiman.

Even so, Candy could not bring herself to turn and see them.

The rear doors were closed and there was a hiss of pressure from the floor. The carriage gave a small lurch and immediately left the surface. The team of reptilian steeds drew it down with powerful strokes of their tails and the underwater procession started to head out to sea.

A sense of embarrassment reached through Candy's fear and she was a little ashamed of her unsightly display of weakness. She had seen and endured many strange things on Pangaea but nothing had come close to the terrifying visage of a Kronosaurus. Land based dinosaurs were still masters of a realm she was comfortable with, but there was something so vulnerable about being in the water. It was not a human's natural environment and it made them easy prey to those who had so magnificently mastered it.

Determined that she had now been taken to the limits of what this world could throw at her psyche, Candy moved back and stiffened. With a resolute snap, she opened her eyes and remained where she was. She unfocused her eyes to blur the terrible creatures cruising at their sides and instead of concentrating on wicked teeth that were the size of her torso she took in their more majestic aspects.

The animals flowed through the water as though made of it and their muscles rippled like the waves above with even the most casual motion. Sometimes they conducted a sweep further ahead of the procession and the speed with which they accelerated almost made them seem to vanish before her eyes. One moment a deadly predator was filling her vision and a split second later it was a dot in the distance with eddies of turbulence as the only thing left behind it.

No man made vessel or indeed anything on Earth could match this speed, and Candy now realised just how vulnerable her world was to the Houses of Water. These monsters could dodge any torpedo or just snatch it from its journey like a dog fetching a stick. They could rip open a submarine as though it were a tin can and punch through any hull. They would be away from an area in seconds, leaving futile depth charge assaults to pound empty water before they returned in a lull and despatched the craft that was dropping them. Nothing would be able to stop them.

"Brave girl. I have seen some Nakatomi and even Mikado break down from their first encounter with these creatures."

Candy felt less embarrassed at the thought of merciless warrior elite of the Houses of Fire dropping their weapons, squealing in despair, and covering their eyes. She could only imagine the reaction to them on Earth where people had not even been desensitised by the image of something as commonplace as a real live Tyrannosaurus.

Eased as to the visage of their escort, Candy turned her attention to the world around her and saw another carriage pass by to the left. It was heading back up towards the docks so it might collect another of Hachiman's Warlords and Candy could see others waiting further out in the hazy middle distance.

The Empire had settled the ocean bed with ease and every-where she could see rocky outcrops and cliffs. Windows dot-ted the spires of stone and people were readily visible inside.

As they continued out to sea she saw underwater mining and drilling, small factories, and other strange signs of civili-sation whose reason eluded her. It was clear now that the Houses of Fire ruled and defended dry land and the Houses of Water were just as domineering and efficient beneath the waves.

Suddenly, the herds of fish, the farms, and the mines all vanished and only unblemished underwater wilderness re-mained. Brilliant coral and dazzling tropical fish created a rainbow of colour, shape, and pattern as beams of sunlight continued to rain down from above and create great shifting columns of golden radiance.

The Kronosaurs suddenly veered aside and vanished when the carriage began to approach a great ridge over which could be seen light. The sources where numerous and powerful and together they generated a great golden haze such as might be seen in the night sky around a major city.

The underwater steeds drew them up and over into a huge undersea valley in which dwelt the palace of the Toyo-tama-hiko.

Everywhere the seabed was covered in twisted coral cov-ered structures and towering floral plumes. Rocky outcrops had great bulbous windows set across them and these re-vealed that the spires were hollow and accessed a vast under-sea domain that extended deep beneath the ocean floor.

Elegant coral stanchions climbed from the rock and many of them clasped a great glass sphere, the bottom of which was open to allow access to the sea. In these isolated transparent cabins were individual chambers where people could be seen at play. Extravagantly dressed priests moved amongst the sublime females that dwelt within, and these elite donned or removed their diving apparatus as they travelled amongst the rock-anchored bathyspheres.

The waters about the palace also teemed with life in the form of mermaids. The women were sealed within rubber outfits that shimmered and sparkled in the light. Their arms were folded up behind them and were contained within the slick suit to leave the limbs as little more than a bulge. Their legs were similarly contained and several long fins were attached to the costume while a single large tail offered them a means of propulsion. As they moved and swam, the fins trailed through the waters like long colourful streamers.

The mermaid uniform was comprehensive save for the head. The uniform ended at the neck and their scalps were shaved smooth and free of any encumbrance save for their gag. The smooth mouthpiece seemed to have a small grille at the front and two discreet vents at the side from which poured regular clouds of bubbles.

The women curled around in the waters and darted playfully amongst the coral and other shoals of legitimate fish. Systematically, they would circle around and rise under one of the cabins to acquire breath before returning to the waters.

Candy could see guests and priests in the countless bathyspheres and they were feeding or petting the women as they arose for air. Some tossed treats into the waters or fed them by hand because the women could spit out their strange mouthpieces, snatch the food, and then gobble the device back up before it sank. Other citizens of this land joined them in the sea and Candy could see scuba divers chasing or playing with the mermaids while others strode along the seabed in weighty suits.

The carriage was drawn down towards a cluster of tall towers that were all covered in recessed windows and a fantastic array of coral. Mermaids saw their approach and abruptly flocked towards them to investigate. As some mermaids rose for air, they had the craft pointed out to them by occupants of a bathysphere. These guests then sent them forth to find out who the mysterious new arrivals were and the women readily obeyed.

Candy knelt and watched in awe as the multitudes of contained women flowed sleekly alongside them, peeking in at the Warlord before darting off to gain new breath and inform the curious.

The steeds drew them towards the towers and then into the heart of the small undersea city. In all the numerous windows could be seen activity. Elegant concubines of the Kami were serving and being used by priest and deity alike. Common chores were being undertaken and stringent bondage or arbitrary discipline applied.

A monstrous column of rock arose before them and from the lower areas sprung outcrops that held great orbs of glass. These hemispheres were pressurised to create deep-sea docks and she could see that they were heading towards one of the larger examples.

The driver brought them under the dock and then let his team simply stop. The buoyant carriage started to drift upward and broke through onto the surface. The waters flowed down the windows like rain and thinned to grant a genuine view of the port.

A huge pair of golden doors existed to one side with a marble platform arrayed before them. This took up a third of the massive hall, the rest of which was open water, and the doors allowed entry into the great mountain palace rising upward behind them. Warriors in dazzling armour stood in rigid and ordered lines and their mother-of-pearl armour shone in the light.

A walkway extended telescopically from the docks and reached the back of the carriage. There were some clicks and

Hachiman span around and snapped to attention. Candy shuffled to follow him as the doors opened and offered them a route back onto land.

As soon as they stepped out, the warriors bowed most deeply and then the great doors began to swing open. A tall and athletically built male was swathed in plain robes and he marched at the head of a procession of extravagantly dressed courtesans, all of whom bowed much deeper than the male leading them.

"Reverence and greetings, Warlord Hachiman. My master, Toyo-tama-hiko, welcomes you most joyously to his palace. I am Hirata, his Mikado, and I am privileged to escort you to your quarters."

Hachiman said nothing and merely followed as the Mikado turned, straightened, and led them away. The courtesans fell in behind and Candy could see the excitement in their eyes. They were ecstatic at the prospect of attending Kami from the surface and Candy also noticed the odd envious glower when she passed them. By marching a step behind the man that was the focus of their lust and expectations, she was inspiring a level of attention rivalling that paid to the Warlord.

They were shown to a wing of great splendour where the courtesans took up positions throughout every room so they could instantly attend every need. The Mikado announced that he had to welcome the other Warlords and that the slaves would see to their desires before he bowed and left them.

The chambers had been carved out of the rock and then polished until it resembled marble mirrors. Staggered layers of shelves had been gouged from the wall, resembling small ledges upon which was an array of esoteric apparatus and instruments. Before she could loiter on these toys, she was presented to a small elegant cage next to the vast sprawling bed.

The door was opened and she was shown in before it was

locked behind her. Candy knelt demurely and watched through the bars as her master was shown to the bathroom. This chamber was still visible to her, so Candy sat and watched with jaundiced eyes.

In the middle of the next room was a replica rocky pool. A series of layered stones arose from the floor and then rolled up to the wall. Warm water trickled from several discreet holes and flowed down the rocks, creating small steaming waterfalls that filled a grandiose pool.

Standing within the waters were three naked maids with heads bowed and sponges in hand. Another trio were kneeling before the bath and Hachiman stepped amongst them so they could remove his armour and allow him to walk up the rocks and then sink into the ornate bath. The sight of them easing sponge and hand across his physique quickly curdled Candy's thoughts with lust and her hands clenched against her thighs. She tried to think on something else, and even not to look, just so she wasn't torturing herself with fantasies of pleasures that the chastity belt would not allow her to pander to. She also began to understand Lady Uzume's vicious mentality a little better because the sight of other women relishing the sublime anatomy of the Warlord was inspiring serious fury.

Eventually, Hachiman emerged and strolled onto the bed before indicating to Candy and then to an item of restraint on a shelf.

Her cage was opened and two of the courtesans brought her out and started to undress her. Already armed with the correct keys, her chastity belt and collar were all stolen before she was given a token application of clothing.

A pair of white patent thigh boots was zipped up her legs and matching vinyl opera gloves were quickly drawn up to her biceps. The shimmering plastic skin creaked with her motions as her arms were taken up and she was offered to a new form of security.

The strong steel device was formed around a dense collar. The item reached out with flowing rigid arms and these struts then created two thick shackles. Several small anchor points had been welded about the arms and collar, and after her neck and wrists were entered and captured she was shown up onto the bed. A large white ball gag was pushed between her teeth and buckled about her head and with their duty complete, the women stepped back.

Hachiman merely threw her down, hoisted her hindquarters, gave her a vigorous spanking and then ravished her with gusto.

Candy filled the room with elated squeals and as her master neared climax, he grabbed the struts that held her wrists and pressed down. Her face was squashed into the covers and she had to fight to strain even hints of breath through the material. Hachiman fired himself upwards and each slap of his hips to her rear shoved them upwards. The strength of his drives made her pussy throb with delight and in seconds her thighs were flicking to attention as orgasm neared. The blankets then resonated as her scream of ecstasy flowed against them. Her owner thrust himself into her and Candy clawed at the bed as she fought not only for air, but to endure the pleasure.

Hachiman jolted free to bring a final virulent spasm from his possession and then he simply brushed her elevated rear aside and dropped back. Candy managed to pull her face up and rasp weakly for breath. She clamped her thighs together and her body twitched as she savoured the feel of his cock within her. With ankles entwined, she shuffled forward and propped her chin up on a pillow. Orgasm from masturbation or cunnilingus was intense and sharp, but nothing was as deeply satisfying as the bone shuddering power of climax from coitus.

Once she had acquired a little comfort, she simply lay and watched the inert form of her master as he slipped into sleep with his manhood still jutting into the air. The flesh glistened with her moisture and the eyes of the other concubines were all locked to the same enchanting sight as well. Candy wondered for a time how many others had been rewarded with the ministrations of that succulent manhood. Was Hachiman a devoted lover, spending the coin of his endless years on one mortal at a time, or did he thrust into a willing body as the whim took him? It was an important question for Candy because it would determine whether he would grow weary of her charms in a short time, or be there, immortal and untouched by the years until old age claimed her. He was a patient and implacable being, so she happily convinced herself as to the latter and ignored the nagging worries about all the current intrigue.

# CHAPTER ELEVEN

Candy was left to snooze beside her master but barely slept at all. For most of the night she lay on her back and stared up at the ceiling, unable to bring her arms in or do anything save lay on the sheets and enjoy the occasional feel of Hachiman reaching over and groping her body in his sleep. She thought through everything that she had heard time and time again, trying to locate clues or anything else that might help her unravel the web of deceit and prepare herself for the truth.

A small bell gave several tiny chirps and Hachiman stirred. The sound of footfalls reached Candy while he sat up and absently let a hand wander around her breasts and tickle her nipples.

"Apologies if I have disturbed you, Warlord Hachiman," said the Mikado. "But an initial meeting has been prepared so that the Warlords of Water may welcome their honoured guests in person. Would you like your slave made available at this meeting?"

"Yes," he said firmly, and after grabbing one of the struts, he dragged Candy upright.

A leash appeared in the Mikado's hand and was immediately clipped to the front of her personal set of steel stocks.

"Come with me, slave," he ordered, and gave a brief yank to ensure she slipped from the covers and tottered after him.

Candy was escorted down the passages with her hands still held out by her neck. She sashayed on her heels and wondered what the Warlords of Water would be like. Would this be an erotic affair as with the briefing? Would she be servicing a Kami while bound tightly in some brutal but delightful configuration?

A towering pair of doors swung open at their approach and revealed a great hall with a domed glass roof. The rocky walls bore stalagmites and proved that it had once been some sort of subterranean cave. The almost organic formations poured down the walls and continued to roll through the rest of the ancient location like frozen waves. The roof offered not a view of the blue sky but of the deep blue sea. Mermaids flowed within it, glaring down with jealous eyes.

Throughout the bulbous and curling natural sculptures could be seen locations where restraints and bondage furniture had been set up. Many of them already had occupants and the hapless slaves were twisted and contorted by metal, leather, wood, and rubber. The creations caused them to offer their bodies to any attention and while some writhed against a particularly callous position, others just waited and ached for attention.

Candy was led through and towards the side before being brought to what was to be her resting place. However, her first glimpse assured her that would find little rest on such a creation.

The primary piece of the furniture was a horizontal copper pipe that looked like it had been cut in half down the middle. The semi-circular three-yard pole was held between two glittering pale stalagmites with its smooth arched outer surface facing upward. A large stern ring was set on top of each supporting rock formation and one of them had a pair of dense shackles already locked to it. The other ring bore two tightly curled lengths of spring that gave way to dangling coils of slender chain.

Glancing down, she saw another pair of matching rings. They were situated in the floor a short distance out to the sides and these rings already had a spring and a stout chain attached to them. The gleaming links broke into two and connected to a pair of hefty *D* rings and these were situated on either side of a copper coloured fetter. Already waiting by these bonds were two crouching priests.

"Straddle it," stated the Mikado.

Moving carefully to ensure she kept her balance; Candy approached the pole and could guess that her arms were not destined to be in front of her because this pose would obscure access to her breasts. So, facing the springs with a hint of trepidation she stretched up a vinyl-clad leg and slid it over the cool copper pipe. She shifted sideways and managed to perch herself on tiptoe. The rounded surface of the pole was now pressing between her legs and as soon as she was aboard the priests grabbed her ankles. Candy gave a mew of shock when they pulled on her feet and made her legs reverberate with stress. They snapped the fetters into place and the strength with which they had hauled out the restraints became immediately obvious as the springs sought to retract. Her inner thighs coursed with havoc and Candy flung her torso from side to side in a bid to gain some slack. However, the springs were fierce and she could not ease the power they levied on her lewdly parted limbs. Her pudenda instantly began to ache as the pull of the fetters drew her down onto the pole with callous force.

Candy clenched her teeth and furled her hands into fists as a dull brutal pound started to emerge in her pussy. She instantly stifled all resistance because every motion only made the effects worse. Even a slight shift of her legs caused escalation in one area of her pussy when the pole barged more forcefully into her.

The stocks about her neck and wrists were opened and the item was set aside. Her wrists were swiftly grabbed and pulled back to enter the cuffs at the rear. With her chest arched upward by the pose and her legs splayed wide, Candy moaned and fought to stay still. Yet she could not help writhe and fight to get free when the chains at the opposite end reached up and their springs elongated before the clips snatched her nipple rings.

With the contrary forces of her arms and her breasts fighting for supremacy, and each leg equally desperate for an ease of its pains at the cost of the other, Candy was summarily deserted to the evil rigours of the position. She chewed on her ball gag and her whimpers joined the soft delicate threnody of all the other slaves who were currently bound and presented in this ancient location.

The position was a maddening one. Every instinct demanded that she move to alleviate an area of monstrous discomfort, but to do so only made it worse in another area. Every attempt left residual distress that started to gather and strengthen until she was shaking with travail and dripping with sweat, and it was worse for knowing that this was not her true torment rather just the means to serve her to it.

The interior of glove and boot became humid and the wet vinyl slithered upon her with every twitch and flex of her limbs. She could feel perspiration pooling in toe and finger as lines ran down her torso and gathered on her brow.

A gong sounded and the doors opened to reveal Warlord Hachiman and his fellow Kami of Fire. Her tear filled eyes panned up and down his form as he marched in, dressed in loose robes with a serene expression on his face. He did not even notice her as he turned and stood at the head of his entourage.

The Mikado walked in, bowed deeply, and stepped to the side to announce the ruling elite of the underwater domains. He introduced them in a formal queue and did so with bold piety.

"Our honoured guardian of the sea — Naka-tsu-wata-dzu-mi."

The protector of all that rode the ocean waves was a giant of a man, with a broad chest and a strong jaw. His head was shaven and his eyes were dark and penetrating. He was exceedingly muscular and wore dark leather leggings. The tight second skin dwelt beneath ornate sections of silver armour that were attached to thigh, shin, and around his waist. The man stopped and both parties bowed to each other before rising to attention and regarding each other with a fixed and unwavering glower.

"Our revered master of the waves—Uha-tsu-wata-dzu-mi."

A feral man now entered with drawn and acute features situated beneath a shoulder length mane of dark hair. He wore a suit of emerald armour that was formed from interwoven fish-like metal scales with a dark ruby coloured breastplate. Rectangular plates adorned his shoulders and flanks, and solid sheaths of plate mail embraced forearm and lower leg. All present bowed again and returned to their former stringent stances.

"Our beloved ruler of the harvest—Soko-tsu-wata-dzu-mi."

The next Warlord was a slender man who carried a harpoon shaped staff to assist him in compensating for his slight limp. He had a kindly face but it was one that bore a severe expression. A white moustache dropped down onto his long black beard and he had adorned himself with flowing pale robes that were embroidered with countless intertwined images of the deep.

"Our glorious master of the rivers—Midzu-chi."

This Kami was a tall and magnificently built male with a long mane of thin black hair. He had chosen to fix it into a high ponytail with acute sideburns that reached to perfectly trimmed points at the corners of his upper lips. His naked torso revealed his smooth tanned skin and he wore only a wide belt and a flowing black robe.

"Our most honoured and revered divine deity. The Supreme Warlord of the Great Houses of Water — Toyo-tama-hiko."

The ruler and owner of this astounding palace was a robust and handsome male in a suit of gleaming metal armour whose elegant and perfectly sculpted sections mimicked the quality of scales to a near life-like degree, making the metal skin appear to be his own. His shoulder length dark hair hung about his acute features and a flowing cloak of red poured behind him.

"The Great Houses of Water extend our humble hospitality to our honoured guests. May the blessings of Sun-Goddess and Moon-God be upon the Kami of Fire." He said calmly.

"The Houses of Fire are honoured to be amidst our brothers of the deep," replied Hachiman.

The formalities ended and the various powers lightened their attitude and started to talk casually while wandering into the cavern. Other servants entered to bring them food and drink, or items that they wished to use on the concubines on offer. Candy tried to listen to their various conversations, but it was difficult to hear over her own rasping breath and the moans and cries of those that were being used for the pleasure of the immortals.

Suddenly, deep powerful drums started to ring out along with a dancing rattling bell and an occasional whistling flute. During the lull, Taiko drums had been brought in and now the massive instruments were filling the chamber with a raucous and chaotic melody. The power of the largest drums made the area tremble and Candy distinctly felt the quaver of the pole between her legs as it responded to the mighty sound waves.

She listened to the energetic tunes and tried to focus on them to distract her from the infuriating nature of her pose.

She pulled upright a little to try and quell an annoying ache in her shoulders and her nipples throbbed with internal hatred as they were stretched by the springs in front of her. With a despairing sigh she sagged and just gritted her teeth.

A cool hand cupped the underside of her breast. The sudden grope made her move back a little and this caused her nipple rings to again be tugged upon. The fleshy tunnel seemed to swell from within as the transfixing metal was drawn away and she instantly threw herself forward until her arms snapped taut. The sudden reaction made the continuing dreadful ache between her legs acquire fresh strength and also exaggerated the scathing torment in her shoulders. Candy's head lolled down and she whimpered softly.

"This is yours, Hachiman?"

"Yes. A current favourite," came her master's voice. The strength of his tones was easily discernible over the booming drums, clattering bells, and wailing flutes.

The Supreme Warlord of Water moved out into her field of vision and let his hands run up and down her torso and onto her thighs.

"Would I be wise to guess that she is not of Pangaea?"

"Wise indeed."

"So I assume that this is the specimen you paid so much for and fought so valiantly to acquire?" offered Toyo-tama-hiko.

"She has already proven her value to me," rebuked Hachiman with a most casual air.

"I do not doubt it," purred the Warlord and his hands squeezed her assets as his thumbs tickled her stretched nipples. Candy gave a purr of bliss that dropped into a murmur as she inadvertently flexed and pulled herself harder onto the pole.

The armoured form of Toyo-tama-hiko stepped out before her and his eyes scanned up and down her body before following her rippling legs to the fetters. He held out a hand and received a device from an unseen servant.

The black plastic cylinder had a button and a small, elevated dial set just before the handle grip. A thick electrical cord extended from one end and the other bore what appeared to be an overlarge light bulb.

"I had not expected to find so many of the Water Houses already here," said Hachiman.

The Warlord emerged on the other side of the pole and revealed a brief ornate stave in one hand. The tip sported a brief bushel of thin rubber tendrils and in his other hand resided a rod of translucent flesh-like rubber. Candy could see silver bulbs deep within the vibrator whose structure curved up at the tip like a smooth beckoning finger. The base of the toy had several small controls set upon it and was fed by another electrical cable.

"Just a small gathering of the Kami who have been entrusted with the security of the Empire's water. Sometimes it is wise to be aware of what one's subordinates are doing," came the Warlords reply and Candy could almost hear the implication that it was just as wise to be aware of one's rivals as well. The two were locked in a verbal sparring contest but it was not one to unearth secrets, rather it was to covertly inform and probe, to explain and explore without any overt word.

Toyo-tama-hiko turned the dial on his instrument and a strange cranking growl emerged from within it. Cyan arcs of energy started to spill from the filament and lick the interior of the glass. The portable plasma sphere wafted towards Candy's stomach and she instinctively tried to shift back, earning herself another bite of pain in her pussy and additional flickers of strain on her stretched nipples. When the glass reached her, a tiny spark of static charge jumped from the surface and licked her skin. The sharp distress made her jerk and when she pulled with her legs she made her loins thud with anguish. Candy cried out onto her gag because even though the effect of the strange toy was fairly minor, the pain her reaction had brought was less easily withstood.

"And how *are* matters with your Great Houses?" asked Hachiman.

With a flick of the small whip he laid the rubber strands to Candy's exposed inner thigh. The thin tendrils deposited an annoying flash of heat that made her mewl. When he applied another trio of swats she again wriggled and punished herself further.

The small whip was infuriating because it was harsher than the warm background heat of a spanking but did not have the delightful vindictive fury of a crop or cane, or the stern might of a flogger. It was like a persistent mosquito, one that annoyed even as it disciplined.

"Fair. Idleness breeds complacency," was Toyo-tama-hiko's simple rebuke.

The Warlord lifted the bulb and the angry incandescent teeth of the device continued to leap into her skin, making it glow from within as the fierce sensation was channelled into her. Candy struggled and chewed on her gag as the sphere continued to etch a scratching sharp feeling up her torso and towards her breasts.

"Intrigue is often encountered as an additional flaw when such inactivity reigns," said Hachiman, the words being an almost absent statement as he prepared Toyo-tama-hiko's target for him. The tiny whip slapped to her breasts, alternating from one to the other and making the flesh ripple with each vexing swipe. Candy jolted and when she dropped back down she gave a yell as her crotch seemed to swell from bumping herself upon the pole.

"At least intrigue can sharpen the intellect. Idleness just enfeebles and my forces would benefit from action," said the Warlord with an equally light sigh. The implication that

Hachiman's forces saw more regular action than those of the Water Houses was not lost on Candy or the Fire Warlord, but suddenly she had greater things to occupy her thoughts. The electrical wand began to reach around her breasts, dodging the chains and etching angry violet lines into her skin. No bruise or welt was left behind, the vexed skin was just left a little flushed. However, the lack of damage did not mean that the toy was not difficult to withstand. The insubstantial nature of the attack was maddening. A physical weapon felt real, it marked her with lingering contusions whereas this toy just tormented her with strong static blasts that denied her any treasures that she might marvel at and trace to savour the recall of their creation.

"Action can be a curse," stated Hachiman and started to levy his whip to her inner thighs and her rear.

"A statement we of the Water Houses rarely get to explore. Perhaps your agent could explain it?" he asked and drew the wand away.

Candy tried to steady her breath and also stay still. Her instincts howled for her to try and escape, to fight her bonds, to try and break free of this accursed pose, or simply beg and plead for mercy. She clenched her jaws and battled to remain stalwart. She was bound before two of the most powerful beings in this world and could not sully herself with such gross displays of frailty. She had withstood the desires of countless cruel beasts and so this light play should be a delight to her. Keeping her devotion to her master in her heart she turned her thoughts away from escape and focused them on the conversation and the sensations she was being bequeathed.

The Warlord of Water knew of Lady Uzume's quest and was using it to see if there were other motives behind her recent undertaking. The focus he applied to the words suggested that he found the proximity of her destination to the Eastern territories suspicious. Perhaps he thought that Lady

Uzume was taking a force to mount war on the Provinces, to gain experience and refine the abilities of Mitama and Wani prior to the invasion of Earth. Battle experience would be valuable and the duty to recover a stray arrival would be an ideal excuse to gain it.

"Stray arrivals permit us to mount expeditions, but the lands beyond the Empire offer little challenge to our forces," said Hachiman, implying that he was indeed sending Uzume for battle readiness exercises and then dismissing this reason behind the sheer lack of threat the Provinces offered their forces. He was supplying a fake cover to lay over this falsified reason, hiding Uzume's imminent failure beneath obfuscating blankets.

The grinding noise from the toy grew in volume and the light within the bulb became brighter. Candy gave a croak as it started to rise up towards her breasts again. This time it touched a chain and the wriggling influence of the charge poured along the metal and churned about her nipple rings. Candy arched and cried out as the power of the toy entered her teats. The journey along the chain had greatly diminished the effects but the feeling of it actually inside her nipple was much more vivid than any outward attack. Candy's howl became a gurgling moan when the soft head of the vibrator reached in and its hooked bulbous tip brushed her lips aside and levied itself to her clit. A touch to the controls caused it to break into a speedy shiver.

"Even this sweet treasure from the other side was hardly a feat to snatch," he added, spryly changing the subject to add more weight to the lie. By deserting this topic, he suggested that Toyo-tama-hiko was correct and now had no wish to delve deeper into the matter of his training ploys.

"She was a stray?" asked the Water Kami, who had either accepted this was true or knew that Hachiman would reveal no more on the subject.

Toyo-tama-hiko brought the bulb closer and let the charge leap from its surfaces and pour directly into Candy's nipples. The stretched morsels thundered with new mayhem and any attempt she made to try and get them away from the spiteful Warlord only made the chains pull and her nipple rings distend her trapped tips.

"The will of Izanagi and Izanami chose to leave her in the Wastelands."

Hachiman pressed a control and the vibrator slowed its rate. The device now surged with slower but much more powerful beats that channelled rhapsody into her punished pussy. The bliss was a most welcome treat and it offset to the savagery of her pose and Toyo-tama-hiko's continuing abuse of her nipples.

"And no doubt her awareness of this world and her experiences have been broadened by her brief time in the barbarian lands. Just as your forces taste of foreign lands and foes and are improved because of it," said Toyo-tama-hiko.

The Warlord was not to be dissuaded so easily and was pushing the conversation back towards what Lady Uzume was *really* up to.

Hachiman turned the vibrator a little so that it entered Candy and began to spread more of its succulent vibrations into her pussy. Candy fought to stay still. Her legs wanted to thrash and flex as the toy continued to pleasure her, but any response would only subtract from the ecstasy. Normally she loved to thrash and struggle against her bondage but this time they had engineered her position so that she had to commit to enduring her punishment without even twitching.

"Combat is rare and even when it occurs it ends very quickly. I am sure that any pirates on our waters barely manage to fire a bolt before your cavalry rip out their hulls from under them," said Hachiman, and smiled as he saw Candy begin her ascent towards orgasm. Even against the punishing pose, the steady delightful throb of the toy was not to be denied. Her breath started to deepen. Her chest rose and fell as the glowing bulb continued to wander about her breasts and torso, offering an excruciating itch wherever it went. Candy sank her teeth into the gag and actually feared climax. The convulsions of succulent release would be terrible on her spread pussy and her stretched nipples. It was hard enough to stay still as it was and she would be powerless to deny her reactions against a pain-charged bondage orgasm.

Candy tried to focus on the conversation and misery of the electrical attack, to try and keep herself in the forerunner to orgasm without letting herself embrace the pleasure and tumble recklessly into it.

"Our military could almost be accused of being too effective. There is little challenge here on Pangaea," said Toyo-tama-hiko.

The blatant nature of the words clearly aimed their dialogue to the very heart of the matter. Both knew that the other was informed of what was coming and suddenly their words were rigid, like iron, hiding subtle inflections and any clues. Each regarded the other with a firm and uncompromising countenance and both their toys came away. Toyo-tama-hiko touched the button on his implement and it deactivated immediately.

Candy went as limp as she could against her bondage. Panting for breath, her pussy was throbbing with pain and churning with bliss while the rest of her resounded with residual havoc. She was a diversion to the Warlords—something to absently torture as they discussed politics and strategies.

The feeling of being so whimsically tormented by such mighty figures was oddly reassuring and Candy began to find a new and strange sense of satisfaction in her position and abuses. She was a trivial thing, an organic bauble whose cries were just part of the melody in the room. Just as the musicians played their drums, these two warriors played her in a similar fashion.

"Times change," said Hachiman.

"And immortality gives us an infinite supply of that commodity," replied Toyo-tama-hiko.

"But our immortality can be withdrawn."

"Failure cannot be tolerated in a deity and so it is not an option," said Toyo-tama-hiko and then gestured to the servant that had delivered the wand. Candy detected movement beneath her and heard a scratching sound that she briefly feared was another wand, but then she realised that it was a flint.

"But our subordinates are not as perfect as we," said Hachiman, "Their errors would reflect poorly on us. While our forces are idle and unchallenged, failures are trivial and hardly worthy of note. If the action you crave were to ever arrive then failures would shed all such levity."

Her master had exposed his reservations concerning the coming conflict. He was a wise leader and a pragmatic ruler. He knew that at present, in this time of peace, where the Empire was invulnerable and terrified all in this land, failures were tiny and trivial. Reprimands for a bad decision carried little wide-ranging effect. If full-scale war with Earth began, then great actions would carry equally great ramifications. Did Hachiman prefer the peace? After all, he was a god. He was immortal and all-powerful. There was little reason for him to risk everything to acquire nothing. In essence, what else could he possibly want from life?

Candy's deliberations turned from the conversation and back to her brutalised pussy. It had taken a moment for her to notice but now she could feel warmth spreading between her legs. As she looked around as best she could, she could see an amber glow directly beneath her. Candy gave a shocked gasp and clenched with fear. A candle had been set beneath the pole and it was pouring its heat up into the cupped groove of the copper pipe.

"May we live in interesting times?" said Toyo-tama-hiko, using the ancient curse to offer his assent and perhaps reveal his similar fears concerning the future. Were he and Hachiman of equal mind? The other Houses were lesser in stature. They wanted to expand and enjoy the wealth and pleasures that the ruling Great Houses of Fire and Water took for granted.

Toyo-tama-hiko touched the cut-off button on his toy. The wand returned to growling life and again filled with light. He turned the dial, and the implement gathered more brilliance and grew louder. Candy whimpered to see it so full of punishing life.

"I do not fear interest. When one is sufficiently prepared, interest can be sustained without fear of flaw or catastrophe," replied Hachiman and began to lambaste Candy with his small whip. "The rash are the first to let the edge of the cliff go unseen."

"To their cost," agreed Toyo-tama-hiko and let the bulb travel onto Candy's spread thighs. Her legs rippled with effort, and this pulled her onto the pipe, which was now growing hot and starting to pain her. Some swats to her breasts from Hachiman's whip made her squawk and struggle more distinctly.

"And I am a miser of the greatest magnitude when it comes to investing the sum of my longevity on risky and unnecessary ventures," said Hachiman.

Candy arched and swayed as the vibrator returned and hooked itself into her pussy. It threw dedicated bliss into her pussy even as the heat of the pipe started to make her loins tingle.

"Yet conquest is in our blood. We must expand or

stagnate."

Toyo-tama-hiko turned the wand higher still and let it travel more freely. He arbitrarily let it chew on her arms and her shoulders before he swayed back down her chest. Candy squealed and jolted, her cries becoming corrupted as the whip returned to her flanks and the vibrator changed to a rapid setting that made it become a blur of frenzied oscillations.

"The Fire Kami know what is in our blood for we are those who most often see it spilt," said Hachiman.

Her owner drew the vibrator around to tickle her vulva before he again let it slide in and rage against her clitoris. The heat between her legs was growing more distinct and was now starting to hurt. It was not yet strong enough to burn, rather it was like holding a cup of coffee that was way too hot, save that when the object was pressed against her most intimate regions the result was much harder to abide. This sensation was especially harsh because every twitch and throe brought by discipline or teasing only exacerbated the experience by making her press herself to that very same source of reviled heat.

"A distinction that may not be yours alone for long," added Toyo-tama-hiko, offering her master that his own forces would be at risk in the coming conflict and that he knew the value of ensuring preparedness. The supreme assurance in his voice was not inflated and there was a rigid backbone behind his words, as though he knew that his position was solid.

Candy's focus began to waver as a terrible orgasm began to loom. She wanted to pay attention to their words, to use the interesting verbal wrestling match to keep from losing herself to her desires. If she allowed herself to drench herself in the session she would lose all awareness of their conversation. She tried to tell herself that she was acquiring important information that may be of use some day, working in the manner that Candice had protected her stature and position on

Earth. However, she secretly knew that if she abandoned herself to the stringent affair she might do herself some serious damage as she crushed her pussy to the burning pole and lurched around to abuse the rest of her supplicant body.

Her loins were being scorched but there was nothing she could do to stop the approaching climax. She was a submissive creature and was bound and controlled by two august powers who were absently torturing her. Her masochistic urges could not help but delight in this ill-treatment and even though she knew an orgasm would bring an unendurable additional degree of dire ferocity, she could not stop herself. Her master's toy was within her while his rival's roared angry tongues of energy into her skin. Candy tried to resist but knew she would lose, as she always did. When the Kami wanted something, they made it happen — as Toyo-tama-hiko had said when he remarked that deities did not fail.

"Unfortunate that the Houses of Air and Earth are unlikely to attest to the colour of their own vitality," said Hachiman.

If their positions were so obviously secure, threats might come from the Houses that would look diminished when compared to their perfection. An army without defeat looked far more impressive than a full harvest or a long period of uninterrupted power generation.

The pain between her legs was now as powerful as the level of pleasure Hachiman was installing. She tried to mouth words, to make her displeasure known even over the gag. Scarcely had she managed to formulate a few syllables when Toyo-tama-hiko took away her efforts. He grabbed her hair, held tight, and started to let the bulb wander about the front of the gag. The angry spears of power lapped at her lips and made her squeal before he let go and returned to the rest of her body.

"Then we must be equal to any task that arises and tread carefully," said Toyo-tama-hiko and there was a fleeting and suspicious pause before he continued. "Especially because we have no clue as to what lurks in the shadows of the future."

Even with her lips tingling with painful flutters of anguish, Candy had noticed that there was an unusual emphasis on his final words.

Hachiman was stalled in his conversation for a moment as he looked through what Toyo-tama-hiko was implying. Did they fear spies? Candy knew that there was a secret police force within the Empire. Were the Warlords communicating in the open, using innuendo under pleasant discussion to help each other against other threats? What was Toyo-tama-hiko trying to tell her master? Whatever it was, Hachiman seemed to understand and he immediately slowed the rate of the vibrator. The slower, more potent surges dragged Candy into orgasm. She tried to stop herself but now she was defenceless against their designs.

Candy screamed at the very limit of her lungs and quaked as though mimicking the action of the vibrator. The wand came away and the whipping stopped, leaving her with the heat and the bliss in her genitals. She bounced herself on the pole and her legs shook with strain as she was hauled through a most nightmarish release. Words to beg Hachiman to show mercy flew around the gag but were unintelligible. The pleasure was more unendurable than the pain. At least she could handle the distress, focus and manipulate it, let her masochism feed on it. She was supposed to yearn for pleasure and savour it when it came, but this was too much, it was too corrupted by all that they had applied to her on this accursed burning pole.

When the vibrator came away, Candy was almost delirious. The cave was a shifting realm of blurred lights because of the tears filling her eyes. She slouched against her bonds and offered spasms to the continuing ferocious forces that possessed her. Every twitch punished her loins but likewise every tiny movement against the hot copper made her croak and thrash as her hyper sensitive loins reacted to every tiny touch and shift. Candy devoted herself to being still with all her remaining strength. She needed to calm down. She needed to recover.

The heat that had ravaged her crotch was easing, suggesting that the candle had been blown out but the after-effects of such an eldritch orgasm were fading at a much tardier rate, especially because the stimulation was not ending. Every confused shuffle revived the climax, restored her painful bliss, and undid all her efforts to become placid.

"I have found this conversation most gratifying, Supreme Warlord," said Hachiman.

"As have I. May there be more in our future."

The two were allies as well as rivals, and something incredibly important had been exchanged between them. There were subtle plots and schemes but in the end, they were both dedicated to survival and were working together on the most important matters to ensure it. It was then that Candy noticed the similarity in their features. When they both wore the same expression of satisfaction, she saw it. The family resemblance was subtle but striking. Candy realised then that they could well be brothers, but a moment later she corrected herself. Because of their immortality they could be father and great great grandson, but whatever the connection, they were certainly blood relatives.

Priests unfastened her fetters and then her hands and breasts were freed. When she was lifted up, Candy jolted to attention and screamed as the weight on her long crushed and abused crotch was taken away. Her thighs clamped together and squeezed as though to restore some pressure and ease her withdrawal from the pole.

As she was laid onto the cool stone, she sobbed and whimpered freely. The dreadful ache in her body was now being eclipsed by the anguish between her legs.

Candy remained on the ground at the feet of the two Warlords. If their conversation were continuing, she had no idea. All she could feel was the stamping woe between her legs and the pain haunting her body. As the ghastly intensity began to dwindle, she embraced herself and quivered. The potency of the session was now hers to relish. She had survived it, not been damaged, and had extracted moments of unparalleled albeit corrupted rhapsody.

In a split second every lingering contusion and ache became a heady aphrodisiac and her convulsions transformed into spasms of arousal as she mulled over and luxuriated in the barbarity of her trial.

Recovering on the smooth stone floor, Candy listened to the drums and cuddled the brutal delights of her encounter with the two Warlords. She had taken her first tastes of life in the underwater realm and was now thirsty for more.

# CHAPTER TWELVE

Xiao Lin continued to thread a path down through the rocks and stepped out onto a slim ledge. The rocky shelf ran along the upper reaches of a low cliff until a tumbling waterfall ended it abruptly.

The slender and lethargic cascade fell into a wide glittering pool that dwelt below her. The waters were murky, choked with minerals from the mountain streams that fed it.

The barren cliffs encompassed half the lake but a solid wall of vegetation enclosed the rest of the covert location. The trees and plants had thrived from being so close to the water and they had grown so dense that accessing the lake by any other route than the cliffs was almost impossible. There were wild predators in the tangled depths and by removing the visual compass that was the sun or landmarks such as the mountain peaks it made it easy for a traveller to become lost.

Xiao stripped off her trousers and shirt, kicked away her shoes, and quickly jogged forward. She threw herself out into the air and gave a high pitched squeak of delight as her stomach seemed to rise within her, tickling her innards before she landed in the chill waters.

She vanished into the opaque depths and exhaled a little so that she continued to sink. When her feet touched the lakebed she kicked up and rocketed back toward the surface. Xiao exploded from the waters, collapsed aside, and sank once more. When she again bobbed to the surface, she continued to tread water and watch the ripples from her landing expand out towards the shore. In some ways it was a fitting metaphor for her life. Every movement she made disturbed her environment and affected every life about her.

Xiao flicked her head back, throwing her sodden mane of blonde tresses over her head. She had considered cutting them off in a bid to disguise herself as a boy and head away from the border to seek her fortune in the Wastelands. The problem was that she was not exactly inconspicuous. She had just turned eighteen and the curves that had caught every eye since her childhood were now coming to full fruition. Her breasts were like magnets for male eyes, and no matter how baggy or rough her attire, how she tried to conceal them, it just seemed to tease with a hinted promise of what lay beneath. Her features were subtle and alluring, defying any attempt to mar them with dirt or dishevelment. Then there were her eyes. Emerald green, they shone in the light and were wreathed by eyelashes that seemed to beckon like fingers.

No one else seemed to understand why Xiao hated the attention and the few other women in the camp thought she was just playing hard to get, tantalising those around her by feigning indifference and even disdain towards those interested in her. It was a source of serious contention for the wealthy Provincial merchants and nobles who travelled out to the border to see this young beauty that had so many tongues wagging and so many hearts fluttering with desire.

Their designs on her had until now been stalled by her father. He operated under the strict morals of his old life and swore that she would not be married off until she was eighteen. It was an outlandish stipulation in Pangaea but he would not waver on it. In fact, the only time he had ever given ground to the customs of his new world was the taking of his wife's surname to replace his own of Johanson. Yet Xiao suspected that he had done so more to fit in with the predominantly oriental heritage of the area than to accept the tradition.

Now her time was up. She was of an age he deemed acceptable to be given away. New suitors were no doubt already on their way with coffers full of sturdy metal coins to win her hand and own her body.

Xiao's parents were simple miners. Her father was now too old to work the small shafts that had been drilled into the rock faces and so with her mother, he panhandled on the streams next to her ten brothers. No matter how often they tried, her parents were never blessed with another daughter and so they were stuck with one who didn't even want that gender.

Her father had been a young military man from the other world, one cast through during some sort of global conflict about fifty years ago. He had thrived here, and his adventurous youth had resulted in wealth sufficient to buy a native Pangaean wife and settle in semi-retirement in the mountains to start a family. It was an almost unheard of eventuality in these parts.

Xiao suspected that the initial isolation of their home was deliberate so that her father would not have to keep fighting to keep his valuable spouse from the clutches of others, but previously undetected metal deposits in the area soon meant that a small and thriving mining settlement quickly manifested. Fortunately, by this time, he had gained enough sons to back up and enforce his monogamous marriage and make sure the family remained together.

Then Xiao had been born and her very existence placed a great strain on the family. People were insanely jealous of a man with two females at hand. Several times abduction had been attempted.

It was obvious why they wanted to sell her off to a suitor. Her father was too old to continue to handle kidnappers and her brothers were getting tired of it too. Inspired by their father, they wanted to make their own way in the world, not be a bodyguard to their sister for the rest of their lives.

Nevertheless, they were not the only ones who wanted out.

Xiao floated on her back and started to idly paddle back towards the cliff. The squawk and chirp of the forest beasts dulled when her ears were submerged, and she stared up at the cloud-flecked sky with longing.

This was a great big and wonderful world. She wanted to explore. She wanted to travel and have adventures like her father had. His bedtime stories of peril, daring, courage, and cunning had not only left their inevitable mark on his sons, but on the daughter who had overheard them too. She wanted to emulate him, something a rich husband was unlikely to allow, especially after paying the exorbitant dowry her family would demand. Rather than adventure she'd be little more than a breeding machine surrounded by guards in an exquisite palace that in truth would be her prison.

Xiao flipped over and grabbed hold of the rock. With a strain of effort she dragged herself up and onto the sharp incline that fed back to the start of the ledge. It was an easy climb largely because of experience. Few others knew the secret route to this place, so she used it to escape the eyes and be alone and naked for a moment.

The rock was warm to the touch after having been soaked by the sun all day and when she reached her clothes, she was almost dry. Xiao settled back in the sun, stretched out her limbs and stroked the smooth stone. Luxuriating in the open rays and her complete nudity, she squirmed a little and a hand slithered in to start to touch her own skin. She closed her eyes and gave a soft murmur as her fingers circled her nipples and slowly worked their way up to the tips. Her back arched up and her other hand voyaged across her stomach to make the skin tingle. Amidst a long self-indulgent moan she parted her legs and let her hands reach down and take hold of her inner thighs. Xiao bit her lower lip and started to move her digits inward as the others tightened their hold on her thigh in anticipation of what was to come.

A deep rumble rolled through the air. Xiao opened her eyes and found that the sky was still fairly clear so either the thunderstorm was some distance away or there had been a seismic event. Tremors were not rare in these mountains, especially because of the collapse of a shoddy or derelict mineshaft.

Xiao swiftly pulled on her trousers and looked at the sky again to recheck for any dark clouds. She found nothing.

As the thunder continued, another strange noise reached her ears. It sounded like someone clapping squares of wood together with swift and steady beats. The eerie music echoed across the mountains and was joined by others who played at a different rate, distributing chattering bursts rather than the steady and deeper sounding song.

Intrigued, Xiao started to walk back towards the village. The thunder started to abate but the clattering chaotic music continued. Then she started to hear the shouting and screaming.

Xiao stopped in her tracks and her pulse quickened. Her limbs trembled and a sinking feeling manifested in her stomach. Something was very, very wrong.

Unable to turn away, she chose not to head down onto the road and instead continued up towards the escarpment that surrounded the main village. It was a risky route because not only was she left alone and in the open, but also the surface rocks were loose and often slippery from morning dew. However, right now, she knew that there were greater dangers abroad than lustful males or a rockslide.

The shelf that would allow her to peek down on the village was near. On the other side was a viciously steep hillside where tufts of wild grasses held the stone in place against the elements but seldom against human travel, making it an ideal defence. Xiao lowered onto her belly and started to creep forwards towards a small bush that might help hide her when she stole her surreptitious glance.

Black smoke was starting to curl up into the sky and the sound of fire was growing more distinct. The strange music was now less prevalent, and the anguished cries were diminishing. When she saw the village, her breathing stalled and her eyes widened in absolute horror.

The other side of the valley was much less steep and considerably lower than this one, and metal plated monsters had flattened the trees that normally covered it. The titanic beasts snarled and growled. Gore still stained their wicked teeth and some stood in the crushed remnants of a cabin or just watched the unfolding carnage with a cruel passion. Brilliant banners cascaded from towering poles on their back, but the language was none she recognised.

Even with the metal skin, Xiao knew what these monsters were, but also knew that such terrible predators did not come this far into the mountains. These animals needed the regular giant prey of the herds that roamed the plains. Only on one other occasion had such a terrible creature come this far from the Wastelands. It had been pushed on by the desperation of being crippled in a territorial dispute with a rival and could no longer catch food on its own. Even so, three villagers had died in the slaying of the threat.

Another factor that made her question whether these were the same beasts was that each wore a saddle and in it was another demonic form. The riders were not Lizards, but were definitely not human. They also carried firearms, but ones so complex and intricate that she could scarcely recognise them as such. The weapons she had previously seen in her life had been relics from the other world. They were generally old, unreliable, and were sported more for prestige and intimidation than actual use because few could waste precious metal on bullets. Arrows were far simpler, almost as effective, and far more trustworthy.

Several buildings were aflame and others had been damaged by the passage of the beasts. Slaughtered bodies were everywhere. The assault had come so quickly and been so merciless that for a moment, she could see no survivors.

Suddenly, a villager broke cover and ran down the valley, heading for the woods at the base of the mountain. One of the riders took aim and a brief growling chatter racked the form with crimson plumes that sent him sprawling into the dirt.

Xiao gave a brief bark of chagrin when she saw the murder and then her heart skipped a beat.

One of the diabolic riders spun in the saddle and fixed its contorted screaming face in her direction. The two stared at each other for a moment and emerald human eyes met featureless devilish silver ones.

The rider wrenched at the reins to turn its steed towards her. When Xiao saw the colossal creature face her and its jaws stretch wide to reveal teeth the size of short swords, she gave a scream, jumped up, and started to run.

She had to get back up the mountainside and back to the family cabin. If she could warn her family, they could take cover in her father's old mine shafts. In them, he had hidden a few relics from his soldier days, and these might help drive off the attackers if they tried to follow them in. Separating them from their steeds would make them vulnerable because after all, there were only six of them. Whether they were mortal was a problem to consider another time because first she had to escape.

Xiao scrambled over the rock and ran as her lungs burned with an arctic chill and her pulse thumped in her veins. Sobbing and panting, she continued her pell-mell dash across the land. She had hoped that the loose stone might stop the monster from pursuing her but already she could hear the ground shuddering impact of its feet. It had made it up the slope and was now in pursuit.

Xiao wove amongst the boulders, trying to obscure herself from her hunter and lose them in the twists and turns of the area. Even if she could make it to the nearest family, she would have access to their tunnels. Her fright and jeopardy were compelling and she couldn't even think of who the nearest neighbour was, so she just kept running and hoped that luck was with her.

The deafening sound of the beast at full gallop continued to grow louder, but Xiao could not look around to see how close it was. If she did, she knew that she would be paralysed with fright and devoured an instant later.

A slight sting took her in the shoulder but she ignored it. Then a dreadful numbness started to spread from the point of impact. Fearing a gash that was resulting in grievous blood loss, Xiao risked a glance. She was perplexed to see a small metallic tube with a bright plume of red and yellow fur coming out of one end. A yank pulled it free and revealed the tiny spike that had broken her skin and left a small pinprick behind. When she cast it aside, the manoeuvre offset her balance and she tripped over a rock and collapsed to the ground.

Xiao fought to rise but her arms did not move. She struggled to crawl into cover, but her legs just floundered. With a final defiant scream, she watched darkness encroach in the corners of her vision and spread forward like evening shadows to consume her sight and drop her into a dreamless void.


Lady Uzume looked over the diminutive form that was laying on the rock and purred with supreme contentment. The girl had given her quite a chase and already she was excited about what she could do with her. An untrained captive, reluctant, inexperienced, and all hers was an intoxicating prospect. Even the delightful Candy had been processed by the Temmangu, and this girl would not bear rings, or a collar, and wouldn't even be able to speak the Imperial tongue. This virginal prisoner would struggle and fight, resist and revile her captivity and Uzume was exhilarated at the thought of breaking her. The notion of presenting her master with a concubine that had never been touched by another House crossed her mind, as did keeping her all to herself. No other being would taste this succulent morsel. She would be Uzume's private toy for the rest of her life.

Uzume dragged at her reins as her steed sought to move in and gobble up the inert snack.

"Woah there. She's for my hunger, not yours."

The Tyrannosaur gave a grumble of disappointment but had already devoured a dozen locals during the first moments of the attack and so did not continue complain further.

Uzume removed the small magazine of blanks that were needed to propel her tranquilliser rounds and slapped the far more lethal drum of hollow point ammunition back into place.

The sanguinary pound of another steed grew quickly in volume and paused when the rider drew up at her side.

"Report," she barked, never moving her eyes from the languid girl. A hand involuntarily strolled down between her legs and she found herself rubbing her loins as she contemplated a sudden rota of twisted debauched deeds.

"We have some herds to the south. Ranchers by the look of it."

"What breeds?" she asked.

"Bipedal herbivores. No armoured species."

"Human survivors?"

"A couple of escapees that we'll track down as soon as the village is secure, and we have a number of local domiciles to contend with."

"Ignore them. I want the escapees to tell others of what happened here, and I want locals to investigate and see what occurred. We'll let our mounts feast on the herds and then move out at dawn," decreed Uzume.

"Back to the main column?"

"No, I will head back alone and send Wani reinforcements. The Stray may be in these mountains, so head deeper into the range and start a search for it."

Uzume knew that the survivors would bear news of the attack and it would spread quickly. The Provinces might fear an Imperial assault coming in over the mountains and so they would mobilise quickly to hold them there.

She supposed that if they *were* intending to invade, such a route would allow Mitama forces to move into Province territory unseen. The only drawback would be that if they should be noticed it was hard terrain and could result in a bottleneck. Hopefully, if the Provinces realised this, they would press their advantage and not delay.

By the time the Wani and supplies reached this area, the forces she had sent to scout should have been attacked and wiped out by energetic Provincial reprisal. This would allow her to decree that the local forces were far superior in number and strength, took the Stray, and used the weapons to defeat the recovery force. The murder of elite Tyrannosaur riders might cause enough indignation in the Empire to gain the results Hachiman was after. Outrage would ensue, fear that the Provinces were getting too strong would spread and war would then be inevitable.

Hachiman would get what he wanted, and Uzume started to climb down from her steed so she could gather what she was after.

# CHAPTER THIRTEEN

"What is her name?" asked Toyo-tama-hiko.

"Candy," replied Hachiman.

By referring to the heap of recuperating submissive female at their feet it brought her back to the real world and out of her the realm of stark and succulent memories.

"Such alluring curves. I would very much like to see how she performs in the water," said Toyo-tama-hiko.

"Then allow me to loan you to her. If for no other reason than to let us focus on the matter at hand without this enticing distraction."

"My thanks, Warlord," he said and then turned away before speaking with a deep authoritative growl. "Imbe. Transform her into *Midzuha no me* and send her out to join her sisters."

Two men appeared immediately. Both had the ideogram of the Supreme Warlord tattooed on their chest and entwined sea dragons surrounded this image. Muscular of limb, they had waist length ponytails of dark hair and wore only a pair of form fitting leather shorts.

They briskly untied her and without further comment she was drawn out of the room and into the winding caverns and passages of the palace. Candy was glad that she was to be processed by lower grade priests. She needed a break from the rigid and utterly impeccable façade she was required to keep while within the presence of her master and his compeers.

When alone with Hachiman she felt a little more free to

expose frailty and defect, but when her lapses might besmirch his image due to the presence of other Kami, she felt that she had to forsake her own pleasures and focus her entire self on composure and conduct. With mere Imbe, she could wail and curse, talk back and earn herself the discipline she so fervently craved and do so whenever the mood took her. The thought of being able to complain and berate her escort flashed through Candy and crafted a most torrid feeling. It was a sense of naughtiness, of nefariously committing herself to disobedience for no other reason than to earn chastisement. When basking in the aura of immortal Kami she had to live up to their expectations. Yomi was always there, waiting for her, and that meant she would never see the Warlord or Lady Uzume ever again. That in itself was one of the most frightening aspects of that dreadful place. However, her escorts were mere Imbe and probably lacked the authority to sentence the slave of an honoured guest to the underworld.

Candy decided that she was going to have some fun with them. She could resist without fear of dooming herself. She no longer had to bite her tongue, and was eager to indulge this power before it was again taken away from her. She was about to be sent out into the ocean and a last indulgence of her freedom before it was lost would be a delightful memory to take with her into the watery depths.

The room to which she was delivered was another private dock, one that clearly facilitated the delivery of newly created water concubine into their new environment.

A pool of calm water about six yards wide was set in the floor to the far side of the oval cavern, and Candy could see light rising from some sort of aquatic tunnel stretching outward under it.

The left side of the room was replete with identical racks of the same style of costume. The cascades of brightly coloured rubber hung like discarded chrysalises and each seemed to have a slightly different pattern or colour scheme to create individuality for every water female that was manufactured here.

The right side of the chamber bore several alcoves with decorative embroidered curtains set across the fronts and before them were two items that grew from the smooth stone floor. One was a simple toilet and the other was a wide and very low pillory with only two openings. The stocks were set horizontally and were hoisted from the ground by two supports that were only a couple of inches high. Set a short distance ahead of the device was a dangling chain that vanished into a hole in the ceiling and culminated in a pair of dense leather shackles. Another chain on the opposite side of the stocks held a thick leather belt.

Candy was brought to the pillory and her ankles inserted into the apertures before they were locked in. With her legs spread quite far apart, she was supported by one of the Imbe while the other fetched the loitering cuffs.

She grimaced as her arms were brought behind her back and when her wrists met, they were pulled straight up to bend her over at her middle. The cuffs were quickly applied and the Imbe stepped away so he might gather the belt and buckle it about her waist.

"Time to offer yourself to us, slave," uttered an Imbe as he wandered to the wall. One of the curtains was pulled aside to expose various items lurking in the shadows within. Candy tried to catch a glance and see what might be intended for her, but a lever was pulled down and instantly there came the sound of covert mechanical motion. A winch in the ceiling snagged the chain that was holding her arms and hauled it in. Candy gave a cry as the effects of her own bent arms yanked her face down.

Up and up went her hands and she toppled forward in a bid to ease the sudden rending flare of grief in her shoulders.

The belt dug into her waist and lodged against her hips to stop her falling forward and when the lever was raised, the winch stopped.

"Stop! Please! Stop!" roared Candy.

"A little more, slave?" said the Imbe and briefly yanked down the control lever. The winch clicked on another cog and Candy issued a squawk of anguish as her arms moved onward another terrible degree.

"Dammit! No! I can't take any more! Please! You're breaking me!" she implored.

The distress continued to well and the words to continue begging appeared in her throat. An inverted glance to the Imbe made her breath suddenly stop when her previous commitment to rebellion rushed through her. These were minor servants of the palace, and she had a degree of immunity from lingering consequence. They could not harm her permanently and could not condemn her. She was on loan from a Kami, so there was no reason for her to bite her words or pander to them. Candy's lust-charged stare rolled up and down their physiques and she decided that she wanted them to punish her. She wanted these priests dripping with resentment towards her. She wanted to anger them, leave them speechless at her behaviour.

Just as the Kami tested her tolerances and pushed her boundaries, she wanted to see how far she could push these priests and see how strong their fealty to their master was.

"I told you to stop, you idiot!" she barked, fuelling the volume of her demand with the pain in her contorted shoulders.

"Such a wild creature," commented the other Imbe. "Give her another notch."

"No! Don't! Don't listen to him, I-" the words transformed into a croak and then a wail as a flick of the control imposed another terrible measure to her ordeal. Her shoulders and arms were curdling with pain and her legs trembled beneath her, but any attempt to wilt only escalated the distress on her limbs. She pulled at the cuffs and fought to push herself forward a little, just to ease the pain in her joints. The belt refused to give her any leeway and another touch to the lever turned her grumbles into a scream.

"You stupid priest! No wonder you're just Imbe! You're damaging Warlord Hachiman's property!" she snarled as tears and saliva dripped onto the floor before her.

"What? Just by doing this?" he replied.

An added measure made Candy cry out.

"Are you absolutely sure? Just with this simple tug of a lever?"

Another click was applied, and this met Candy's tolerances.

"Oh God, please. I'll be good! I'll do whatever you want. Just give me a little slack. Please. My arms are about to snap!" she protested.

Now that she felt fully bound and unable to move in the slightest, she wanted to encourage some other forms of use of her body. Also, she needed a moment to acclimatise to her travail. The pain was feeding her masochism and she was starting to feel the onset of intense arousal. If she continued to focus on the prospect of what she could create for herself here, she would be able to take everything they could offer and find delight in it. She just needed a moment to prepare herself.

"Good. Then we shall proceed, slave," said the Imbe at the controls.

He deserted his post after grabbing what appeared to be the end of a length of hose. The thick black piping poured from the alcove and he approached Candy's rear.

"Wh . . . what are you going to do?" asked Candy while turning her head one way and then another to try and spot what was at the end of the hose.

"Ready you for your transformation, slave," he coolly

answered and Candy arched against her restraints and gasped as something stole entry into her rear.

The slightly pliant intruder slithered into her and then suddenly broke into life. The instrument began to swell and stretched her insides against a swiftly growing orb of influence. Candy levied her muscles against it to spit it out and her sphincter responded with a shock of angry fury as it was stretched more than it wished to be. The device was small upon entry and her rear had not been dilated. The item growing within her was now too big to easily be passed.

Candy tried again but she was forced to clench and gobble the orb back up when her orifice resounded with rancour from being stretched upon just the first portion of the intruder.

The plug continued to inflate, and Candy struggled against her bonds as her channels were mercilessly forced to accommodate it. The process only stopped when her rear was at an almost unbearable peak of anguish.

Gasping for breath, Candy gave a controlled push but again, the size of the item meant that she would have to work at getting it out for some time. She flexed her rear and the huge orb moved into her and away from her tight hole. The feel of it creeping deeper made her shudder and she reversed her attempt to again push it to her opening until it throbbed, whereupon she sucked it back in. The stark sensations made her quiver and inspired her to continue with her ploy of pushing the Imbe.

"Get this damn thing out of me!" she bellowed.

Candy gave a squeak when she felt cool water spreading into her. The interior hose was pumping her full of fluid and she found that this was not water, rather it was some sort of viscous substance that she could squeeze and feel move against her. The steady influx reached deeper as her flexing tracts and inverted pose allowed it to trek on and follow the twists and turns of her canals.

"I won't be pumped up like this. I won't!"

The cool gel was distinct within her, and it was a delicious and alien sensation that only further engendered a ferocious libidinous state.

"Quite a mouth on her, is there not?" said the one who had installed the tube.

"Perhaps we should see how else she uses it?"

The swell of the fluid as it was introduced began to push the plug against her sphincter and this almost watertight seal meant that none of it escaped. Candy had to flex and roll her innards to ensure she swallowed the douche because any attempt to tighten up or resist caused the steady pumping orb to push harder to her opening. Only by acquiescing to the relentless anal tide could she ease her lot. However, even as she made her bottom obey their demands, the rest of her hungered for more.

"I won't! I refuse to be used by such lowly servants of a weak House!" exclaimed Candy.

She gave a wail as the hose was grabbed and the inflated orb used to punish her rear. The Imbe continued with the pull, hauling her open until she screamed for him to stop. He let go and Candy promptly sucked the plug back in.

"Leave me alone! Untie me and let me go this instant," she roared.

The other Imbe grabbed her hair and hauled her head up. Rasping for breath after the abuse, she regarded his stare with venom.

"You dare speak thus of the Great Houses of Water?" he snarled.

The sparks of heat in her scalp charged her with fresh impiety.

"Houses of *piss*! I spit on you," shouted Candy. The priest tottered back as though he had been slapped across the face.

"You . . . I . . . w . . . such dishonour! How can the Warlord tolerate such a barbarian?" he stammered with utter disbelief.

"I respect my master. You're worthy of nothing but my derision."

"You will be punished for this grand insolence!" roared the priest.

Candy's mind raced with possibilities, and she knew now that she would be brutally treated, just as she wished. She wanted to be taken past her limits and yet still be able to holler and curse with facility, but she also wanted to be fucked, and she knew just how to play the Imbe to acquire what she wanted. Their fury made them vulnerable and open to exploitation, and if there was one thing Candy had brought with her from her other life as Candice, it was the ability to exploit intense emotion and manipulate it to grab her acquisitions. Previously it had snatched companies and carved positions of authority. Now it would acquire a raging cock and a vicious whipping.

"Am I supposed to be afraid? Water Imbe are renowned as bumbling amateurs in the ways of discipline. Only their skills are coitus are less well regarded."

"Never have I heard such lack of respect!"

"Well, get used to it. I have plenty more. Although I don't want to use any big words that might confuse you, so I'll just tell you to go fuck yourself," she growled and tucked laughter within the words.

The Imbe darted away and she could hear them fumbling in the alcoves. Their hands were clumsy because of their rage. Candy closed her eyes, took a deep breath, and readied to embrace what she had sought. She knew it would be long and terrible, but if she found that sultry state of masochistic bliss it would all be worth it, and even if she did not, the longer and more savage this encounter was the more delightful it would be in retrospect.

"Then you are advised to get used to this," growled one of the Imbe.

Two cool metal prongs pressed to Candy's buttock and a sudden charge rushed between them. Her leg flashed to excruciating attention and her shriek rushed freely from her throat. The other Imbe pressed another pair to the opposite inner thigh and the flesh responded instantly. The skin howled from being savaged and the muscles and tendons burned from overt use as they were compelled to flex to a degree even her own mind could not demand.

"Where are your insults now?" purred an Imbe.

The prods both pressed to her rear and made her lurch against her restraints. A trickle of goo emerged around the bulb and began to move down her leg.

In the wake of the shock, she sagged and then mewed as her arms were twisted from her wilting position. She straightened back up and felt her anus pounding from the pressure of the orb as it barged against her rear. Candy pulled it back in to ease her predicament and savoured the slick trickle that was running down her inner thigh.

"Insults? The only insult is your skill at punishing me. Untie me and I'll do the job properly by myself, you incompetent cretin," was her hoarse rebuke.

The prods summarily pressed to her calves. Candy wailed at the top of her lungs when she was encouraged to stand on tiptoe save that the stocks denied her. The rims of the pillory gnawed at her jolting ankles and her body lurched against its containment.

The prods jumped back and then touched the backs of her thighs. After another grievous dose of maltreatment, they pressed again into her rear and then finally returned to her inner thighs.

Candy dropped and the effects on her twisted arms went unnoticed as the world slithered before her. Tears dribbled from her eyes and a layer of panicked sweat was forming across her entire physique.

"Stooooop! Pleeeease!" she squealed. A caning or whipping had been her intent, not this ghastly electrical brutality.

"You were not so polite a moment ago, slave," commented an Imbe and she saw them step beside her. Each held a yard long pole with one end appearing to be a large square counterweight in which the battery was no doubt contained, and after an insulted section with two grips, the device spat out two copper prongs on the opposite end.

The forks wafted beneath her hanging breasts and Candy fought to draw herself away. The residual pain in her legs was making her frightened of the prods and she greatly regretted her previous words.

"I apologise, I did not mean it, I was . . . wait, no, don't. Not my breasts, I'll do-"

Candy's throat stretched forth and her eyes screwed shut. Her scream pained her own ears as they pressed the prongs into the exposed female flesh. The prods curdled her breasts with a potent fulgent wrath, and she lurched against her restraints. More gel escaped her rear and the force of the orb against her rear was hidden until the prods came away and she managed to gather some semblance of awareness of her surroundings. The pain in her bottom was detected and she quickly hauled the orb back in.

As the sphere nestled into place, she could feel the fluid now being sucked free of her. The tide had reversed and the swollen tunnels of her body were being drained. The feeling was a delicious one of being drained by a mechanical influx as she was punished for her brattiness. Candy trembled and words escaped without conscious thought.

"You bastards, you're nothing to me," she managed to mumble as her view of the room tilted and swayed around her.

Candy flashed back to attention when a forked weapon pressed into her side and the other shoved into her armpit. When they came away, she dropped and hung in a phased stupor. Gasping for breath, she could feel the distinct spots where the prods had touched, and all around these areas the muscles were pounding with heat from their struggle to obey the charges.

"Is that it?" she managed to huskily mumble and then offered a cracked chuckle.

Her body was alive with pain, but her mind was drenched in prurience. The exertions the prods demanded were creating a giddy high, one that Candy knew she had to feed.

She briefly felt the hose start pumping a fresh enema into her and then this sultry slithering insertion was lost to her as a breast and a foot were touched by the angry weapons. Candy jolted and was lost within a maelstrom of suffering that parted to reveal a sensational and warped ecstasy. The sheer potency of the input was exhilarating. The more she was punished, the more bliss she found, and this physical euphoria was matched by a psychological relish. This delight came from cursing the priests, making them abuse her even more cruelly, making them torment her until she was almost deafened by her own cries, and still she wanted more.

"So, when is this punishment going to occur? Or are you going to keep tickling me all day?"

It took a maximum effort to string the words together, and it was even harder to stop from begging for more abuse rather than reviling them in order to acquire it.

The prods shoved into her shoulders and made her shudder and shriek. When she descended from the peaks of misery that the prods bequeathed, she felt her belly being distended by another full measure of the douche.

"Do you want to suck my cock?" asked an Imbe.

"Never!" she snorted.

The prods targeted her breasts again and Candy hollered at the top of her lungs. They left the devices in place for a longer duration, one that caused Candy to run out of air. Her face remained frozen, and the scream trailed off. She just hung and shuddered as she tried to fuel her answer to the prod but there was nothing left.

The weapons came away and she collapsed against her bondage, remaining ignorant of the additional testy bother in her shoulders caused by just hanging in her restraints and having the twisted joints be her primary support.

"Tell me you want to suck me in apology!" he snarled.

"Me? Suck a mere Imbe's cock?" she uttered and again managed to find enough strength to taunt them with a mocking laugh.

Candy flew to attention and her howl reached a new and powerful peak when the prod nestled between her legs and shoved into her pussy. Candy's sight glazed over as tears obscured her vision and again her breath was spent on her shriek until no more remained. When the prod came away, she dropped and struggled to catch her breath. She hauled vast amounts in and then threw it out as croak before rapidly grabbing another.

"Tell me, slave!" snarled the Imbe.

"I . . ." she managed to offer. Her senses were reeling and her ability to process this treatment was becoming corrupted. She wanted more. She wanted to go further. Her masochism was a terrible creature that brooked no denial. However, Candy was not sure that her body could meet the demands of her appetites. She had not felt this fear since her time with Lady Uzume and the Mikado in the Chamber of Sun. This time she had voyaged further, but now she had to try and take a step back before the beast within her consumed the last vestiges of common sense. She was again on a precipice of algolagnic indulgence and had to calm down before she accidentally hurled herself off of it.

"Yes, tell me! Tell me, slave! I want to hear you beg!"

"I . . . want . . ."

"Yes," he growled, his animus now being warped into anticipation of breaking her spirit and making her submit.

"I want to warn you."

"What do you mean?" he exclaimed.

Candy steeled her resolve and shook her head from side to side, casting away the muggy confusion caused by the session. A wry smirk appeared on her lips and she suddenly fixed the priest with an impish glare.

"If you're as physically endowed as you're skilled in discipline, well then it may take me awhile to find that tiny appendage!"

"Again. More! Make this slut beg!"

The charged fork leant itself to her pussy and again Candy was made to shriek and dance against her bondage. When it came away, she snatched a breath and then vent it as an imploration.

"I want to suck your cock!"

The words were not from fear of more torture, but from fear that if she did not stall her raging thirst for this abuse, she would not be able to stop herself again. She would continue to insult them and resist until her body just shut down when it failed to meet the demands her masochism asked of it.

The Imbe grabbed her chin and hoisted it up. Candy realised now that during the last shock, her cuffs had been lowered and she was now able to rise a little and facilitate their intentions.

"Beg! I want to hear you beg!"

"Please! I need to suck your cock!" she wailed.

The prod returned and scorched her pussy with waves of unendurable mayhem.

"More! Say it again!"

"Oh please! I have to suck your cock! Fuck my mouth! Please! I beg of you!" she screamed.

The Imbe before her dropped his prod and grabbed her beneath the chin with one hand and cupped the front of her throat with the other. Candy's maw was already open and so he easily fed himself into her. As she instinctively swallowed, he took advantage of her enervation and rushed into her throat. Candy jerked and gurgled as her breath was stolen. The hold on her throat allowed him to dive down into her and her oesophagus convulsed and grabbed at his member.

Before she could resist further, Candy's breath rushed out from around his shaft and her body jolted to a fixed and rigid stance. The other Imbe was pulling out the anal plug!

Squealing for mercy, Candy felt him pull and let go, then pull and let go. Each tug grew in strength and made her entire anus explode with a feverish pain that easily rivalled the effects of the prods. Fearing that she would be horribly wounded, she fought to get free, but her struggles only made her sway and rock, and the cock down her throat responded to the manipulation and grew harder.

Fighting for air and to get free of the hand that was pulling at the orb, Candy's eyes were filled solely with the image of her oppressor's stomach.

The Imbe drew back a little and the feel of him emerging from her throat was a most eerie one. She managed to get some breath, which she instantly spent on a shriek as a single long pull brought her sphincter to a mordant pinnacle of woe before the bulb popped free.

Her scream was stolen as a stiff manhood again rushed down her throat. Holding her chin and her throat to ensure a straight path, the Imbe laughed and started to thrust. His abdomen pressed to her face and he wiggled slightly before drawing back so he could charge back in.

Candy felt as though she were no longer in her body. Her

mind had been separated from all control, and only intense sensation ruled it now. The Imbe fucking her throat decided when she could breath, and the one that had stolen her plug now took his own toll on that commodity when his penis jumped into her much stretched rear.

Thrashing wildly, she felt his hips slamming to her buttocks, and the dream-like nature of this event became even more surreal as she felt the gel pouring from her body. Already cleansed by at least one douche, Candy could feel men invading rear and mouth as a gurgling font of thick treacle rushed from her bottom. Even as she was filled with manhood, she was being internally emptied of the pressure of the douche.

The Imbe behind her dropped his prod into the small of her back. Candy flashed to attention as the charge rolled out though her whole body. The two priests gasped with pleasure as her throat and rear clenched and squeezed their invading organs. The pain was merged with pleasure as she felt them dive into her, and the tightness of her openings made the feel of them stealing access all the more succulent.

Candy's entire anatomy was in such a confused state that she was not sure if was orgasming or not. The searing zenith of pleasure and pain was so confusing that she could not properly catalogue it. Whatever it was, it was a soul-shredding event that she could barely withstand. If she could have, she would have spent her strength on begging them to stop. Her mind was being washed away on a flood of input and she was terrified that she would not be able to find a way back. Withdrawal from such impossible heights should be fatal because surely no human could drop from this pinnacle and survive.

The Imbe before her convulsed as his cock twitched and she felt fluid warmth being sown along her throat. The sensation made her cavort more energetically and this caused the manhood between her buttocks to copy the action. The feel of their near simultaneous climax brought about a similar response for Candy, and for a moment, the pleasure finally overwhelmed the pain and she was consumed by orgasm that fed on and was enhanced by the rigour of her trials.

The rhythm of the Imbe slowed and they withdrew from her body. The belt around her waist opened and the shackles were unbuckled as the stocks opened. Candy collapsed as an inert heap. With eyes clenched tightly shut, she simply lay on the floor, shuddering and muttering to herself. Riding a wave of impossible delight, Candy just held herself and prayed for strength as the potency of her ravishment and abuse continued to thunder through her.

"Now how do you regard the Houses of Water, slave!"

"They are mighty and skilled, master," she managed to whisper.

"Show your reverence in the proper manner, slave."

Candy opened one eye and saw a foot before her. She managed to stretch her neck forward and offered it several idolatrous pecks.

"Better. Much better."

"Although there is nothing more submissive and weak than water, for attacking that which is hard and strong, nothing can surpass it," stated one of them as he restored his shorts.

"You called us weak. Mocked our standing. But the water has quenched the fire, and eroded the defiant, has it not?"

"Yes, master," she agreed with a tremulous tone. Her defeat was total, and she felt glorious because of it. Everything she had wanted from this encounter, she had found, and was now ready to continue her journey. The unrepentant had been made docile and now was ready to become a mermaid.

# CHAPTER FOURTEEN

"Stand down," barked Lady Uzume.

The ranks of muzzles lowered as the cavalry obeyed. The Wani also shouldered firearms and sheathed swords at the command.

Her meteoric ride across the plains had been misinterpreted as danger and the whole column had sprung into defensive action to protect the incoming deity.

Lady Uzume drew her steed up beside her second in command. Masuda snapped to attention and then bowed in saddle as much as his safety harness permitted.

"Your orders, Lady Uzume?"

"My escort has cleared a path into the mountains. Send a battalion of Wani to reinforce their position and cavalry elements into the surrounding area to help search for the Stray. We will co-ordinate from here and follow them in once the area has been secured."

"As you desire," he stated formally and turned his own mount around to instigate the directives.

Uzume pulled up next to her howdah and the troops atop it immediately activated the door release. The drawbridge extended out on two dense chains and the portcullis started to grind upward. It exposed the set of dense double doors that were the only point of access into the dinosaur-borne fort.

She unbuckled her harness and unfastened the unconscious form of the girl from behind the saddle. Scooping her up, Uzume stepped over and jumped onto the extended drawbridge. Her mount sagged immediately as it was allowed to rest. She had ridden it a little hard all the way back. Her eagerness to establish the girl in her howdah before she regained conscious had been more paramount than the health of her steed.

Several Mitama jogged over on foot to climb up the beast and take it away. Uzume hoisted the girl over one shoulder, marched to the doors, and quickly entered. The sound of the defences being re-established commenced immediately and ensured that they would not be disturbed.

In a day or so she would continue on towards the mountains. By then, her forces would have been dealt with and this victory might help rally the Provinces. Defeating Mitama would bolster morale and encourage unity and commitment in the foe. The force she had left behind would never retreat or surrender, and so their demise was certain. When this was reported back to her, the retrieval force would continue onwards regardless and this would strengthen her position because Lady Uzume putting her divine self in jeopardy and taking on an army that had already defeated her elite would counter any accusations of cowardice. The Wani battalion would then bear the brunt of the Provincial task force and with depleted numbers against a superior force, Lady Uzume would have to retreat.

Outrage at the Province's killing of Imperial warriors would hopefully be sufficiently intense to eclipse anger at her defeat while remaining strong enough that Toyotami-hiko would still renew his offer of recruitment. However, she was still concerned that it might not be enough to promote war.

Her plan was in motion and would not require her attention for a time so she could busy herself with some selfish indulgences. She laid the girl down and went to get changed. The tranquilliser was a stubborn one that lurked in the system for some time. The prisoner would be out for a few more hours and then she would meet her new owner and begin her new life as Lady Uzume's personal sex slave.

Uzume was also excited because she had the almost unique chance to be vulgar with her slave. There were no priests to maintain the image of being regal Kami around, and even the guards atop the howdah would not be able to hear her over the wind and booming steps of the mount.

Her ability to speak the Provincial dialect was a little rusty, but she was certain she could communicate with her captive and where language failed her, a cane across her impudent rear would convey her intentions.

Xiao started to claw her way out of the darkness. She started to feel aspects of her body again and slowly managed to haul her eyelids up. At first she thought her limbs were still paralysed, but then she realised it was because she was tied up.

She gave a sudden jolt and found that she was indeed stringently contained. A dense wooden pillory held her hands a couple of feet out away from either side of her head. The apertures that enclosed around wrist and neck were padded with soft leather and the bright red wood had been carved with swirling dark patterns that flowed all across its smooth surfaces. A stout wooden beam lanced down from the base of the stocks and merged with the floor to hold the contraption aloft. Another beam connected to the lower slat of the pillory and the thin padded surface supported her torso. It ran through her cleavage and left her breasts hanging on either side before it stopped just before her loins. A wide, inverted *V* held this end up and the triangle of wood was also padded. Her lewdly parted legs had been strapped down at ankle and upper thigh, the belts pressing her limbs into the leather. Her toes wiggled against the struts and were unable to even graze the floor.

Xiao pulled with all her strength but could do nothing to break her bonds or slip free of them. With a resigned sigh she relaxed against the soft material and looked around at her prison.

The walls were constructed of dense hardwood planks and a series of arrow slits allowed sunlight to stream in and provide illumination. Four wooden pillars rose around her and they supported an equally strong ceiling. Everywhere she could see small metal eyelets fixed into the timbers and she was awed by the amount of the precious material that had been squandered here.

Xiao winced when she saw several racks upon which were fastened weapons. Curved katana, several longbows, some quivers of arrows, and several barbed spears were situated next to another rack upon which were hung the intricate and advanced weapons she had seen the devil riders using.

A slight feeling of nausea was still residing in her belly, but when she saw the beams of light moving with the sway of the room she realised that it was from motion and not the poison. Xiao wondered if she were at sea and if so, where she could be heading. The strange thing was that she couldn't hear the lap of waves against the hull, the creak of ropes, or the snap of canvas sails as they fluttered against the wind.

Her father had worked as a hired sword on a whaling junk in his early years, defending the massive craft from pirates. Although they were armoured and equipped to capture and kill monstrous aquatic predators and other prey, reavers often found the sluggish vessels easy targets. He had talked of the sea and this craft bore none of the traits he had pined about in his bedtime stories. Perhaps he had been exaggerating, as she often believed he did.

Thought of her family brought Xiao's attention back to them. At least she had performed one last good deed for them. She may have been a burden to them, but the delay caused by her capture had to have warned them and by now they would be in the mines. Her family had to have detected the dreadful charge of the Tyrannosaur and her father had often told her the tale of his involvement in a joust upon such creatures, so surely he would know what it was and had reacted accordingly.

A steady tread appeared to her right and by craning her neck around as much as she could, she could just about see a set of tight spiral stairs rolling up and down onto other decks. Expecting to see some filthy and rag-swathed pirate or another of the demon riders, Xiao was taken aback by the radiant creature that sauntered casually into the chamber.

The woman was young and tall, with an elegant, lithe physique. She had powerful oriental features but they were different to the various Provincial castes she was familiar with. Her perked eyebrows extended out into raised curls and dense shades rimmed her eyes before reaching out towards her ears. Contained between the two extended lines of makeup were blue and red shades that had been woven so precisely as to almost look like tattoos. Her lips were painted a vibrant red and her dark eyes were scathing in their intensity. The stranger had jet black hair that was tied back into a high ponytail and this was held in place by a barbed ring.

The skin of the stranger was pale, suggesting that she rarely went outside. Xiao knew that this was not unusual for women, whose value and rarity often had them kept locked away for their own protection, but this woman did not move like a captive or a concubine because each step was bold and uncompromising. She moved as though all creation bowed to her whim and Xiao trembled to be held prisoner before her.

The manner of her attire was also worrying and Xiao had never seen anything like it. Polished red leather clutched to her arms and legs. The gloves did not have fingers, and this let her slender fingers emerge and reveal her black and pointed nails. Her feet were perched atop wicked heels that clicked against the wooden deck with every step. About her waist was a brief corset that was laced at the back. The crimson band rested on her trim waist rather than drew it in and the front bore a strange black ideogram that had been stitched into place. A skimpy thong of red hide hooked arms under the corset and plunged down the front before sliding up between her rear. Her breasts were free and silver hoops could be seen transfixing both rouged nipples. Xiao had never even heard of any woman wearing so little, let alone being so comfortable in such a state of undress.

In one hand dangled a belt that transfixed a large red orb. The other bore a black leather paddle that repeated the ideogram as a raised emblem in the middle. The alluring stranger simply stopped before Xiao and cast an impassive glower over her form.

"Who . . . who are you?" she managed to stutter. Her fright at being helpless before such a strange entity was making her whole body quake. Xiao had no idea what was happening, where she was, or what was going to befall her. She had been cursing her fate and dreamed of escape but this was not what she had in mind. Perhaps fate was punishing her after hearing her curses and not being specific with her demands.

"I am Lady Uzume, and you will call me "goddess" when I permit you to speak, mortal slut," she said. Her voice seemed soft and calm yet there was an inner well of power inside it that made every sound potent and conclusive.

"G . . . goddess? . . . Th . . . then that means . . . oh Gods . . . no! NO!" she exclaimed as a broad and wicked grin started to creep across the tyrant's face.

"Yes, slave. I am Kami!"

Xiao screamed aloud for help, bellowing at the top of her lungs as the woman closed in and stretched the belt between her fingers. Lurching against her bonds, she was livid with terror as the woman pushed the orb into her shrieking maw and then buckled it tightly about the back of her head. Xiao gurgled and tried to spit the ball out as it craned her jaws wide, but the belt had already been established.

"I see you've heard of us," said the woman with a dry chuckle.

Xiao broke into a sobbing fit and cringed in horror.

"Not the Empire," she screamed through her mind. "Anything but the Empire."

Only in the darkest of times when hope was thin, and only in the company of those one knew and trusted implicitly was the word "Kami" every spoken of. Xiao's body seemed to drain away, and she felt a faint trickle escape between her legs as a lugubrious tempest enveloped her.

Far to the west, over the untamed expanses of the Waste Lands where dinosaur and western barbarian roamed and killed as the whim took them, there existed a wall that no living being dared look upon. It stretched across the land and beyond it was a paradise that was as sublime as it was terrible. In the lush and verdant realm lived a demonic immortal race. The Kami were devils, entities that stole the souls of the wicked and subjected them to hideous torments and depravities beyond mortal comprehension, and did so for all eternity. Sometimes, the vile monsters would tire of the doomed and the wretched, and on these occasions they would emerge from their hellish heaven to seek fresh fodder. Invariably they sought the just, the pure, and the innocent, who they would then corrupt and debase over the years before their soul joined the ranks of the damned as a legitimate member.

Xiao wept uncontrollably as she realised now that such a being had captured her. The stories had terrified her and now that she knew them to be accurate, her fear was complete.

"Let's get this out the way first," growled the woman.

She snatched hold of Xiao's hair and with callous motions

started to weave it into a stern plait that hauled at her roots. Once she had tightened it into a more curtailed format, she stepped back and admired both her handiwork and her captive.

Muted pleas rolled against the gag as Xiao bucked and struggled against her bondage. As though waiting for her prisoner to become convinced that she had no way to escape, the stranger just watched.

When Xiao sagged in resignation, she strolled around the stocks and approached her rear. The leather-clad palm of the Kami dropped against Xiao's buttock and then stung the other. Xiao jerked and gave a long mew that rose to a squeak when another pair of slaps scudded along and clapped to her cheeks.

Her captor continued to lambaste her with strong sweeps, applying her full hand to the peaks of the quaking flesh. The room echoed with the sharp sound of each slap, and every impact fuelled a struggling annoying tingle that quickly manifested in the abused skin. The more she was slapped, the more powerful this distress became until Xiao was crying out against the gag for the woman to stop. Every fresh impact now brought a flash of ardent distress and Xiao threw her hindquarters from side to side to try and avoid each attack. The belts against her thighs stole away even the paltriest movement and the woman could target with absolute precision until Xiao was screaming against her gag for some hint of mercy.

For a moment, Xiao thought her keening hollers had acquired a result but the brief quiet ended with a deep hum and then a solid slap as the paddle landed with stunning force to the summit of her rear. The raised emblem upon it struck the flushed rounded tops of her buttocks. It was terribly distinct because most of the weapon's impetus was focused on this area.

Xiao flew to attention and shrieked against the ball gag as the horrible sensations spread through her cheeks. The spanking had left her terribly sensitive, and the solid broad swipe of the paddle was now a monstrous thing to bear.

The woman just laughed and offered a trio of hand spanks to the other buttock to keep it ready to accept its own mark.

"Ready, slave?" she crooned.

Xiao thrashed madly in an attempt to escape the ghastly repeat of her ordeal.

"Here it comes," teased the woman known as Lady Uzume.

She squealed and sobbed, fighting to do anything to make her stop. She couldn't bear the suspense and equally couldn't bear another application of the paddle.

"Right on your arse!" she hissed, piquing Xiao's fear. "Right . . . .now!"

The paddle swung round in a two-handed swipe that brought it to her bottom with fervent brutality. The flesh rippled and then the detonation of pain raged through the abused region. Xiao howled afresh as tears tumbled down her cheeks and the heinous mark seemed to swell upon her skin and send throbbing waves of anguish out across her whole rear.

"Delightful," commented Uzume and stroked the shivering skin before tracing the emerging contours of the ideogram.

"You savour that for a moment while I go and get some more toys for you."

The villainess turned around and wandered back upstairs, leaving Xiao to gasp for breath and try to come to terms with the awful pulse that was haunting her rear, as well as to fear what else was going to be done to her.

The sounds of heels on the steps became a countdown to her return to suffering and Lady Uzume appeared with an ornate wooden chest in her hands. She set it down on a nearby table and lifted the lid before she started to carefully unpack the contents. The table was out of Xiao's easy sight and so she had no idea what was coming.

"So what had a little morsel like you out in the wilderness all alone? Hmmm? An illicit rendezvous away from prying eyes? Was that what spared you a front row seat at the massacre? Was it your libido that allowed you to miss the destruction of your village?"

Xiao struggled anew as the sound of her heels again came close to her rear.

"Were you fucking some undesirable? Acting like a whore when no one was looking?" hissed Uzume and Xiao shrieked as the woman pinched the lips of her pussy together and applied a wooden peg to enforce this closure.

"Oh but we're not done securing this wanton hole just yet. Who knows how many people have thrust into it."

Another peg was added and the compression made the sensitive region course with a terrible chilling throb. Her thighs shuddered and her hands pawed impotently at the stocks. Xiao bellowed for the woman to take them off, but the viper just taunted her with another grim chuckle and added a third and then a fourth peg.

Xiao dropped her head down and stared blankly at the floor as the nightmarish pincers continued to make her suffer. She could not believe that this sort of abuse were possible. How could someone enjoy doing this to someone else? Lady Uzume was a sadistic demon who assumed Xiao to be some sort of prurient fiend. She considered if this were the reason for her capture. Could the Kami only steal away those who were morally impure? Were the innocents actually safe from them?

Xiao battled to form words over the gag. It was infuriating because the pain was garbling her words much more effectively than the jaw-stretching ball. She struggled to spit it out, to fling her head around and cast it free. She had to tell Uzume that she was wrong, that she was a virgin and had always let a good and chaste life. If she could reveal this, then she could not be taken away to the Empire and they would have to release her. At present, she was ready to assent to any theory or any tactic that might get her out of this hellish domain.

"So this pet slut wants more? Is that what all this commotion is about?" accused Uzume.

The woman listened to the enhanced and incoherent pleading for a moment and then wandered back to the chest.

"Well, if that's what you want, then that is what you shall have."

Xiao screeched for clemency and her cries stopped briefly when she heard the creak of leather at her side. She then flinched when she felt fingers touch her hanging breast. The fondling was delicate and sensual, quite unlike the woman's usual attention. Lips touched her nipple, and this made Xiao jolt from shock. A tongue swirled around the peak, and she groaned from the soft pleasure it bequeathed.

The bliss suddenly became agony when the tongue withdrew and was promptly replaced with another peg. The implement crushed the engorged teat and the same hideous pulse that was stamping in her pussy immediately began to afflict it.

"There we are. Now would you like one on your other nipple?"

Xiao threw her head up and bellowed her disagreement.

"Of course you do, so let's get to it shall we?" sighed her abductor.

The sound of her wandering back around made Xiao whimper and go slack against her restraints. The woman was an evil tyrant who wanted to tease her, mock her, and then make her suffer. Xiao was completely at her mercy save that the woman had none. How could such a bleak fate have befallen her, and every second she was here carried her further from her home and any chance of salvation. If this sort of behaviour were causally inflicted on their vessels, she could not even imagine what awaited her in the bleak lands and infernal palaces of the Kami Empire.

"Let's get it all nice and stiff before we decorate it though."

The hands traced delicate whirls on her mamilla and then the lips and tongue of the woman returned to kiss and suckle. Xiao wished that there was some way to control her body, to stop it responding to such caresses, but the woman was as skilful in making her form respond to pleasure as she was at riddling it with pain.

The nipple stood up exactly as Uzume wished and was summarily clamped between ghastly wooden pincers. Xiao howled as the effects took hold. An identical and terrible beat started to throb in the tip, and it resonated through her breast and chest.

The pegs on her sex had lessened in effect as circulation was impeded and the pain deepened. The shocking initial distress was gone, but the steady stamping pound that echoed through her loins gathered new power with every minute, becoming more and more infuriating the longer they remained on her.

"There, that's much better, isn't it?"

Xiao just wept as she shuddered from the effects of the implements.

"What next though? Decisions, decisions. Such a dissolute creature deserves something special before we really get to work on her. But what could that be? Ah, I have it!"

Her malefactor once more returned to the table and began to collect her tools. There was a sparking sound, and a hint of amber light stained the walls. This preceded a strange squelching noise.

Uzume stepped back to Xiao's side and then made her squeal when a slick pliant object was pressed to her rear. It felt like some sort of balloon and even though she clenched with all her might, the viscous gel that was spread upon it allowed it to steal entry with ease. Xiao thrashed madly as she was defiled, but the small item was already within her. Every wriggle made it shift within her and the feel of the slick sac moving inside her body was a horribly intimate one for her.

Xiao roared for Uzume to take it out, that she could not bear such trespass. The flaccid finger suddenly swelled when the woman began to pump it up and it was then that Xiao felt the tiny tube that was connecting the intruder to some sort of external device.

Xiao screeched while the thick balloon continued to grow within her. She threw her internal muscles into the fight to get it out and the swelling orb barged against her sphincter and started to stretch it.

"No, no, no. Bad slut!" mused Uzume and pulled on some of her pussy pegs. The abuse revived their former effulgence and made Xiao tense. The body wide reaction applied to her insides as well and the emerging orb shot back into her when her rear jumped to attention.

"That's better. Now you keep that inside you."

Another trio of pumps made her tracts churn from the stretching power of the orb. Every convulsion made it horribly explicit within her and now, when she tried to eject it, she found that her orifice coursed with a pain she could not withstand.

Xiao flew into a panic. The woman was still pumping up the toy and it would only continue to hurt her more unless she could endure an even worse pain and get it out. Besieged by this predicament, Xiao applied one dedicated shove in order to regurgitate the intruder. The bloated sphere started to open her rear as the slick lubricant dribbled from her opening and ran over her pinched loins.

Holding her breath and straining, her face went red as she felt the anguish escalate with every portion she managed to expel. She was almost there, but the pain in her bottom was virtually beyond endurance. If she could just reach the widest point then the balloon would pop from her and she would be free of it.

Spatters of fluid decorated her back. They felt almost dry and then they thrust their scorching power into her soft skin. As the line of wax continued to hound her hide, her drastic spasm caused the balloon to shoot back into her. The return of this monster into her canals made her squawk in horror and another trip of pumps made her fear that it would burst her from within.

"There we are. If you want it out now, then feel free. But I think you'll keep it in you because you're such a pain hungry little bitch, aren't you?" murmured Uzume as her freed hand caressed Xiao's thighs and sides.

The accusations that she was a depraved entity were maddening, but Xiao was powerless to refute them. Could it be that the punishing of her captive's body was not enough for this despot? Did she want to mistreat her insides as well, and then compliment her sadism with the brutalising of her mind with these crass imprecations?

The candle started to deposit single droplets across the field of her back. Each torrid landing made her flex and squall until it cooled and hardened to her skin. The spots to her flanks made her dance more energetically and all the while Xiao fought her internal nemesis.

Levying her tracts to the massive orb, she pushed until her rear could take no more and forced her to suck it back in. Sometimes a drop of wax on her lower back or buttock made her prematurely end these attempts to stretch her rear and force her to devour the balloon before she had finished. Slowly, she started to expel more and more as her anus reverberated with misery from this self-inflicted abuse.

Xiao paused to catch her breath and winced when a couple of waxen drops landed on her upper shoulder. She knew that this was her chance. She was sure that she could get the monstrous bladder out on this try and readied her efforts to do it one go. It would hurt a great deal but continued internal companionship was far worse.

With a cry of strain she applied her efforts and the sphere started to emerge. Xiao wept with relief when she felt it escaping, and suddenly she added extra strength to her battle.

A peg on her pussy came away and the orb charged back into her when she jumped to full rigidity. Feeling had galloped back into the compressed flesh and announced its displeasure with a hurricane of malicious travail. The skin seemed to swell, as though it were going to explode, then waves of woe spread out from the region. It was as though there was too much pain to be held in one spot and so the excess was spilling into the rest of her.

It took a few minutes for her to recover from the removal and as soon as she had regained her senses, she again threw all her commitment against the ball. Of course, in the time squandered on screaming from the pegs removal her rear had forgotten its last few instances of being stretched and it was harder this time. Nevertheless, her tolerance was at an end. She had to remove at least one aspect of her tortuous ordeal.

If she were not compelled to scream, she would have launched curses at the Kami miscreant because again the loss of a peg made her squall and spasm and gobble the orb back in. Another couple of pumps improved the misery inside her body and made it even harder to try and eject the balloon.

Unable to simply let the sphere remain within her, Xiao recommitted to the fight and each time she did, her efforts were negated with the removal of a peg and then the objective made all the more insurmountable with some extra inflation.

The loss of nipple pegs had the same effect as before but now she was too exhausted to continue. The bloated device was just too entrenched within her to be expelled. She couldn't stretch herself to such degrees and now just had to accept its companionship. Her throbbing nipples and loins were making her more amiable to the intruder, their loss having brought enough relief that she felt she could now cope with it.

"So, out of effort, are we? What a shame. Oh well, I guess I'll have to extract it myself."

It took a moment for Xiao to realise what had been said and then she was again slamming herself against her bonds. She felt the woman pull on the pump and the tube began to tow the balloon towards her aching orifice.

"Here it comes, slave. Get ready," she warned with obvious merriment.

Xiao shrieked as the balloon began to haul her wider and wider, each millimetre bestowing new and intense agony to her poor abused rear.

"No? You still want it?"

The anguish in her bottom made it hard to operate her muscles so when Uzume simply let go, she could not muster the power to eject the toy and it glided back into her body and nestled within her. Xiao sobbed in defeat. The woman was implacable and was going to make every second of this ordeal as acute and unbearable as she could.

"Or do you? Shall I remove it? Yes? No?"

The balloon began its voyage and again began to draw her open wider and wider.

"No, I think not. I think you like it in you. You like people thrusting into you, don't you. It's in your nature. Having things come out, well, it's not your way, is it slut?"

The despot again let go. Xiao bore down on the balloon and continued to push. The item moved out a little more and empowered by her success she added even more strain.

"Yes, I think I do indeed like it in you."

A finger leant to the bulbous orb and even token effort was enough to defeat Xiao and cram it back into her. She hollered with apathy as her attempt was thwarted and she was made to engulf the accursed balloon in her body again.

"But it's getting late, and I could do with some rest before we start afresh tomorrow, and your love of all things inflatable has given me an idea, so . . . out we come."

Uzume grabbed the tube and just pulled. Xiao vibrated within her bondage as the drag opened her more than she could take and as her piercing shriek flowed over the ball gag, her sphincter finally rode over the equator of the ball and slithered down until the item finally popped free of her.

Giddy with elation and possessed of a wonderful sense of achievement and relief, Xiao panted for breath and watched her tears and dribble drop away and land on the floor beneath her.

"Not a bad beginning, slave. Tomorrow we'll have a full day in which to see you whimper, so make sure you get plenty of rest in there," she said, and with another mocking laugh, Lady Uzume headed upstairs. Xiao squeezed her eyes closed and prayed to wake up safe in her room before tomorrow came.

# CHAPTER FIFTEEN

O ne of the Imbe grabbed hold of Candy and pushed her down onto her knees as the other approached with a full catsuit of black latex. After liberally applying powder to its interior they opened the back and began to haul it onto Candy's body. The eerie fabric clinched at her form and made her shudder with delectation. It was like being consumed by some sort of thick impermeable monster.

Her hands and feet entered featureless socks and mittens and Candy was alarmed when the front was pulled up because within the breast cups she found an interior pad that was armed with row upon row of small blunt spines. She realised that the ripples of the water would manipulate these spines and lightly punish her every motion. She could also feel other, less stringent versions against her pussy. These pliant nodules were pressed to her loins and she could feel them shift with every clench of her thighs or shift of her hindquarters.

Candy whimpered as the catsuit was zipped up and when the cinch on her chest grew it caused the small teeth to gnaw on her breasts. She grimaced again when the Imbe turned her arms around and started to capture them within a ferocious sheath.

Sealed away from the outside world, Candy was lowered to the ground and her tail was brought forth. This sleeve was embellished with brilliant stripes of turquoise and red and it trailed matching fins from its length. At present the streamers just flopped on the floor as though deprived of life, but when entered into the water they would billow and flap in her wake.

Her legs were delivered into the tube and the hem was tightened just below her breasts as other belts were hauled in about her hips so that it would not slough off with her movements.

An armless top was brought down over her head and the light grip pulled her bound arms even more forcefully into her back. The top was attached to the tail and Candy's transformation from naked mammal to rubber-trussed fish was completed save for one addition.

"These are to help you see," announced an Imbe.

Candy struggled as the other priest applied a brutal arm-lock and captured her head in the hold as the other opened a contact lens case. Her eyelids were held open and despite her best efforts to resist, she did not manage to stop them dropping a set of clear plastic cups onto her eyes.

Blinking to make the uncomfortable items settle into place, she caught only flashes of her delivery to the open pool. The Imbe presented her to the shimmering waters and a sudden moment of concern struck her as to whether she could function in this alien environment.

"Wait, I-" she began, but then they simply threw her out.

Candy struck the waters and vanished beneath the surface. For a moment, she panicked and this caused her to flounder and sink a little. She strained her arms to try and get them free so they could help her, but the sheaths and garments stopped her. Her face broke the waters and she snatched a gasp of air.

"Help! I can't do this! I'm d-" she began and the words ended when a wave crossed her face. She jolted and managed to cough and hack before she sank down again. She could see the Imbe standing impassively at the water's edge, flagrantly ignoring her travail.

Candy threw her willpower to her trial and quashed her

fright. Animal instinct would kill her if she didn't suppress it.

Still coughing under the water from the tiny measure she had accidentally inhaled, she fought to hold her breath and concentrate on figuring out how to operate within her uniform. Candy conducted some simple beats of her tail and was driven back towards the surface. She gasped for air and hacked vehemently while she gasped and mewled.

All that was needed to keep her afloat were some tardy beats of her tail. The large fins were an excellent means of propulsion and little effort was needed to maintain her position. With her head above the water, she regulated her breath and finally stopped coughing.

A final glance to the Imbe saw them smile at her success and then they presented her with her gag.

"And this will help you breath," one of them stated.

Trusting their words, Candy swam forward and reached forward with her lips. She locked her teeth into the accommodating groove and the Imbe buckled the item around her head so that she could not lose it. The other mermaids she had seen all willingly held these items and it appeared that the strap was a training consideration for newly created water concubines.

"Go now, and be with the other Midzuha no me," he said, patted her head, and then with the other priest at his side he began to wander away. There was no way for her to follow them, and so all she had was the aquatic world awaiting her beyond the palace.

Candy found that she could breathe through the strange mouthpiece and exhaled fully before stealing great massive inhales to oxygenate her blood as much as she could. Hoping that she had enough air to make the journey, she arched over into the waters and dove down.

She beat her tail with strong strokes and was sent rocketing out down the long underwater corridor. Towards the end, she could see a small dome with an air pocket in it and she surfaced there to acquire another series of breaths before streaking out and into the open waters.

The ease with which she moved had other rewards for a submissive mermaid. Each shift of the water caused her breast cups to grind into her, but this slight misery was emphasised and used to heighten her pleasures as the ranks of rubber nodules against her pussy shifted and danced tantalising fingers to her flesh. This quiet ecstasy initially made it harder to swim because of its distracting nature and tendency to induce a lust charged convulsion or twitch. However, once she got into the steady rhythm of swimming her rate grew faster as every thrash of her legs send a delicious methodical movement against her sex.

Candy launched herself downwards and arose into one of the bathyspheres where she acquired breath and then continued onwards. She had barely made it a few yards when she climaxed. The jolt of rhapsody made her arch and thrash against her suit. Her breasts throbbed as her reactions were translated into a sumptuous distress that raged against her nipples and skin, emphasising her delight as she suffered and elated in her odd aquatic predicament.

The bliss was so fierce that she accidentally breathed in, and to her surprise she found herself drawing in air rather than water. Whatever the gag was, it had some sort of high capacity rebreather invested in it, one that replenished itself automatically when she entered a bathysphere. Candy decided to test her theory before she committed to any further exploration and so she arose back towards the air pocket. When she emerged, she inhaled more gently and could hear the steady hiss of the mouthpiece refilling its tanks. When she ducked her head back down, her first exhale expelled the tiny measure of water that had entered before the gag sealed its refilling vents and once again she was funded with air.

Sinking down again, she swam around in circles, practising her strokes and feeling the delicious caress and spiteful grabbing of her breasts. Round and round she went until it started to get harder to draw in a full breath. Candy now knew that the rebreather had roughly a five-minute capacity, more if she kept her exertions light.

Exultant that she would not be so open to the horrors of drowning, Candy refilled her tanks, thrashed her tail, and shot out into the open ocean. It felt glorious to have been so transformed and now that she knew more about her lot and what she could do, she felt even more excited to experience it.

Confident in her ability to at least function in this strange underwater world, Candy began to head out away from the main palace and towards the great fields of bright glass orbs that rose from the coral like frozen air bubbles.

She could see people of every nationality lounging amidst the regal splendour of the brightly lit interiors and along with other mermaids, she cruised past and watched them at play. The citizens and guests bound their land-based brethren or had them service them in whatever way they desired with a casual command or an equally indifferent summons.

In every aquatic bubble could be seen faces locked in agony and ecstasy and Candy then felt the true burden of her uniform. It aroused her, teased and pleasured her, but it offered her no access to other people and experience was what Candy was truly hungry for.

Like all the others she swam under the sumptuous rooms and arose into their pools to refill her tanks. The contact lenses allowed her to focus and operate easily in the ocean, but if she kept them free of water for more than a few seconds, when the water ran off, her vision became blurry and distorted. Whether this was an accidental by-product of their design or a deliberate measure to keep the mermaids in their designated environment was unknown but from what she knew of the

Kami, Candy leaned towards the more strict explanation.

After several hours of reconnaissance, Candy found that she had travelled a great distance and that the palace was now little more than a silhouette on the seabed horizon. With diminishing air, she spotted a near deserted bathysphere and closed in towards it.

The other mermaids seemed to be avoiding it and she became even more wary when she spotted several of them close in on the underside where some small treats floated on the surface. However, when they saw the occupant, they immediately headed away to a different location.

Candy regarded the figure and found him remarkably unthreatening. His arms bore a number of spiralling colourful tattoos that depicted sea serpents, dragons, fish, and other ocean styles. The images reached up onto his shoulders and then flowed down onto his chest to embrace a depiction of the Supreme Warlord of Water. The priest had long dark hair but was otherwise naked. He was sprawled on some cushions at the edge of the access pool and was casually throwing out treats from a bowl next to him. The rest of the bathysphere was strewn with other cushions and divans save for a hatch that had to feed into the rocky outcrop that anchored the orb.

Candy regarded the scene one more time and when she felt her breath becoming laborious to draw, she was pledged to approaching. She swam down and looked up at the small oval nuggets that were floating on the calm surface. A small shoal of tropical fish had started nibbling at the untouched rewards and more were following the morsels that were sinking down towards the ocean floor.

With a curling motion she swam upward and caused the fish to scatter. She brushed aside the treats and broke the surface. Her rebreather gave a covert hiss and she paused to take a quick look around before her contacts misted over.

There was a sudden flurry of movement as two men

jumped up from beneath a pile of cushions. Stretched between them was a net that they summarily cast out over the
waters. Candy spun around and tried to dive but the weights
on the corners of the net had caused it to sink down beneath
her. The ropes threaded along the perimeter were yanked and
this closed the net beneath her, catching her in a pocket of
mesh.

Candy beat her tail but could do nothing as the net closed
tighter and the two attackers began to haul up their catch. She
left the water and was pulled up onto dry land.

"A fine specimen indeed. Inari, lay her down over here,"
announced the man who had been donating the treats. He
kicked some pillows aside and cleared a space for their captive.

"I agree with you there, Dii, but she's obviously not to
clever," chuckled Inari and drew her into the gap. Inari was
taller than Dii and had a shaven head that exposed water ser-
pent emblems that reared at his temples and streaked down
his neck and onto his upper arms. "Mio, help me get her out.
Or were you asleep under there again? Do you need some
time to wake up before we begin?"

Candy looked to the third priest as they operated the net
and working with his partner, started to open the mesh and
draw her out of it.

"I wasn't sleeping. I was resting my eyelids," retorted Mio.
He was more muscular than the others and had a white goatee
and short pale hair. Only a few token emblems adorned his
forearms, signifying the lowest ranking priest in the room.
"Besides, if you two wouldn't stop grabbing every female fish
that pops her head up, maybe we wouldn't have to wait so
long between catches. Ever heard of using restraint?"

"Oh we'll be using restraint alright," muttered Inari as he
surveyed her form. "But why did she come here? Is she hungry for our attentions? Do we have a masochistic fish on our

hands?"

"No. That's not it. Look at her gills. This one is new to the water." Dii indicated her mouthpiece. Mio reached in and took hold of it. He tested the strap with a brief tug to confirm that she could not spit out the rebreather.

"So she's a new-born Midzuha no me," said Inari, and knelt down on her rear to press her into the floor and stop her from escaping back into the water. She felt his hands grab her hips and assess her curves with complete freedom. Candy knew she had been duped, and was now surrendered to whatever fate these men wanted to subject her to. The fact that she had been trapped, and that other mermaids had avoided them out of experience and fear, suggested this was going to be a fierce encounter.

"One who hasn't learned to avoid enticing bait," said Mio, and moved around to settle before her face so he could regard her features. He reached out, grabbed her chin, and hoisted her head up to look into her eyes. He instantly saw the worry displayed there.

"Oh you are right to be afraid, water concubine. After this, you'll not fall for the same ploy again. I assure you."

Candy felt something being fastened around her ankles and after it tightened to the bunched extremities her legs were being hoisted into the air. She saw that a rope had been set to a conical ankle sheath and this was now dragging her up. When she looked upward, Candy found that the priests had set the coil over a ring in the upper reaches of the bathysphere and were hauling up until she swung out over the water.

The men took the excess rope and passed it through another ring that was near to the entrance hatch. They started to pay out slack until her head vanished beneath the waters, whereupon they tied it off.

Mio placed his hand to the section of rope that was stretched between the rings. By pushing down he could now draw her free, or he could dunk her simply by letting go again.

Inari reached out, caught her, and unfastened what they had referred to as her gills. The item came away and she was released to swing out over the pool again.

"I'll do whatever you . . . oh no, please, no!" exclaimed Candy as she saw Dii and Inari draw long and weighty canes from beneath the cushions. She struggled against her uniform, knowing that such barbarous devices would easily defeat the dense rubber shell.

"Water concubines do not talk back!" snapped Dii, and hurled his instrument out at her. The weapon struck her across her rear and before she could cry out, Mio let go of the rope. Candy dropped and jerked to a halt so that her shriek emerged as a cloud of bubbles and an underwater tone.

Another trio of stern swipes ate at her rear and made her thrash from side to side but she could not curl up enough to get free of the waters.

She was towed upward and her lips left the pool. Candy spluttered and gasped for breath. Her hindquarters were throbbing terribly, and she strained as much as she could to try and break free of her uniform. It was now maddeningly frustrating to be bound so tightly because these sadists could act with liberty.

"Do you have anything else to say, concubine?" asked Dii, and tested her obedience with another swipe that slammed across the upper reaches of her thighs. Candy jolted and issued a long squeal as the skin swelled with infernal feeling.

"Anything at all?"

This time his attack caught her breast. The weighty rod made the flesh ripple and unbridled sorrow poured into the welt. The spines also dug in to emphasise the effect, and the resulting heartfelt cry devolved into a series of whimpering gurgles. Tears began to drop from her face and fall into the waters.

"She weeps like a novice. Perhaps this was not such a sterling catch after all," commented Inari. "I mean, look at this shameful response."

Bamboo greeted her rear as the other strut sank into her chest and brutalised her breasts. Candy screamed aloud and roared for them to stop, to show mercy, but again her words vanished beneath the waves and as soon as she was submerged they started to attack her with greater venom and speed. Candy could not take this, they were treating her with utter disdain and she prayed that her owner miss her and send for her. She tried to stop her cries, but the savagery of the beating demanded them. Streams of bubbles escaped her lips and she fought against her uniform with all her might as they continued to force her to squander her breath. Candy battled even harder as the panic of the dunking started to possess her and rival the pain that they were imparting with every cruel swipe.

Mio hauled her up and she gasped and coughed for breath. Suddenly she was back beneath the water and the men were beating her again.

Hachiman's cruelty was a token of his affection, each cruelty proof of her revered status. These men assumed her an incompetent novice, a weak being who deserved nothing more than their contempt and they were announcing this disdain with every merciless stroke.

Crying out beneath the waves, Candy saw other mermaids beneath her. They were watching her agonies with wicked glee. She had fallen for the ploy, and they were savouring the errors of their aquatic sister. Perhaps some of them had fallen for this trap in their early days and were now delighting in seeing another endure what they too had been made to take.

Candy was drawn up and the women became distorted smears of colour beneath the choppy surface of the pool.

"I . . . I'm . . .n . . ." she began, trying to inform them of who she belonged to. The name of the Warlord might temper their abuse and make them stop. If they knew she was Kami-tso-ko to the Supreme Warlord of Fire, they might cut her down and either ravish her of make her service them.

"Quiet! Your imperfection is infuriating! How did the Temmangu ever allow you to set your foot within a Great House?" snarled Dii.

Candy followed Dii's glance to Mio who was now grinning broadly. All three were blatantly erect — their enjoyment of her obloquy being a profound one.

"No! Wai-" she began and lost valuable air on pointless cries as she was dunked.

The canes returned to her body and seemed to come from every direction. The pain of their punishment was devouring Candy and there was nothing she could do to stop them. She felt utterly abandoned. All she wanted to do was go home, to once again sit on a leash at the feet of her master, but until she was reclaimed, she was at the mercy of any who could grab her. This was indeed a most important lesson and she vowed that if she made it through this trial, she would be more cautious in future.

Candy was dragged up and she was almost delirious from the abuse. She wanted to shriek "I'm no water concubine! I'm the property of Warlord Hachiman!" but all she could do was mewl and sob and then squeak as they continued to attack her with scoffing venom.

Lost within a monstrous storm of cane blows, Candy's inverted world turned over and over as she dangled and repeatedly suffered for their amusement. This rampant confusion caused her not to notice as they drew her in and reapplied her gills. Only when she felt them attending her feet did she become aware that they had actually stopped chastising her.

"Back you go, Midzuha no me," said Dii, and her title was

issued with a sardonic snarl.

Before she could curse him, she was tossed aside and landed in the waters. Exhausted, she sank down and drifted towards the ocean floor. The cold of the water reached in through the layers of rubber and soothed her many vibrant welts. Candy tried to swim but the movement caused her suit to ripple and she squealed against her gill as the breast spines moved and other areas of her attire tightened onto her contused skin.

Employing small and stolid movements, Candy managed to limp her way from the three men, and cast a final hateful glower back at them. She saw them watching her and they just laughed at her resentment before returning to collapse onto the cushions and attend their arousal with masturbation. With her screams still echoing in their ears, they chuckled and talked of her reactions and implorations, pounding fists to their raging shafts as they did so.

Her resentment burned within her almost as potently as the throbbing weals that criss-crossed her body, and Candy made her way out to a different sphere, one that looked uninhabited. She refilled her gills and then sank back beneath the waves.

Candy's loathing of the three priests was mighty within her, but then it began to transform. She was a slave to the Kami Empire. She was here to obey and to please them. However, she was a slave within one of the Great Houses and her time with the trio had shown her just what a privilege that was. She had a duty to her master, a duty to take whatever was handed out to her, to relish every act, every opportunity to experience or please even the lowliest priest. Candy had become bloated with a sense of her own importance and her encounter with the three priests had graphically reminded her that she had no authority, no power, but also, no responsibility. If she just surrendered herself to the whims of all within the Empire, she would fulfil her role. It seemed that some part of that lost being called Candice had sneaked back into her. Warlord Hachiman, Lady Uzume, Toyotama-hiko, she had been amongst the greatest powers in the Empire and they had used her freely. The pride she had felt in being theirs had made the encounters intensely arousing and she had found bliss in the cane, in the whip, in being bound, contorted, penetrated, and subdued. She had regarded Mio, Inari, and Dii as unworthy of her. She was Candy, a slave to Hachiman himself. She was destined for greater servitude than to these inferiors. She snarled inwardly at this mistake and promised to crush her old prideful self. At present, she was Midzuha no me, just another rubber-clad water concubine. Others had been in this role longer and were more experienced, while she had learned this the hard way. From now on, Candy would be dedicated to this role, and not dwell on her return to her master. Until that treasured moment, she had to prove her love of him by embracing this existence.

Candy saw a small shoal of mermaids trailing behind a strolling figure. Dressed in a billowing green diving suit, leaden weights were fastened around his belt. A silver dome of one-way glass contained his head and connected to air tanks via a pair of corrugated pipes. The two oval tanks were held within an ornate harness of gold and were decorated with pearls. The diver's erect manhood jutted from a vent at the front of his suit and stood out like the prow of a ship against the waters.

The mermaids were circling around him, obviously anxious to attend the wanderer. When he paused, they barged and jostled to reach his crotch whereupon they spat out their gills and devoured his manhood with alacrity. As though oblivious to their frenzied oral attention, the diver would then continue marching, leaving the victorious mermaid to dive down and try to recover her mouthpiece. After a few quick wriggles she caught the item and then flipped it back up so she could arch around and devour it.

The sight of such frenzied oral competitiveness was most intriguing and Candy closed in so she might join in. She watched the other mermaids vying for the divers attention and studied how they tried to defeat their rivals to be in the right spot to service him when he stopped. When sufficiently appraised of their tactics, Candy then swam in and joined in the frantic undersea fellatio melee.

A shoulder caught her in the ribs and drove the wind from her lungs as a mermaid knocked her aside and darted in, but the diver was not stopping and so her efforts were wasted. Low on air, the woman had to cede her prime place to another and head for a bathysphere.

A second woman slammed aside two rivals and stole the position, but again, the diver continued his steady march and so eventually, she too was brushed aside to make room for another.

Candy decided to make another attempt and squeezed in between two retreating mermaids. Another mermaid arose beneath her and with several powerful beats of her tail she barged into Candy and thrust her up and away.

Even as she was manoeuvring back around to try again, the diver stopped and the poised woman darted in, dropped her gills, and locked her lips to his shaft. Her head darted back and forth, attending him with fanatic devotion until he again started to walk.

Candy could not see the purpose of this affair. The women did not have enough time between stops to accomplish much, so just what was the motivation behind this bizarre contest?

It was then that she saw the real reason unfold when the diver continued towards a vacant bathysphere and arched his back to regard the entrance pool above him. The reef that rose up and held the sphere had the rungs of a ladder set up it, allowing access for walking travellers. Standing in the rays of light dropping down from above, he suddenly grabbed one of the concubines by her tail and began to ascend with her. The woman went limp and Candy saw her rubber skin quake with anticipation. The woman had been the most gifted of the oral supplicants and had won a place on dry land.

The other mermaids broke away and swiftly swam up to jealously circle the sphere and watch as the diver dragged the mermaid out and dropped her on the ground.

The diver surveyed his choice and began to unfasten and remove his equipment. His helmet came away and Candy saw the features of Soko-tsu-wata-dzu-mi, lord of the seabed, and now she knew why the mermaids had been fighting so eagerly. This premise gained even more weight when he began to draw his chosen female free of her entire uniform. The woman was elated and immediately abased herself before him, kissing his feet and shuddering with joy. Tears of reverence were in her eyes when he finally lifted her features from the floor.

Candy could see that the woman had just been promoted for her valiant attention to him. She was now *Idzu no Midzuha no me*, a blessed concubine, one who was now permitted the honour of walking on the land of the Great House.

After her previous abuse, Candy had been craving pleasure, but had not managed to succeed. A chance for elevation out of the shoals had slipped through her fingers, and she realised now that she was in a completely new world, with new rules, new opportunities, and many new pleasures.

# Chapter Sixteen

The room stopped rocking and Xiao could hear sounds of activity from without. The chamber suddenly lurched and swayed and plummeted downward before a muffled crash caused everything to shake. Xiao squealed against her gag in panic and fought to get free. Had the ship run aground? Was it under attack? Mortal calamity ruled her as she imagined the room slowly filling with water and drowning her by inches.

Silence descended and the faint signal of activity from without managed to reach her ears over her own racing breath. Xiao finally figured out that she was being borne on the back of a sauropod. The massive herbivores were valued sources of mass quantities of meat and also invaluable for heavy lifting and towing because most of them could throw a good ten to twenty tons of body weight into a task. They were also more docile than the smaller armoured breeds that people often used to pull carts or the bipedal breeds that made excellent mounts.

Xiao had only ever seen a howdah once before. It had been during a trip north to the coastal town of Botau for the new year festival. Several dignitaries from other settlements were in attendance and many of them rode in small palaces that had been built upon the backs of these great beasts. Xiao had marvelled at the shimmering jewel bedecked creations and had always wanted to ride in one. She had never thought that this wish could have led her to such a miserable end.

The night was long and arduous. Trussed to her mockery

of a bed, her inability to move stopped her from gaining any real sleep. She was used to tossing and turning, a habit brought about by her concerns and frustrations about the future. Every time she started to nod off, from habit she tried to turn and was thwarted by the straps of the pillory and each time it jolted her back awake.

The dull rays of the sun started to seep in through the arrow slits and the beast arose and recommenced its journey. A short time later, Xiao trembled when she heard the staccato click of high heels on the steps.

The sadistic vixen strolled down into the room and set down another small chest next to the first one. Completely equable with Xiao's bondage, she let her hands run over the contained form and appraise its vulnerability.

Uzume stepped before her and unfastened the gag. Xiao stretched her jaws and licked her lips to try and get rid of the ache that had been haunting the corners of her mouth all night long.

"What is your name, slut?"

Xiao's tolerance for these insults had been eroded by sleep deprivation.

"Don't call me that!"

The woman's hand lashed round and stung Xiao's cheek. The extremity curled back to deliver another attack and Xiao cringed and tried to shy her face away.

Uzume placed a hand to her brow and pushed back to crane her prisoner's face up. The woman was grinning with malevolent delight and started to mock her with an implied assault, delivering her hand at Xiao until she squeaked in fright. She then stalled her attack an inch from her cheek and drew it back again. Six times she was teased with the promise of another slap and only when she was sobbing apologies for her rash words did Uzume spank her cheek once more and then let go.

"So did I offend you? Well then, just what would a dumb slave from the hills like to be called?"

Uzume gave a stark cackle and put her hands on her hips before cocking her head aside and waiting for the answer. Xiao's former rebellion was gone. The heat in her cheeks had driven it from her along with the fear of how the woman would chastise her if it continued.

"Why are you doing this to me?" she whimpered with eyes lowered so as not to regard the frightening malice in her captor's expression.

"Because it amuses me. Now, unless you want me to gag you again. Tell me your name."

"Xiao Lin. Just . . . just please . . . don't gag me."

Uzume sighed.

"I asked you a question. I did not ask you to beg. If I want you to beg . . . Oh I'll make you!"

"I'm sorry, Goddess, I-"

"I can see I'm going to have to teach you to stay silent."

"Wait, no . . . I . . ." stuttered Xiao as the woman twirled around and shuffled back. Aghast, Xiao struggled to try and fend her off, but her hands were too far apart to help her.

"In you go, slave."

Xiao tried to duck her head down, but Uzume just crouched and then hoisted her rear, catching Xiao's nose in the cleft and then pushing her face up. Uzume pushed back and buried her features between her buttocks, cutting off her breath and making her livid with distress.

Uzume wriggled her hips from side to side to relish the feel of Xiao's panic and then leaned down a little to set her nostrils free. She stared agog along the contours of the woman's back as she snorted for breath against the smooth fragrant skin of her oppressor.

"You speak only when I say you can. And you limit your words to what I want. Understand?"

Xiao tried to nod. The hint of movement was distinct enough against the woman's bottom that she discerned her agreement.

"Good."

Uzume pushed in again to stifle Xiao's breathing. She fought to get free or find some avenue of access to air but her struggles only made the villainess groan wantonly as she felt the captive face writhe.

"Only when I say so, slave. And keep your words to the answer and nothing else, unless you want more of this," warned Uzume and continued to keep Xiao's breath restricted.

Spots flashed on her eyes and her lungs hauled futilely at the butt of her kidnapper. Suddenly Uzume stepped forward and let her prisoner gasp for breath as her mind recoiled at what was being done to her.

"Anything else to say?" crooned Uzume while looking over her shoulder. Xiao remained silent and just focused on catching her breath.

"Excellent. I see we are making progress. So, we were going to find out about you, but because you'd rather irk me with disobedience, I can see we will have to set that aside for another time."

Uzume fetched a cane and stood before Xiao. She examined the long wiry strut in the morning light and then conducted some hateful slashes. Xiao gave a terrified shudder as she watched her captor rip at the air with the bamboo sceptre and her lips trembled while she fought to hold back a deluge of imploring words.

"Open your mouth," ordered Uzume.

Having seen the venom with which her captor would employ the cane, Xiao's jaws snapped open instantly as she readied to accept the gag. Instead, Uzume held the cane out and slipped the middle of it between her teeth.

"Hold this," she stated and quickly moved back to the table.

Uzume again appeared before Xiao, and this time she held a long leather-bound handle. One end culminated in a large metal ring and the other set loose a great cascade of long leather ribbons.

"I am going to beat you, slave. And if you drop that cane, it will replace this whip," she hissed with a lustful tone.

Uzume moved to the side, trailing the weapon over Xiao's face. The leather fingers strolled over her features and head and then travelled over the stocks and along her bare back. She felt them slither aside and drop away from her hip.

Carried in both hands, the weighty flogger flashed down and launched overhead before descending into Xiao's back. The pounding attack filled the room with the deep slap of the tendrils to her body and Xiao gave a snort of answer to each stroke. The weapon threw a mild discomfort across the whole of her back and her reactions were more to the noise than the actual effects. However, as the strokes continued to fall, her skin started to become raw and intolerant of the continuing deluge.

The onslaught started to become painful and then quickly became more distressing as she was lambasted with a steady and endless rhythm. Xiao bit harder to the cane and fought to hold on as she gasped and grunted with every new stroke.

The misery in her back was quickly becoming more than she could handle. Every time Uzume thrashed her, the blow made her body lurch and her need to scream grew stronger. Garbled squalls raged over the cane but the woman ignored them and just kept beating her. Xiao prayed that she grow tired but the physical fitness of her captor was acute and she did not slow or tire in her barbarity.

Was Uzume going to beat her until she dropped the cane? There were no parameters to this assault so this might well continue until she was forced to fail. It seemed in keeping with the savage mentality of the woman, and as the blows continued to come, Xiao considered whether she should just spit it out and get it over with. If a caning was to be her fate then she should get to it sooner rather than later.

There was another aspect to her desire to spit the cane out. Her head was rushing with a strange intoxication. The lethargic process that had finally carried her into pain had also kept her endorphin flow steady so that there was now a sublime torpor swirling within the storm of anguish. It was confusing her, making her wonder if some sort of Kami sorcery were afoot, and the urge to go higher and explore this sensation was making her consider the cane as the means to launch her into these unexplored regions.

The monotony of the flogging ate at her thoughts and finally, in a desperate attempt to end the abuse, her teeth moved apart in a series of small jolts until the cane fell free. No sooner was it gone than she stared with horror as it dropped away and bounced on the ground. The flogging stopped and Xiao immediately regretted her action.

"I'm sorry, Goddess. Give me the cane . . . I mean, in my teeth. I'll hold it. I won't drop it again, I swear!" she howled.

The woman said nothing. Xiao stared at the cane with horror and wondered just how many licks of the stern rod she would receive for her crime.

The gloved hands of Uzume reached over the top of the pillory and grabbed Xiao's face. Before she could react, she was pulled up and a large ball was being forced between her teeth. Xiao gurgled and fought to stop the insertion but Uzume was not tolerating her defiance and just crammed it in.

The weight of the ball made itself felt in her mouth. Even though it was padded with leather, the core must have been made of a dense metal or stone. Xiao was about to spit it out when she saw the two cords emerging from between her teeth. The two strands reached down and swayed as Uzume ducked down and started to move them under her.

Her teeth ground on the ball when a pair of padded jaws simultaneously snapped to her nipples. Xiao roared aloud and jerked in response as the powerfully sprung clamps continued to compress her hapless teats. She instantly gurgled for mercy when she saw Uzume reach over and retrieve the cane.

"If the threat of the cane won't keep that stupid mouth shut, then I'm sure having that weight hanging from your tits will do it!" growled Uzume.

Xiao lifted her head up and sucked the ball in. Her jaws were already smarting from fighting to hold it in, and her saliva was not helping either. The fear of having this burden dangling from the cords that now fastened clamps to her nipples was potent, but would it be enough to keep her stalwart against the ravages of a caning?

The first stroke crossed her rear with a solid thwack. Xiao jolted in her restraints and issued a long and high pitched scream of response. The scorching line seemed to swell within her bottom and explode with a misery that continued to hound her for a hideous duration. Uzume merely waited and watched as she suffered and was forced to hold the ball while the effects of the stroke ebbed to more tolerable degrees. A split second later another swipe of the cane crossed her cheeks and made the flesh ripple.

Xiao howled and then broke into sobbing fits as the power of the cane made itself felt. Holding to the ball in the immediate aftermath of the stroke was easy but when it's awful potency faded, so too did her strength and it took a great deal of effort to keep her jaws clenched. Her whole body was forced to rigid attention with another stroke, and then melted into a languid heap as the agony faded. Again, her jaws were no exception and after the stern bite to the ball amidst a stroke, they wanted to go slack when the scorching mayhem slowly settled into a dull and infuriating throb.

"I am going to give you twenty strokes, slave. A punishment for dropping this weapon. Maybe next time you'll try harder."

Xiao gave a horrified croak as she was informed as to the extent of her discipline. She was sure that she could not survive such abuse, but Uzume did not wait and delivered her first swipe with cold-blooded fury. Xiao screamed aloud, and her cry was given new volume when a second line was drawn across her proffered rear.

Her head dropped down and her body bucked as the third landed. Xiao ground her teeth to the orb and just gurgled and croaked as the fourth and fifth strokes came. The rate of the caning was swift and Xiao was glad of the increase because it meant that it would be over sooner. Throwing her rancour into the ordeal, she bit down and just roared in pain as the weapon slashed into her shaking rear. Deafened by her own squeals, when the caning eventually stopped, she barely processed that the trial was over.

Holding to the heavy gag, she sobbed with relief and joy as she realised that she had actually succeeded.

"Oh who cares. Let's keep going, shall we? I want to see how long you can hold out."

Xiao started to wail in disapproval but then the cane transformed her garbled words into a distraught squall.

"Yes, that's it, slave. Scream."

The strut hounded her rear with stroke after stroke, it's every application as unbearable as the previous. Xiao shrieked and fought to get free as she was assailed and finally, her grip on the orb began to falter. Now she was having to suck it back in during the brief pause after a stroke, and sometimes it almost popped free when her screams flowed against it.

"It'll come out now, slave!" panted Uzume and before Xiao had a chance to respond, three swift and merciless strokes crossed the upper reaches of the backs of her thighs. This pain was like no other and the orb tumbled from her lips. Even so, her face remained frozen in a static shriek of utmost dismay.

The cords snapped taunt and the clamps wrenched at her nipples. The ball bounced in the air and then dropped to hang from her and stretch at the captive nuggets. Xiao shrieked as the effects of her failure were imparted in full.

"Goddess, please! Mercy! Show mercy!"

Uzume stepped out in front of her and crouched down. Already the terrible pain of the last three strokes was fading and exposing a vicious strain of pleasure. The soaring high that she found herself being subjected to was emphasised by the rending pain in her nipples, as though the continuing abuse was fuel to this depraved bliss.

"Oh! Goddess! What's happening to me! Make it stop! Pleeease!" she screamed as tears rushed down her cheeks and her thoughts seemed to curdle. The feelings were alien and terrifying because of their might.

"Take it, slave. Take it for your Goddess," muttered Uzume and moved closer to embrace Xiao's head. Against all reason, Xiao buried her head into her tormentor's neck and sobbed freely. The Kami soothed her and petted her as she wept and fought to withstand this event.

"There. Just let the pain control you. Just as I do. You are mine, slave. I'll mould you as I see fit, and you'll adore me for it."

"Yes, Goddess," burbled Xiao and filled her nose with the fragrance of the woman.

"Now, I'm going to take the clamps off in a moment, and you'd better make sure you show the proper gratitude or back on they go."

Uzume lowered and took hold of the devices.

"Ready, slave?"

Xiao swallowed for strength.

"Yes, Goddess."

The clamps came away and each tip instantly raged with crushed misery.

"Thank you, Goddess!" she screamed at the top of her lungs, and then felt her oppressor caress each breast as her lips pressed to hers. The soothing embrace possessed her, and Xiao found herself returning a wildly passionate kiss with the woman who had tortured her. Her tongue rushed forward against Uzume's, and their lips slithered upon one another. Murmurs and groans escaped during the exchange as Uzume continued to tickle and stroke the dangling breasts of her prisoner, and Xiao lost herself to the wanton kisses of her abductor.

Uzume pulled away and Xiao just melted into her bondage. Her head draped down, and she stared with unfocused eyes on the floor. Huffing for breath, she heard Uzume rise and head out of the room, leaving Xiao in a contradictory state. She hated the woman for what she did to her, but in that instant of tenderness she had been overwhelmed with adoration.

The only other female that Xiao had encountered at length was her own mother and Uzume could not have been more different. She was young, gorgeous, experienced, independent, lethal, and bore considerably authority over powerful people. Uzume was as terrible as she was beautiful, and in the aftermath of her session, Xiao felt quite abandoned to her lot as the sublime deities property.

# CHAPTER SEVENTEEN

Candy was now insane with need. Every orgasm she acquired from the effects of swimming was a hollow thing, one that just fanned her desire for some actual attention. Every time she was crippled with the onset of climax, she darted around, anxiously looking for a way to get out of the water and back onto the land.

After several hours, in sheer desperation, she trekked back to the location in which she had been so bitterly misused. She wanted to be strung up again, to dangle, be dunked, and barbarously caned, anything to distract her from her frustrations but to her dismay the three priests were gone. She thrashed her tail and tried to find them, hoping that they had just relocated in order to trick fresh prey but they were no longer in the fields.

Several times she tried to get close to a diver or another swimmer but the women that were after that same attention were far better swimmers than she and were not intending to miss the chance to try and earn a promotion. Each time she tried to get close, she was driven away by the jealous veterans of the deep.

Cursing her inadequacies, Candy continued to cruise through the coral beds and try to get noticed. Nevertheless, the mermaid uniform hid all but the most distinct feminine curves and left those entombed in them to display their allure in action, and Candy was most certainly no expert in aquatic debauchery.

Suddenly she spied a bathysphere that was lurking

surreptitiously amongst a kelp bed. Candy slithered through the obscuring veil of green and gained a look inside.

The middle of the room bore the access pool and a dense door was set against the stone exterior. The four levers that surrounded the pressure door were open and the thick oval portal was left ajar to expose a descending spiral staircase. On either side of the riveted metal frame were some tall wooden cabinets with handles shaped like nautilus shells while set around the rest of the wall were piles of cushions and some low, comfortable chairs. This sphere was obviously a perverse play space because placed around the rippling pool were three solid items of furniture. Not all of them were vacant.

There was a polished wooden box that was banded around the edges with iron. From the top emerged an oval rubber balloon with an abrupt pipe jutting from the front. Obviously, a slave was pressed into a tight ball within the box and only her head was allowed to emerge, and even then it did so into the crushing embrace of an inflatable hood.

The second item was a collection of pillories. Three sets of stocks were set in a row so that the girl who was served up to them was trapped on all fours. One set of stocks caught her ankles and the next grabbed her just below her knees. This left her rear thrown up into the air before she was arched back down and a conventional set of stocks near the floor trapped her wrists and neck. The girl was petite and fishnet stockings enhanced the delicate curves of her legs. The stockings were held in place by a suspender belt, and her blonde hair was tied into a single plait before this was pulled back and fastened to a ring at the top of the stocks that were charged with capturing her throat. With her head hoisted up by her hair, Candy could see the ball gag distending her jaws and the blindfold that was fastened in place to leave her with sound as her last unimpeded sense.

The last item was an "A" shaped wooden frame and

wooden legs propped it up. Steel rings lined every side and this item was the only one currently unoccupied.

There were only two guests in the chamber. One was a man of powerful build with close-cropped red hair. He was clad in a form fitting latex catsuit that reached into leather riding boots and a pair of leather gloves. About his waist was a belt that was laden with a number of different sized leather utility pouches. He was standing beside the slave in the pillory with arms folded across his chest. His eyes wandered from foot to head and back again as though he was contemplating performing something complicated and was trying to figure out all the nuances before he began. The latex skin rippled with the motion of even the most minor tensing of a muscle and the zip at the front of the catsuit swelled as his arousal tested the garment's ability to hold him back.

The other occupant was a woman. She was tall and lithe, with an eruption of black hair that cascaded about her features. Dressed in a sinister fashion, she wore dark saturnine makeup that accented a black leather mask. The item was small, covering from cheeks to eyebrows and offering a feline countenance that included a pair of small, pricked ears. A black leather corset squeezed her into an elegant hourglass figure and a pair of leather shorts clutched to her hindquarters. There was a brief glimpse of nylon-clad thighs before leather thigh boots covered the rest of her legs and set her atop tall heels.

The woman was laying at the edge of the pool with her head propped up on her hands. Her shins were lifted up and her boots entwined. She bobbed her feet idly back and forth and continued to extend her offer. The lounging female was continually puckering her lips and presenting kisses towards the water. It was an invitation that Candy could not resist.

Candy moved her eyes across the pert leather-clad rear of the woman and then assessed the strong enticing contours of the male. She knew she had to accept this offer.

The previous bait had been food and this time the offer came in the form of physical attention. It was a mode of nour-ishment that Candy needed the most.

Taking a final deep breath for courage, Candy committed herself to the scenario and turned away from the view. She slithered down through the kelp and focused on the light pouring down from the entrance pool. She crept through the shifting veil of plants and saw the woman above her. With a flutter in her heart, she started to ascend.

Her face emerged through the waters and the woman re-garded Candy with a broad grin.

"Well hello, little fish," she crooned.

Candy beat her tail and moved closer. The woman reached out with one hand and unfastened the gills. The item was drawn out and set aside before the same hand curled around the back of Candy's neck and drew her in for a kiss. Their lips met and the woman's tongue sought entry. She complied with a ravenous haste and their slick organs curled and swirled.

Candy stopped moving her legs and just hung from the hold while she continued to savour the exchange. To finally feel some attention after so long was utterly splendid and she started to stretch her legs back to make the nodules caress her loins.

The woman moved back a little and looked into the eyes of the new arrival.

"Does this little fish want to play? Does she want to come out and be with Ochi and I?"

"Oh yes," spluttered Candy. "Yes please, mistress."

"Mmmm, I like your accent, fish," purred the woman and ran a digit around Candy's lips before placing it in the middle of her bottom lip.

"Suck," she stated flatly.

Candy opened her mouth and engulfed the digit. She

locked lips to the smooth skin and began to rock her head against it. She could feel the woman stroking her tongue as she attended her finger.

"How is she, Iha?" asked Ochi.

Candy glanced aside and saw him walk around the bound slave, trail a gloved hand along her elevated rear, and begin to wander over. The steady deep beat of his boots echoed in the quiet of the chamber.

"I'll let you know," uttered Iha and then removed her digit. She pulled herself back up onto her feet and Candy watched her tower over her while she floundered in the water.

Ochi joined her and glared down at the new arrival. Candy felt like an insect before them. She was below even their feet, staring up across divine mountains of latex and leather.

Iha placed her hands to her corseted sides and tapped her fingers to the dense boning. Candy's eyes locked to the shining mound that presented itself between Ochi's potent thighs.

"Where shall we put our fish?" she wondered.

"I believe we already have a most accommodating cushion. She can provide us with the necessary support, but we will definitely need something to stop this fish from wriggling."

"Oh, I believe I can help you there," muttered Iha.

The woman stepped back and started to elegantly unzip her thigh boots and then draw them off before she removed her shorts and then her tights. Ochi lowered into a crouch to the sound of creaking latex and his strong hands grabbed Candy by neck and bound arms. With an unusually easy haul, she was drawn from the waters and dropped over his shoulder. Hanging down his back, she was delivered to the slave in the box.

Iha flipped her tights over her own shoulder, donned her boots, and sauntered towards the same location. The bulbous head of the captive shifted as she detected the approaching heels and footfalls of those who had so comprehensively trussed her.

Candy was set down so that her tail was at the foot of the box. Ochi then draped her over the pliant orb and her torso poured down the other side of the small prison. The helmet had been inflated to such a crushing degree that it was almost solid and it easily supported Candy's entire body weight.

Ochi held out a hand and Iha dropped her tights into it. He immediately opened out the legs and after stretching them to their limit he wove them around Candy's hindquarters so he could tie them into knots and fasten her to the trapped head of the slave.

Iha took hold of Candy's jawline in both hands and hoisted her up. After pulling her outward, she regarded her with an iniquitous glare.

"You think you can distract her while I work?" asked Ochi as he grabbed her hips and pressed his groin to her rear. Candy could feel the solid bulge and he moved it against her in steady sways, as though tasting her.

Candy closed her eyes and focused on the feel of that solid hillock against her bottom and dreamed of when it would be unleashed to pummel her.

"Oh I think I can come up with something," crooned Iha.

Iha lowered Candy back until she was flat against the rear of the box and then strolled to the cabinets. She looked up and watched the naked rear of the woman as it rolled and flowed with every step, using the image to keep her libido at full power.

Ochi unfastened her top so he could hoist it, expose the fasteners for her tail, and then draw it down under the tights before gathering it at her knees. The firm grip of the tail still kept her shins pressed together and she could do little to escape now that she was bound to the head of an imprisoned slave girl.

Ochi then revealed that there was a small zipper at her rear to permit him access without compromising the security of her catsuit, and the clatter of metal teeth was followed by a similar sound as he lowered his own zip. Fingers clasped her rear and thumbs dug into the cleft before they pulled apart to reveal his target.

There was a faint squelch as Iha tipped a small pot of gel and dribbled the contents into the exposed crevasse. The slick cold goo dribbled down over her sphincter and Candy gasped and quaked with lust. The woman simply tossed the emptied pot aside.

"That should help you," she said. "As will this."

Iha appeared beside Candy and began to fasten a leather collar about her throat before she knelt down, snapped a leash to the ring at the front, and then presented a gag to Candy's face. The solid leather plate had a large stubby dildo on the interior and the exterior sprouted a much more significant version. The artificial cock was formed from a translucent pliant substance and had rows of small nodules dotted along its entire length.

"Swallow it," she ordered, and grabbed the back of Candy's head before forcing the interior dildo to her lips. Candy eagerly let it.

"Hold it."

As soon as Candy clenched her teeth to the jaw-stretching gag, Iha began to establish the two straps about the back of her head and the third that reached up around her crown.

"There we are. Now that's an impressive sight," commented Iha as she grabbed the massive dildo and used it as a handle to haul up Candy's face. Taking the leash, she pulled it taut, stepped over it, and bent over.

"I want you to fuck me, little fish," she hissed.

Iha shifted back and Candy watched with bewilderment as the dildo sprouting from her gag kissed the woman's pussy and then started to vanish into it. Iha quivered and moaned aloud. She pulled the leash taut and continued to shuffle back until Candy's nose was pressed against her.

"Oh *yes*! Now Ochi! Take her now!"

The words had only just emerged when Candy felt a solid manhood lean against her rear. Offering her no time to get used to his sterling girth, he merely exploited the lubricant and roughly entered her. As soon as he was clearing her sphincter, Candy flashed to attention. Her hips bounced on the inflated orb that was supporting her and her legs sought to swing her aside and escape. Ochi's muscular legs clamped inward and immediately subdued her struggles. His hands held tighter to her hips but now they pushed inward to close her buttocks to him.

"My, aren't we a wriggly little fish?" he commented with a soft giggle.

Ochi continued to rush into her, sinking himself to the root. Candy's reaction was just as vibrant when her tracts erupted from the sudden and excruciating trespass. She then gave a cry when his hips battered her already much punished rear. The latex was hiding the signs of her previous maltreatment, and the pressure of hips to these bruises was terrible to bear.

"There, now you've gone and hurt yourself," he uttered, and started to draw himself free. Thinking that her reaction was due to a virgin rear, Ochi departed and gave her a moment to recover. Candy struggled again. Her rear was throbbing and she feared another entry. She strained her arms, and her torso bucked, but this was turned into an intense pleasure for Iha because the dildo thrashed and darted chaotically around within her.

"Stay still, fish," hissed Ochi and rushed back into rear, this time stopping before he struck her buttocks. His second entry was easier to take and her thrashing eased a little.

"No! Make her dance, Ochi! Make her *dance*," growled Iha, and Candy saw the pussy before her eyes clenching and flexing madly. Iha pulled on the leash and shifted back, craning Candy's head back to the limits of what she could perform.

Ochi jerked back and then slammed himself as deep as he could. The ferocity of his ravishment made Candy struggle anew just as Iha wished, more so because each slap of his hindquarters to her welt covered bottom made each and every contusion reverberate and mimic its former effulgence.

"More, Ochi. *More.*"

His gloved hands began to jump back and flash in to clap to her exposed cheeks. The sudden attacks made her jolt, and this made her clench, and Ochi enjoyed this result with a drastic thrust. He spanked her again as he withdrew, making Candy tighten to his shaft and to inspire her to churn the dildo within Iha.

The flashes of sensation as his palms greeted her rear began to cultivate a heady bliss. Candy began to writhe as the heat of Ochi's ravishment merged with the succulent scent of Iha's arousal. Lines of moisture stretched from Candy's features and nose, and a delicious strand of Iha's juices continued to dribble down her face.

Candy could only wonder as to what was happening to the poor girl beneath her. Trapped in a box, unable to move, all she could do was listen and envy Candy while she was fucked and used for the couple's pleasure.

Iha started to rock forward and then sink back onto Candy's dildo, and Candy tried to turn her head, to pivot the shaft and refine the woman's ecstasy.

Ochi started to hasten his drives and his hands rolled across her bound body, appraising every area of her anatomy. Iha's breath started to rush in and out as she neared climax, and Candy's snorts flowed across her rear.

"I'm almost there. Fuck her harder!"

"Shall I set her to "vibrate," Iha?"

"Yes! Oh yes. Do it now!"

Ochi's hands leapt forward and closed to Candy's breasts. The spines dug in, and the many fresh weals exploded with anguish. Candy screamed against her gag and quaked. Ochi had anticipated a reaction based on the exploiting of the breast cups, but he knew nothing of the caning her breasts had received just a short time ago.

"By the Sun-Goddess! This fish can *move!*" roared Ochi and he manipulated her assets with even more brutality.

The intense reaction instantly threw Iha into orgasm and the woman's hold on the lead tightened to pull Candy in as closely as she could. Her shivering face made the inserted toy judder and Iha shrieked with elation.

Ochi's cock gave a spasm and Candy felt him come within her. He slammed himself to her with added enthusiasm and this only aggravated her welts. The quiver of her bottom and the fierce clench of her sphincter made Ochi bellow and fill the room with the signal of his rhapsody.

Iha screamed with delight and her shriek rose several octaves when Ochi withdrew because this extraction made Candy's rear flash with renewed sensation. As a consequence, when he dropped free, she thrashed and jerked with all her strength, making the dildo churn and assail the woman with vicious delight.

Ochi gave a deep chuckle and then reached through with the head of his cock. He grazed Candy's clit and such was her enjoyment that just a few swirls against this hyper-aroused morsel tossed her into raging orgasm. Her reactions to the ravishment and the pain had been strong, but they were nothing compared to the result of a long desired and hard earned sexual release. The dildo became a berserk rod that made Iha lift onto tiptoe and arch upward. Her squeal was piercing and lengthy and after just a few seconds she could tolerate no more of this overt ecstasy.

The lead was released and Iha collapsed forward. The nodule encrusted toy poured from her and its sudden flight caused the woman to launch upright and arch back with a second orgasmic howl. Candy flopped down the box and Iha fell into a pile of cushions. She pushed her torso up with her arms and clamped her thighs together. Her buttocks flexed and rippled as she gritted her teeth and continued to endure her delight. The soft applause as her hips bounced up and down, clapping her bare skin to the ground, reached Candy's ears as did the moans and gasping breaths of the satisfied woman.

Ochi stopped teasing the captive and stepped back so he might also fall onto another pile of cushions.

"I didn't know Midzuha no me could be so energetic," whispered Ochi.

"That display will have made the others jealous," murmured Iha.

"Well, we can't have that."

Candy looked up a little and saw a number of other mermaids gliding around the walls and watching. Others were peeking up from the waters and had been studying their affair, breaking contact only to wet their eyes.

Ochi arose and moved to the cupboards. The sound of his return ended with a sudden invasion of Candy's rear. It felt like a soft rubber bag was being eased into her, and Ochi's fingers had to stuff it in because it was awkward and flopped about. Finally, the unruly orb was inserted to his satisfaction and her rear zip was hoisted. He lifted her tail sheath, fastened it, and restored her top. Candy could now feel a tube pressed against her and when she looked around she saw the inflator bulb hanging from the end.

Ochi unfastened the tights and unbuckled the gag. He drew the item away from Candy's lips and offered her gills as a replacement. She accepted them and did nothing as he buckled it, lifted her up, and causally flung her back into the water.

Candy winced as she landed on her back and irked her bruises, but then she just relaxed as she sank back down. She exhaled and let her face vanish beneath the water and watched Ochi move over and join Iha. As the two embraced, she smiled broadly and savoured the memory of their energetic coupling.

Candy trembled when the flaccid intruder in her rear suddenly swelled a little. With a spasm, she arched around and found a pair of mermaids beneath her. They regarded her with a wicked frown and then spiralled around and back over her. Their chests collided and their bound breasts squeezed the bulb to swell the inflatable dildo that was trapped within her, filling the toy with water rather than air. Candy kicked her legs and tried to escape but the women wanted Candy to pay for her good fortune.

The bulb slowly expanded and drew in another measure of the ocean. Another breast collision thrust this into the dildo and made the toy grow larger. Candy squeezed her channels, trying to eject it, but it was already swollen enough that when she levied her muscles against it, the base merely pushed to her catsuit and did not escape. She realised now that she couldn't apply enough force to crumple the toy and squeeze it out, in fact her only chance had been shortly after she had been dropped in the water. She had wasted it on savouring the session and now that chance was gone.

Another meeting of rubber smothered breasts made the dildo well again. Candy gurgled as her tender rear started to course with renewed feeling. She beat her legs as hard and as fast as she could, but her technique was not as effective as that of the veteran mermaids. A small shoal was in pursuit and with a sudden lurch of acceleration they caught up and when their bodies met, they squeezed the inflator. The tube let it trail down past her tail, and it was a ready target that the wicked mermaids repeatedly assaulted.

Another impact made her pause briefly as her rear was stretched more than she could easily take and this resulted in another easy expansion of the toy.

Candy sought to lose her pursuers and began to weave and dodge amongst the coral. The concubines were not to be denied their vengeance though and doggedly kept up with her.

She was starting to run low on breath and had to seek more. She knew what would happen but she needed air if she was to continue her flight.

Candy dove around and shot up towards a pool where her tanks refilled. She cried out against her gill when three swift impacts made her anus churn with pain. The dildo was now bloated to a level that she could barely stand.

Diving back, she started to charge away. The women chose to continue their chase rather than refill, and Candy knew what she had to do to get rid of them.

Another inflation made her quiver, and it became harder to swim because of the water-filled zeppelin distending her rear. A quick look around spotted a darker area of the ocean. The bathyspheres were not present and the depth of the area extinguished most of the ambient light. She could also see some sort of crevasse where no mermaids frolicked and perhaps this would be her salvation.

Candy continued towards it as vigorously as she could, knowing that she couldn't take many more pumps. She had never been so filled before and was not sure how much more her body could take. One thing was certain though—she had no wish to find out.

Another crushing embrace made her tail flash to attention as her rear pounded. She again tried to eject the toy but this only made it more distinct against her canals. She had to refill her tanks again, and all the while the mermaids continued to brutalise her with an endless rota of impacts that crushed the bulb and filled her rear with escalating anguish.

Candy tried to lurch around and strike them, to beat them off, but they were agile and she never once made contact. Her attempts just served her up to another sadistic inflation.

Candy gave up on fighting them and continued to limp towards the trench and her overpowering distress served her to another dose of internal pressure. This recommitted her to her quest and she fought her way onwards.

Several of the mermaids broke away and hurried back as their air started to dwindle. With the benefit of a full tank, Candy persevered.

A stubborn pair of mermaids continued to follow and managed to collide again. Candy rolled and curled up. She started to sink as her bottom was pushed to a terrible degree. Each inflation was educating her rear, dilating the flesh, but now it was reaching its absolute extreme capabilities. Another squirt of water made her sphincter shriek with misery and she beat her legs as fast as she could. The final two mermaids broke away and started head back for fresh tanks.

The water started to get a little colder as she continued towards the edge of the precipice. If she could sneak over the edge, she could travel along unseen and then head back when her air was running low. It was risky, but it would stop the women from seeing where she went. If she then travelled discreetly amongst the kelp beds, she might hide her tube and avoid any more inflations. She couldn't think on how she was going to get the toy out of her, or how she would find her owner because right now, everything in her mind revolved around stopping them distending her bottom anymore.

Surrounded only by other fish and the shifting fields of anemones and sponges, Candy trekked onwards. When she eventually reached the cliff, she flipped and with a few strokes ducked down. The sight that met her gaze would have made her drop her gill had it not been secured to her.

An army was in the trench, lurking in the eerie twilight. Regiments of slithering figures moved in perfect unison and charged replicas of hulls and other dummy targets. Armed with harpoons, spears, and other stabbing instruments, the creatures were clad in sections of elegant armour that in no way impeded their streamlined forms.

They resembled normal Wani, save that their fingers and toes were greatly elongated and membranes were stretched between them. Their tails were larger, stouter, and bore several fins, while their eyes were overlarge to compensate for the darkness.

Standing on ledges and other outposts were divers who watched and drilled the water Wani, making sure that they worked as one and without error.

Candy could not believe what she was seeing and then the truth dawned. These were going to be the Midzu-Wani. It was obvious now. The Kami of Water had been mentioned as being the strongest proponents of dividing Hachiman's power. The Warlord held sway over the Mitama and the Wani, and they wanted that power diminished. Previously, she would have assumed that it was out of jealousy but now it seemed that it was a precaution to further weaken his House and make their own stronger.

The coming conflict with Earth depended greatly on dominion beneath the waves. When the Water Wani proved their worth in the coming invasion, the Houses of Water would be the most highly praised and obviously highly rewarded faction of the Empire. The Wani on the land would encounter the full potency of Earth's stubborn refusal to submit, but those in the water would be safe and invincible. Armies of aquatic Wani who could sabotage, invade undersea vessels, destroy ships, come and go as they pleased by river and then lurk in the unexplored depths. Destroyed shipping could be looted for weapons that could be graciously donated to the land forces, making the Houses of Water seem even more magnanimous.

Three Kronosaur cruised overhead and made her duck in against the stone. She merged with the rocks and peeked surreptitiously out to see what was going on. The riders were adorned in flamboyant armour that mimicked coral and was encrusted with gems and pearls that shone in the dim light. A pair of poles arose behind the saddles and each trailed a banner that rippled through the water and portrayed the emblems of Toyo-tama-hiko, Naka-tsu-wata-dzu-mi, and Uha-tsu-wata-dzu-mi. Together, they were the three Warlords who ruled the oceans and the waves.

The three martial powers cruised into the middle of the ravine and then paused to survey the efforts. They pointed out various smaller groups, those who were being trained separately as though they were some caste of special forces.

Candy continued to watch until she noticed that her air was running low. A sudden panic set in and she broke free of her cover. Just as she arose and began to head back, she thought she saw Toyo-tama-hiko turn in his saddle and catch a glimpse of her, but the handsome Supreme Warlord of the waves did not pursue or indicate to the others. More concerned with the pain in her bottom, Candy swam for the remotest bathysphere she could find.

# CHAPTER EIGHTEEN

The sound of an approaching Tyrannosaur reached into the fort and when the portcullis was hoisted it alerted Lady Uzume that she was about to receive a visitor. She could ignore them if she so wished, but knew that the importance of the message no doubt merited intruding on her privacy.

A knock came upon the door so Uzume donned a flowing leather kimono and slipped on her veil. She straightened it to make sure it hid her features and opened the hefty portal.

The two officers bowed until they were almost prostrate on the drawbridge. One was covered in dust and some flecks of red, and the other was her second in command.

"I humbly beg forgiveness for disturbing you, Lady Uzume. But I bring grave news from our outriders," said Masuda.

"Rise and you may speak," she ordered, knowing full well what he was going to tell her because she had in fact orchestrated it.

The officers clambered back to their feet and kept their gaze down. Masuda stepped aside as though to distance himself from the rider who shuddered with the shame of what he was going to have to say.

"Our outriders went to inform the search party of your orders and found that they had been attacked. We explored the area and discovered that an army has been raised in the Provinces. This force surrounded our troops as they continued to search for our quarry. We found no survivors and the army is continuing to muster greater numbers as more settlements send militia and troops to bolster it."

"Explain this!" snarled Uzume and jabbed a finger at the bloodstains.

"We came under attack from their advance riders and then snipers forced us to retreat from battle before the Wani could reach our position."

"Disgrace!" she snarled and slapped him across the face. The fierce blow jerked his head aside and the warrior collapsed at her feet. He remained on the floor, quivering with overwhelming sorrow as he readied to accept his fate. Masuda drew his sidearm and shot him without compunction. He then kicked the chastised soldier from the drawbridge and there was a snap of motion as his Tyrannosaur mount snatched the cadaver from the air like a tidbit and swallowed it whole.

A brief silence fell as the gunshot continued to echo in the foothills.

"So, they have the shipment," she sighed irritably.

"They do not, Lady Uzume," said Masuda.

"Mitama defeated by backward peasants! What is happening here, Masuda? Modern weapons may have diminished your shame. The fact that the shipment is not only lost, but also did not factor in this humiliation heightens it beyond tolerance," she growled fiercely.

The elite warrior trembled in terror at the sound of her outrage. His forces had angered a deity and he appeared almost ready to faint. Only years of absolute fealty and dedication kept him conscious.

"I will end my life imm-" he began with conviction.

"Wrong!" snapped Uzume "You have brought a terrible shame upon us, Masuda. Your blood will not be spilt by your own hand. No, it will be spilled making the barbarians pay in their own. Do my words become clear to you!"

"Yes, Lady Uzume. I conquer!" he bellowed.

"Then do so," she said with cool gravity.

Masuda turned and ran back to vault into the saddle. Without fastening his harness, he drew the monster around and started roaring orders. Lady Uzume took little pleasure in sending him to his death. Masuda was good leader and was well respected by his troops. He had proven himself in several campaigns and whispers even had him heading towards a taste of Lingzhi. He had devoted every aspect of his life to the furthering of the Empire's goals and had done so to exemplary degrees. The reward of being able to partake of a dose of the immortality potion would either allow him to expend another life in this cause, or spend it on self-indulgent retirement with all the fruits of his accomplishments.

Nevertheless, his death at the hands of the enemy would further fan rancour in the Empire and excuse her own decision to retreat.

Uzume watched Masuda vanish into a cloud of dust when his mount galloped away, then span on her heels and strode back inside. She closed the door and heard the sound of the defences being re-established while she slid free of her concealing garb.

After a moment of further contemplation she decided that she needed to clear her head, so she decided to go and torment Xiao.

Uzume grabbed a small stool and walked upstairs. She dropped it before Xiao's sorrowful features and settled upon it. Crossing her legs, she rested her hands on her knees in a demure pose.

"So, where were we? Ah yes, we were finding out all about you."

Uzume hoisted a leg and offered the sole of her boot to the captive girl. She looked at it with confusion, her ignorance of even the most commonplace acts of submission being total. Uzume smiled at the thought of correcting that failing, because failing it was. Slaves had to be ready to endure anything and this wild creature was no exception.

"Lick," she ordered and gave a small lewd shudder when she saw the appalled expression on the girl's face. She was so virginal that Uzume just wanted to ravish her right away, but she kept her desires in check. She wanted to draw this out. Frustrating herself was helping pass the time.

A trembling tongue emerged and stretched out to touch her sole. Uzume laughed when the girl recoiled at the tang of trail dust. She then shed this mirth and fixed the captive with a stark glare.

"I told you to lick! Now do it, you stupid slut, before I cane you!"

The gravity in the words made the girl tremble and she started to take hesitant laps of the footwear. There was something so fragile about this prisoner, and yet there was an inner strength that made Uzume yearn to keep her bound, contained, and in pain. When Xiao was suffering and screaming, she revealed that she was not as flimsy as she seemed compared to when she was merely sobbing and cringing in the shadow of the lash.

The girl was also obviously inexperienced with regard to sex, and even intimacy was likely unknown to her, so Uzume was taking great delight in her crass words and insinuations. This gave her another debauched idea.

"Suck the heel," she ordered, and lifted her foot higher.

With tentative motions the prisoner craned her head forward and puckered her lips to touch the bottom of the stiletto. Uzume slid her foot forward so that the heel entered the girl's mouth and then decided to gouge at her sense of propriety.

"Suck it like you'd suck cock," she uttered lecherously. "I want to see how that harlot's mouth devours men."

Uzume's hands clenched to her thigh boots as she observed the repelled wince on the girl's face. It was as though she had been slapped, and Uzume trembled a little with relish to see such a reaction. The kami-tsu-ko were already trained and even if they were still resentful of their lot, they had been introduced most effectively to what the Empire wished of them. Not so with Xiao.

"Suck it or I'll fuck you with it!" snarled Uzume and her head lolled back as she heard a terrified squeak and felt the girl clamp lips to her heel and start to fawn upon it. Even the most trivial threat made her quake, especially when it involved anything relating to intercourse.

"Yes, that's more like it," she purred while staring up at the ceiling.

She let the girl attend the item for a few minutes and then chose to continue with her interrogation. Uzume dropped her foot back to the ground and quickly grabbed a bag of pegs.

"So, your name is Xiao Lin?"

"Yes, Goddess," was the meek reply.

"How old are you, Xiao," she asked with mock kindness, and started to reach into the bag for her first implement.

"E . . . eighteen, Goddess."

"A tender young thing then."

Uzume removed a peg and clicked it threateningly before the girl's eyes. Her lips tightened and she mewed from seeing the item and obviously guessing what Uzume intended to do with it.

"Ever been fucked?" she said with as much crude venom as she could. As predicted the girl flinched from the question and Uzume rewarded her by promptly clipping a peg to her earlobe. The girl gave a sobbing squawk and shuddered. She threw her head from side to side and her fingers strained forward to try and reach the item, but there was nothing she could do.

"I asked you a question, Xiao."

"No! No, I haven't . . . oh . . . please . . . ow . . . this hurts!

Take it off, Goddess. Please, Goddess," she whimpered.

"Of course it does, and that's why you're wearing it," said Uzume while removing another peg in readiness. "Now, are you sure? I think you may be lying."

Uzume started to trace the tip of the peg around her captive's features. The girl kept her eyes locked to the implement to keep track of where it was and perhaps prepare for its application.

"Is that it? Are you lying to me? Lying to your Goddess?"

"I swear, Goddess. I wouldn't lie to you. I've never been with anyone."

Xiao's face crumpled into a tight grimace when her other earlobe was enveloped within the wooden jaws. Uzume then grabbed another peg and started to tickle the length of the girl's ears with it.

"Are you sure? Not a man. Not a woman. No one? Are you absolutely sure?"

"YES! Yes! Goddess, I swear I'm telling you the truth!"

The addition of the peg to her upper ear made Xiao croak and again fight her bonds to try and access the cruel instrument and remove it. Cocking her head aside, her face reddened with strain but her fingers could not even graze the contraption. Her efforts froze when another peg started to trace the opposite edge.

"What about other activities?" said Uzume, being deliberately opaque.

"I . . . I don't know . . . wait! . . . .No! . . . Please!" she cried as the peg opened and moved into position. Uzume grabbed the girl's forehead and pushed back to pin her into position and let the peg remain open and poised to clamp down on her flesh.

"Tell me the truth, Xiao, or I'll add this one as well."

"I have no idea what you mean! Kissing? Is that it, Goddess? I've never even kissed a boy!" she cried.

"What about a girl," asked Uzume.

"Only you, Goddess!"

Uzume let go and the jaws clamped down onto the upper reaches of Xiao's ear. The captive gave another despairing croak and her head sagged in resignation.

"You think me a girl? A woman? A mere mortal meat sack?" she offered gravely.

Xiao's features jumped back up and utmost imploring ruled her countenance.

"Oh no, Goddess! Of course not. You . . . you're Kami . . . and . . . I . . . oh no! Please, not another one, Goddess, I'm sorry, I . . ."

Uzume ran the next peg along her eyebrows as she stared up at it with tears welling in her eyes.

"I am an immortal, Xiao," she stated forcefully. Uzume used her other hand and pinched the skin, making it swell so she could apply the peg to that ridge. Xiao gave a long despairing moan as she alternatively frowned and hoisted her brow to try and slither free of the mordant implement.

"I am Kami," she added, and then adorned the middle of the other eyebrow. "The embodiment of thought and deed and substance."

Another peg was established on either side of the pair and this left Xiao quivering with distress as six crushing pincers ruled her eyebrows.

"I am Uzume—the Dread Female."

The words culminated in a peg that slid a jaw into each nostril and then snatched a vicious hold on her septum. Xiao gave a decent cry of misery and started to stretch her tongue up, but all she could do was knock the rear of the implement around and have it tug and draw at her nose.

"So I ask you again. Have ever kissed anyone? Male or female?"

"N . . . no, Goddess," she said over clenched teeth.

"Better. What about masturbation?"

The shocked gasp that slipped her lips was an exhilarating sound to Uzume and she decided to start adding pegs there next. The pain she was in and the threat of a constant flow of additional doses made Xiao quicker with her response.

"I don't really. I'm always watched so I can't. Not in front of my brothers."

Uzume was momentarily thrown by the words and as she processed the statement, she added the peg to the middle of the prisoner's lower lip. Xiao quaked and choked back her cries.

Female forms were in abundance in the Empire, but then so too was metal. The lands beyond the great wall were starved of these commodities that she generally took for granted. It was a difficult concept to grasp, that this gorgeous young creature was kept suppressed and hidden, like a fine vase in a display cabinet, one that remained behind glass, appreciating in value until its owner decided to sell it and make their fortune.

It was odd to think that although she was kept guarded at all times, defended from the desires of others, but defended from her own as well. A total lack of privacy was common for Imperial concubines, but that was because they were always being made use of. Although Xiao was not permitted time alone, she was utterly neglected. It riled Uzume, and for a moment she felt a hint of pity for the girl, but then the knowledge of what she would do to her as her own private plaything soothed this fury.

"What do you dream of when you pleasure yourself?" asked Uzume and to add weight to this question she traced another peg up and down Xiao's tear sodden cheek.

"Nothing really, I . . . just . . ."

Uzume pinched her cheek to gather a target and then clipped the peg to the generous measure of skin. Xiao cried out and the parting of her jaws made the flesh struggle to slip the jaws, but the tightly sprung teeth refused to budge and only made the area throb even more potently.

"Tell me what you fantasise about!" she ordered testily.

"I don't, Goddess! I . . . I just like the way it feels. I mean, I . . . no!"

Her other cheek was similarly adorned, and Xiao sobbed and trembled while trying to formulate a response that would not result in another peg. In preparation, Uzume started to caress her upper lip with another item.

"Tell me."

"I want to get away, Goddess. I want to have adventures like everyone else. I don't want to be a prisoner anymore. I want to do what *I* want. Everyone just wants me as a trophy and to give them heirs. No one cares what I think or want!" she cried.

Uzume applied the peg anyway and watched the girl break down and give melancholic sobs.

While watching the funereal response of her prisoner, Uzume dwelt on what had been revealed. The girl had no fantasies. Her masturbation was just to feel the sensation, like eating something sweet or indulging a capricious notion. Sexual fantasy was pointless because her fate was sealed and she would be little more than a breeding partner who saw herself as such and valued her only because she was valuable. It was something that annoyed Uzume about the rest of Pangaea. In the Empire, although slaves were treated roughly, sometimes cruelly, they were still valued. Concubines in the Empire were pleasured and abused so that their owners could gain satisfaction from the impunity with which they used them and from gaining the responses they desired to see. Binding a slave, tormenting them, ravishing them, it was all about indulgence. Even when they were deserted in encasement or pained isolation, the thought of their distress could bring joy at any moment to the person responsible, they could indulge the succulent thought of their plaything struggling against their imprisonment and praying for release. Xiao's eventual owner would not indulge because she was too precious. She would be a bauble, one to give him status and material in the form of offspring.

All Xiao wanted was freedom, and under Uzume's ownership she would have it. Uzume would use her freely, and through this, Xiao would finally have dreams. She would dream of being set free of her bonds, of being allowed to climax, of lapping at her owner's sex, breasts, or heels, and the joy she would take from having these dreams fulfilled would be immense. A single kiss from Uzume's lips or her whip could make all Xiao's hopes come true. It would take time, but Uzume had plenty.

# CHAPTER NINETEEN

With her air rapidly diminishing, Candy made for an air pocket. The closest bathysphere appeared empty, and she could not see any of the vicious mermaids in the vicinity. It was a lonely outpost and there were some tall coral spires blocking easy view of the location.

Candy swam up and refilled her tanks before she simply sank back down amidst the rocks. Her body was exhausted and the vast water swollen dildo in her rear was making her sphincter pound with an anguish she could not reduce. She tried to flex and squeeze it out, or to curl up her legs and find some way to slip the vile toy from her body but no matter what she did, a subsequent move just made her rubber sheath draw inward and pull the ghastly phallus back into her.

Candy spent some time alone. She wanted to make sure that the other water concubines had given up on finding her so she could migrate towards the main palace and hopefully gain someone's eye. Her master had to want to reclaim her at some point, and so if she were closer to the main palace she could more easily be recovered.

She had endured her fill of being a fish. She wanted to be out of the water and back on territory she was familiar with. Besides, the thought of Hachiman's gratitude for exposing the Water Wani made her shiver with lewd anticipation.

Once she was sure that she had stayed away long enough, Candy refilled her gills and started to swim carefully towards the strongest aura of light in the distance. She skulked amidst the coral and crept onwards, always carefully scanning the waters above her for sign that she had been spotted. The tube and inflator were a dead giveaway, and she had to be cautious lest this means to torment her be noticed and then employed.

The water around her seemed to shiver and a sudden roar filled her ears. Candy screamed against her gills and thrashed her tail but it was already too late. A section of the ocean floor had suddenly snapped open and the water above it was plummeting in. At first she feared an underwater earthquake, but at the last moment she saw that the opening was perfectly circular.

Candy plunged down towards the dark abyss and vanished into the hole. As though falling down a well, she looked up and watched the realm above shrink until she was drawn around a bend in the subterranean chute.

The waters rushed around her, carrying her to some unknown location. Lost in the inky void, she relaxed and refused to fight the impossibly powerful current. There was a flash of light that pained her eyes and made her screw them shut and then a moment of free fall before she struck water again.

Squinting, Candy looked around and found herself in a cylindrical aquarium. About four yards across and eight high, she could swirl around within the container and access the air pocket at the top but that was all. The chute that had deposited her closed and Candy moved to the glass to see where she was.

The room was a jagged underground cave with uneven walls and a rough floor. A solid pressure door was the only way in or out, and a couple of dim lights created a sinister ambience. She could see some metal frames in the shadows and perhaps some storage containers but little else.

A look around at her watertight cell found another hatch near the base which fed onto a brief slide and what appeared to be some sort of table with raised edges. It looked a lot like a sorting tray on a crab boat and she wondered if this were either her route back to dry land or the means to be sentenced to a different aquatic destiny.

Hoping that this deliverance meant that she was being returned to her owner, Candy was momentarily thrown when Toyo-tama-hiko appeared. The resemblance to her master and the dim lighting tricked her and made her think that it was he. So much so that she lurched forward and pressed herself adoringly to the side of the tank.

When she saw the scale armour of the Warlord she drifted back and merely lurked disappointedly at the bottom of her tank.

Three priests from the palace stepped out from behind his flowing cloak and readied themselves around the tray. The door was opened and the water poured out, carrying Candy with it. She slid down the chute and slapped onto the table. Their hands were upon her in an instant and pinned her down. She wriggled beneath their holds but could not escape.

Candy looked up and met the libidinous glare of the Warlord. This vision was stolen when the inflator tube was grabbed and given a brief pull. Candy squawked against her gills as she felt the massive intruder shift. Now that she was out of the depths, the weight of this bloated trespasser was far more distinct and was proving a significant internal burden.

Toyo-tama-hiko approached and accepted the inflator bulb. Candy looked up at him with a desperate beseeching expression.

"Well, I wonder where this came from? Still, it is of no consequence. Let's get you emptied out, slave."

He turned the valve and water started to drool from the bulb.

"Come on, slave. We're not taking you out until you empty this," he warned.

Candy moaned softly and clenched. The flow increased and so she tightened her legs together and squeezed more fiercely. She wriggled and pushed her belly to the table as she continued to roll her tracts and press her muscles to the dildo. Bearing down on it gained the best results and time and time again she applied her strength to deflate the accursed toy. It was a strange sense of relief to crush what had for so long pained her and when the flow ebbed to a trickle, a final squeeze caused the deflated sac to slither from her body and finally pop free. Candy dropped as an enervated heap. Spots flashed on her vision from her relentless straining, but the sensation of being able to close her bottom was a most welcome one, and it had been hard fought for.

"Good, slave," commented the Warlord and patted her sodden hair before he turned to the priests. "Extract her."

Candy just lay and rested as they started to open her various layers and pull them off. Her gills were removed, then her tail, and then the catsuit followed it. Her naked skin immediately became cold as the heat of her efforts was stolen on her sweat, and when the spines on her breast came away she gave a tight whimper.

Her panic rose a little as they grabbed her head, and before she knew it, they had stolen away her contact lenses. Candy blinked to remoisten her eyes and then arched and mewled when her arms managed to stretch out and reach her sides. They had been kept restrained for so long that they now coursed with ardent pangs from being moved.

"Oh my arms! The pain!" she whimpered.

"Ssssh, it will be over soon. You are evolving, Candy. Of course it will hurt," said the Warlord and caressed her with a soothing hand that made her flounder on the wet table amidst the limp wet layers of her former uniform.

"Thank you, Warlord," she muttered, grateful beyond measure to be free of mermaid uniform and water swollen anal trespasser.

"It seems that you acquired a lot of attention, slave," he

said and pinched an intersection of weals to make Candy jerk and give a long mew.

"I . . . I was captured a couple of times. Trapped and punished," she replied meekly.

"Well we should let you recuperate for a time before bringing her to the main event," he said and turned to a priest. "Fetch a harness."

One of the men wandered into the shadows and the sound of metal scraping against rock caught Candy's ears. The other priests lifted her up into a seated position and a metal collar was hastily established about her throat. The collar was abnormally dense, almost an inch and a half thick, but the sounds of it against the stone were light, implying that it was hollow. The interior had dense leather-coated padding and the lofty height of the collar set her chin up and greatly restricted the movement of her head. Even against the plush padding she could feel something a little more solid pressing gently into the front of her throat.

Two metal struts were welded to the front of the band and reached outward in a wide *V* shape. Set in the middle and at the end of each strut was another dense and padded restraint. Her wrists were presented to the cuffs and the two metal clasps locked tightly to the joints. Her legs were then drawn apart and entered into the fetters at the end.

Priests grabbed the struts and used them to lift her up. The collars and cuffs kept Candy in a sitting pose with her legs spread wide and they merely delivered her back to the side of the room and attached the ringlet at the back of her neck to a hook that was hanging from the roof. The men stepped back and Candy was left hanging in the air, naked and utterly defenceless.

"You will be stored here for a time to let you recover, slave," announced Toyo-tama-hiko.

The Warlord stepped out in front of her and regarded the

naked physique as it remained open to him. He could have easily taken her should the desire come upon him, but he merely smiled and extended his hand. A small control device was placed in it and he looked over the settings before turning a small dial.

"I assume Warlord Hachiman has disciplined you in his own inimitable ways, so I think a higher setting will be needed to make sure you stay silent, slave."

A button was pressed and a small red light appeared on the control before he handed it back to the priest who had given it to him.

"Say something, slave," he ordered.

Candy began to mouth a word and then the collar exploded with terrible power. The device within the collar felt the resonance of her larynx and forced a brutal corrective jolt into her neck. Candy lurched against her harness and gave a shocked squeal that only made the escalated the intensity of the blast. She snatched another breath to spend on further hollers but in that instant the collar stopped. Candy snapped her jaw shut and curtailed her noises.

"Excellent," said the Warlord with a chuckle.

He glanced across her one more time, and with his priests in tow, strolled from the room. Candy hung in the gloom, her body powerfully controlled, her taciturn state enforced by technological bondage, and her mind full of speculation as to what would happen to her next.

# CHAPTER TWENTY

Lady Uzume stared at herself in the mirror and continued to apply shades to her eyes and paint to her lips. She considered events and realised they were starting to spiral out of control. The plan should have been a simple one, but her wishes were now clouding that which had once been so clear.

She was committing herself to a battle that was assured to end in defeat. Escaping death or capture in such a circumstance would be difficult and yet against all reason and even her master's wishes, she was still going to pledge her personal involvement.

At first, she thought about the consequences of her demise. The first would obviously be total war with the Provinces. Having killed Kami, the Wani would go into a killing frenzy and rip across the country until they reached the sea. The Mitama would follow in their wake and eradicate all that remained. The assault on Earth could then be conducted without any fear from neighbours on Pangaea.

In the wake of her death, another person would be chosen to enter the role of Uzume. It had happened before. Not all the Kami were the original being who had taken on the role. Despite their immortality, accidents still happened. When death did occur, a kami-tsu-ko was usually the recipient because of their sheer anonymity and their lack of connection to any other Kami. Priests had favourites, fantasies, and passions. These could not be allowed to taint the purity and identity of a Kami.

Taken from their lot as a slave, they were given the

unparalleled chance to become a master of what had previously dominated and controlled every aspect of their life. The closest priests to the slain Kami would form a tight-knit elite cadre to re-educate and teach the replacement all they needed to know. They often made sure the new Kami remained in seclusion until the recall of the previous incarnation had faded, and the ability to play the part for the current one was of an acceptable standard. Sometimes, an entire human lifespan was allowed to pass to make sure that not one mortal remained who had met the previous incarnation. Their teachers would then entrust handpicked replacements and end their lives, erasing the last receptacles with knowledge of the reincarnated Kami.

The new Lady Uzume would not be treated any different and would be allocated all the material possessions, authority, and achievements of that role. Toyotama-hiko would still see her as the valiant leader who stood by his Wani and he would still recruit her. It would be easier for the new Uzume to take on this new role and would probably be prepared for it during the time of indoctrination. The new Uzume would not suffer detachment from Hachiman and would barely know him except as a superior officer.

Uzume caught a tear as it started to well and threatened to ruin her makeup. She soaked it up and realised that this was the true reason she wanted to face death. She was Kami. Divine. Her iron will was made of material that could not bend or be denied. Yet inside, there were secret desires that were so powerful that they would erode that willpower from within over the course of the endless years. She had to be certain that she could handle what was too come.

If she survived the battle, it would be confirmed that she had the inner strength to endure separation from her master. But in the heat of slaughter, if her heart simply knew that it could not take that duration, then her sword arm would instinctively ail, her judgement would falter, and she would be killed.

In the event of her survival, at least she would have her new slave to console her during her detachment from Hachiman. Xiao was a wonderful distraction from her inner turmoil and was proving invaluable in focusing her on her lust, or on her duty.

Uzume tidied the slight smear caused by the budding tear, shook off her saturnine mood, and marched downstairs. Xiao looked at her with a dreary expression and trembled as she spoke.

"Please, Goddess. I'm so hungry. I haven't eaten since you abducted me," she mewled.

"Abducted? But you were just lying there in the open — unclaimed. There's a word for that, isn't there, slave?"

"Yes, Goddess," mumbled Xiao.

"Well, what is it? What were you?"

"Salvage, Goddess."

"True. So, I found you, ergo, you are mine."

The girl was already well appraised in the consequences of contradicting her owner and spoke with meek reverence.

"Y . . . yes, Goddess. I am yours. But please, I need food."

"Well, if you're a good girl, we'll see what we can do," said Uzume and started to pull down her thong. "In the meantime, you can eat my pussy."

Uzume stepped over and arched her back to present her loins to the girl. She threw her head aside and clenched her eyes shut in denial.

"No, I won't! Never!"

"Come on. Just a little taste. You never know, you might like it," chuckled Uzume.

"No! Stop! You're insane. You're sick and demented!"

"So I guess I'll have to *make* you like it. But for now, let's compromise shall we?" she crooned and strolled to a table where she snatched up a banana from a bowl of fresh fruit.

Uzume returned and slowly peeled it before her slave's agog eyes. The girl just stared at her with an alluring mixture of hunger and befuddlement. Once she had finished, she held the fruit out towards the girl. She strained her head forward and tried to take a bite.

"No, not yet," warned Uzume and wafted the enticing food before her prisoner to ensure she piqued her hunger.

Uzume pulled over a table, climbed up, sat down before the girl, and spread her legs wide. With a malevolent smile, she started to steer the soft length into her body. Uzume arched her chest and gave a lewd moan as it slid into her already sodden tracts. She pulled it out a little and then pushed it back in to enjoy the steady succulent glide of the organic toy. With the item deeply immersed, she shuffled forward towards the girl's face.

"Wh . . . what the hell . . . no! No!" she cried.

"Come on. Open wide. You just said how hungry you were."

"This is insane! Stop! I beg you! I . . . I . . ."

Uzume rolled her internal muscles and started to eject the fruit. It touched the girl's lips and she recoiled at the intimate tang of another woman.

"No! Pleeease!" she protested as the soft pulp started to flatten against her lips, spreading the taste of Uzume's pussy upon them.

"At least try it."

The girl tried to shake her head away and avoid her fate.

"Well, perhaps I should serve it from another orifice," muttered Uzume.

The girl released a horrified squawk and her mouth jumped open. Uzume dropped her head back and stared upward as she felt the girl's panicked breaths against her inner thighs and the sound of hesitant bites reached her ears.

"Gooood, slave. Eat it all up now," she ordered.

The girl sobbed and continued to meekly take the banana as Uzume let her sex squeeze it free and into the prisoner's mouth. The girl swallowed quickly and broke into coughs and splutters. More pleas emerged over the fare.

"No talking with your mouth full," said Uzume and jabbed a heel against the girl's thigh. She gave a squeak of pain and returned to eating the meal.

The last of the banana slid free and was swallowed. Uzume stood up and watched the girl hang her head in shame. She was weeping softly, the acute derogation having done wonders to soften her psyche.

"Still hungry?" she asked.

The girl shook her head morosely and obviously tried to forget what she had just done. Uzume walked back to the bowl and took an apple. She marched back and dropped it on the floor in front of the girl.

"There. For you. For being such an obedient little slut."

The girl strained forward as best she could. She was anxious to get rid of the taste that was haunting her mouth but could not reach the fruit.

"What? Can't reach it?" mocked Uzume. The girl fought her restraints and refused to answer.

"Maybe I could help you."

Uzume lifted a foot and gently laid her heel onto the apple. She applied weight and when the skin broke the spire drilled through the item amidst a moist crunch. After spitting the apple, she sat back down and extended her leg to wave the fruit before the gaze of her captive. The girl craned her neck forward, but Uzume continued to just tease her. When lips or tongue touched the polished skin, she ducked it back to leave her captive denied.

Eventually, she decided to be lenient and let the girl have her treat. Uzume stood up and with a jerk of her leg she shed the apple. It struck the floor and rolled away as the girl stared at it with imploring eyes.

"First, an appetiser," said Uzume and twirled before stepping back and leaving her heel rising before the girl's face.

Ravenous, her tongue poured against the lofty spike and lapped at the juice and the few morsels that had been pulled from the core.

"Excellent."

Uzume stomped over to the apple and kicked it back towards the girl. The fruit rolled to a halt right before her but remained out of reach. Uzume gave a dark titter as she watched the girl sway and fight to access the snack.

Wandering over, she placed her pointed toe to the apple and slowly applied weight. The girl smacked her lips as drool slipped from her mouth and then she gave a whimper when the item finally collapsed with a wet crunch.

Uzume stepped off the shattered fruit and sat back down. Curling a leg up, she stabbed a heel into a piece and hoisted it up for the girl. Heedless of the shame of eating in this manner, the girl closed her eyes and clamped her lips to the heel. Uzume drew away and left the fruit in the girl's mouth. She chomped on it and swiftly gulped it down.

Her heel descended again and skewered another morsel that she again fed to her prisoner who released a delightfully sorrowful mew as she was made to suck on her captor's heel in order to acquire her food.

Xiao was developing nicely, and for a moment, Uzume forgot all about her own woes.

# Chapter Twenty-One

Candy spent a long and unknown duration dangling in the corner. She rested her weary body and simply chose to hang in the frame and wait for whatever it was that the Warlord had decreed for her.

The frame was reassuring in that it offered her time to recover, but she had been so inundated with attention of late that it quickly became a serious bane. She flexed against the strong arms of the device but could not get free. She wanted to move, to feel something, to do something, and it was maddening to be held so immobile. Her pussy hungered for attention and the recent recall of the gigantic dildo, the breast spines, and the abuses and pleasures that had been heaped upon her now started to plague her every thought.

The quiet and darkness of the room let her mind wander and her latest trials were memories of the most vivid kind. Every time she let her thoughts drift she was again submerging herself in dreams of being bound and used by merciless lovers and cruel sadists. She recalled the mermaids distending her rear with pain, the denizens of the bathyspheres, and the smothering pressure of her restrictive costume.

Her thighs flicked and her body writhed against the struts. She tried to find some way to get her loins to a strut or to her fingers, but she could not defeat the stern harness. Despite this knowledge, she tried numerous times and continually fought to find a way to exploit the pose and give herself some pleasure. She was sure that there was a way, if only she could find it.

The weighty hatch entry opened and a slender woman sauntered in. She had long auburn hair that hung in dense curls about her shoulders and her green eyes glowed like jade when she looked over Candy's body. A collar and her piercings were the only adornments to her body.

The new arrival set down her tray and her hands immediately began to travel over Candy's body. The touch was welcomed except when it traversed her welts, so she decided to inform the girl of this. Because she had been hanging for some time she had forgotten about the collar so the savage device instantly chastised her first syllable.

"Silly girl. You know you're not supposed to speak while you're convalescing," said the maid. "Or is it that you like the pain?"

The woman grabbed Candy's breasts and squeezed at the base so that the flesh bulged and swelled with hostile feeling.

"Are you sure you don't want another shock from your collar?" she crooned.

Candy bit her tongue and her face started to redden from strain. The woman rolled her knuckles and tightened her grip.

"Come on. Give me a little cry. Let me hear you scream, just for a bit."

Her eyes closed as she snorted for breath and fought to stop even the most meagre answer to the abuse.

"Sure? Not even a little whimper?"

The woman held to Candy and hoisted a knee that she started to rub between her captives splayed legs. The joint was rocked against her, and Candy found it even harder to stay quiet.

"Well, how about if you come against my leg?" asked the woman. "Would you like that?"

Candy was astonished at how effective the maid's attention was with such an outlandish portion of her anatomy. Since her arrival on Pangaea, she had been used in many ways, but no one had ever stimulated her with their knee before.

The boredom of her pose caused her to suddenly surge with a need for input. The feel of the smooth joint rubbing in circles against her pussy and tickling her ring was delicious, as was the woman's misuse of her breasts as handholds to steady herself.

Suddenly the servant stopped and lowered her leg. Her staunch grip remained.

"You don't want to come? Well that's fine. If you won't ask me, then I'll just stop," said the maid with a petulant huff.

Candy opened her mouth and her lips trembled as she contemplated what to do. The feel of the shock box was distinct against her throat and she feared riling it with disobedience, but her pussy was now hot and frantic for use. If she were deserted now, she would find the remainder of her bondage even more unendurable. An orgasm might temper her desires, at least for a short time.

If she could placate her infernal lust, perhaps she might actually be able to get some sleep rather than just hang in the corner, struggling against her bondage in a frenzied despairing quest to find some sort of relief.

"What's that? I can't hear you," said the maid.

She let go of the breast and cupped the hand to her ear.

"You want to come against my leg? Yes? Or No?"

Candy swallowed and braced for what was going to follow. Her assent was inevitable.

"Yes!" she barked and instantly wailed as her neck muscles were thrown to rigidity and the pain of the shock immediately made the rest of her body lurch against the frame. Candy battled to stop her cry and managed to bring it down to an anguished murmur. It still did not stop the collar, so she was punished until her breath ran out. Only this managed to appease the mechanism.

Even though the attack had ended, Candy still had to continue her efforts, save that now she sought to stop herself from gurgling or moaning as she sucked in deep gasps. Her body went slack for a moment, and she trembled in her bonds.

"Good girl. But you have to ask nicely," she muttered.

Candy's eyes flashed open and regarded the nefarious twinkle in her stare. The maid leaned in closer so that her breath wafted upon Candy's cheek.

"Be polite, and ask me nicely, slave. Go on. Right now. Or I'll leave you all alone."

Candy swallowed as she moved back and rolled both hands upon her breasts.

"Please! Pl-"

The rest of the petition was turned into a caterwaul of anguish when the collar retaliated against sound. The maid laughed aloud as she watched Candy grind her jaws, croak, and whimper in distress.

Saliva trailed down her chin. She hissed through bared teeth and fought to endure the reprisal. The discipline ended and she wilted against the strong hold of the contraption.

Candy hoisted her weighty eyelids and regarded the maid with a beseeching desperation, knowing that she could not offer her another word. If the woman asked for one more syllable, Candy swore she would faint from the results.

"Good girl. Very good. I'll let you come then, just as you asked for so sweetly."

Candy surged anew as the maid let go of her breasts and slid her leg back into place. This time she held to the struts and rocked the frame so that Candy's pussy trailed along her thigh.

"Mmmm, already so wet. You must either be quite the slut, or you've been kept waiting for this for some time," commented the woman and kept her rhythm steady and strong. Candy's hands furled into fists and her body trembled with the fight to stay quiet. Even a wanton moan would set off the collar and she needed the pleasure too much to risk activating it again. This was a far harder feat than she was used to. It was tough to stay quiet when she was being punished and had been ordered to remain mute, but to willingly stay silent in the face of such attention was harder than she would have ever thought.

"Come on. Let's see you climax! I want to see this horny little whore *squeal*," muttered the woman.

The maid pressed her thigh upward even harder as she swung Candy back and forth. The additional pressure greatly emphasised her bliss and Candy's face became a mask of ferocious strain while she struggled to stay quiet. As she focused her thoughts on the pleasure, she felt orgasm approaching. The succulent swell of warmth was forming between her legs and getting ready to erupt. Her legs shook and her toes and fingers wiggled and pawed at the air. Her breathing started to deepen and she screwed her eyes tightly closed as her jaws started to spread wider and wider on every drastic gasp.

Candy was actually afraid of climaxing in this pose. She knew that she would not be able to stay quiet, and so her pleasure would again be that terribly mesmerising cocktail of agony and ecstasy. Even though she loathed it and revelled in it with equal abandon, each time it happened she became more and more addicted to it. Candy was worried that normal orgasm would soon leave her empty inside, that a standard simple climax would almost be mundane without the impositions of restraint and the catalyst of anguish.

"Oh you're almost there, slave. Are you ready? Ready to scream and be punished for it?" murmured the maid and her hands reached in to again grasp at Candy's breasts. This time however the hold was much more gentle and her fingers flitted and danced upon her nipples, flicking the rings and making the metal tickle the tunnels that bore them.

Candy's jaw widened and her breath rushed in and out as she started to rise towards climax. It was taking all her effort to stay silent. The woman's rhythm was exact and never faltered, making it impossible for Candy to try and stall her bliss.

"That's it. Come for me, slave! Come now!" snarled the maid and applied pinches as she suddenly stopped moving her bound toy and just jiggled her thigh against it. The sudden change and the shuddering tickle made her leap into orgasm and Candy cried out in rapture before she screamed in pain.

"Yes! Yes! That's it!" gasped the woman as she watched wide eyed and enthralled as Candy juddered and bellowed while the collar blasted her for daring to make noise and her body convulsed with waves of sexual release.

The woman forced Candy through a terrible and contrary ordeal of such intensity that once again, she ran out of fuel for her screams. This stopped the collar, but the residual effects of overlong stimulation were not letting her capture new air. When the thigh came away and Candy managed to snatch air, she was actually too exhausted to spend it on a cry. Instead she just dropped against the inflexible arms of the harness and simply wheezed for additional breath.

Her senses were reeling and sweat and tears dripped from her skin as her thighs gave random spasms and her chest heaved. She flicked to momentary attention as aftershocks of delight flashed through her, tightening her physique and making her sway slightly.

"Well, now that we've fulfilled one need, let's fulfil the others, shall we?" said the woman with a light giggle hiding in her voice.

Candy heard a jar being opened and then felt a cool gel being smoothed onto her weals. The servant eased it on with careful consideration and then attentively worked it into her hide. Several generous scoops were applied and Candy stirred slightly when she felt a spoon nudging her slack lips.

"Open up, slave."

She managed to raise her eyelids and saw the woman offering her a measure of food. The white gruel-like substance was bland and had little flavour, but as she started to accept serving after serving, it definitely quelled her hunger and seemed to energise her more than would have been expected. Every swallow made the shock box distinct against her throat and reminded her not to speak.

"There. All done," commented the maid and dabbed a napkin to the corners of Candy's mouth before placing everything back on the tray and then strolling from the room.

Candy watched her departure with adoring eyes. Another stranger had entered her life, offered her new experiences, and then vanished without even having bequeathed a name or asked as to hers. Identity was meaningless in the Empire, and the lesson that only sensation mattered was once again reinforced.

Candy closed her eyes and wondered what was intended for her next, and what those she loved were doing right now.

# Chapter Twenty-Two

Xiao once again listened helplessly as Lady Uzume strolled down from the upper reaches of the prison, set down some heavy items, and then stepped out before her captive. Xiao gave a shocked gasp when she saw the plexus of leather straps clutching to the woman's hips and from her crotch jutted a large black manhood. For a moment, Xiao assumed that the woman had magically conjured herself a real penis but then she saw that it was a separate toy, worn to imitate, but still just as effective on someone as restrained as she.

"Like it, slave?" she purred and grabbed the phallus at its base. Stepping forward, she started to rub the head of the toy around Xiao's face and laughed as she cringed and whimpered.

With a heartless cackle, she quickly installed a ball gag and then sashayed around the pillory. She leaned down and Xiao heard the rattle of chains before she felt cool steel closing about her wrists. The cuffs clicked and tightened and then a much larger one was installed around the base of her neck. The feel of naked steel was an unusual one. The material was too valuable to waste save on the most important and functional purposes. Squandering it on something as strange as restraint was puzzling to say the least and to Xiao it almost felt like jewellery of the most extravagant kind.

The straps on her left leg were unfastened and her ankle pulled forward until her knee was up by her breast before another cuff snatched hold of it. When her leg went limp, she found that it was connected to another chain, one that reached up and linked her wrists and collar. The other leg was similarly captured and Uzume opened the pillory and hauled her languid form from the padded surfaces.

The tyrant dropped her to the floor and closed the cuffs another few teeth to ensure they were fixed tightly to the areas that had previously been enclosed in leather. She then moved a small switch on the surface that locked them to prevent anymore closure, but only the correct key could coerce them into opening.

A glint of metal caught the light and Uzume revealed that small key in her fingers. After deliberately getting her captive's attention she stood up and slid the item into the front of her thong. With a slight wriggle she inserted the item and gave a shudder as its chill surfaces entered her body.

Xiao lurked on the floor, remaining on all fours as the five cuffs kept her in a curtailed squat. She stretched out against the impositions and when the chains snapped taut and revealed the maximum degrees of her movement, she instead looked around.

At the base of the stairs was a wooden bucket and a large scrubbing brush. Uzume marched to it and grabbed a leather stem from which a bushel of long thick straps emerged.

"Well, what are you waiting for? Get to it!" snarled Uzume.

The woman gathered the ends of the straps in one fist and yanked to make them snap together with a sharp cry.

Xiao started to scuttle over to the items and gave barks of pain when she accidentally knelt on the trailing chains. Keeping her legs wide and her hands close together, she dragged the weighty lengths beneath her and grabbed the brush as soon as she arrived.

The flogger flew in an overhead arc and descended across her back. The brutal signal made her jolt as heat spread through the assailed region. Uzume let the tentacles loiter on her for a moment and then trailed them aside. The leather slithered against her skin and fell away before being carried in another full circle. This time they swept down into the crease of her rear and the tips spanked to her pussy. Xiao gave a shriek and jumped up, only to be stalled by the collar. She dragged her hands up with her and then collapsed back to the ground, pressing her cheek to the wood and holding to the brush for strength as the scathing fires in her loins made her sob and chew on her gag.

"Get to work, slave!" ordered Uzume, and the flogger dropped across a wide expanse of her back to push her down towards the ground. The straps remained on her as a warning and Xiao humbly reached up, dropped the brush in the water, and started to scrub diligently at the timbers.

"Come on, slut. Faster! I want this done before sundown!" growled Uzume but left the flogger in place. Xiao scrubbed as quickly as she could, throwing her upper body into each shove as she felt the leather shifting on her back.

An arbitrary jerk carried the flogger aside and Xiao cringed in anticipation of another stroke.

"No delays!"

Uzume stepped behind her and after using the side of her boot to offer a light kick into Xiao's bottom, she laid the weapon to the base of her back. Xiao's hindquarters sank towards the ground, and she recommenced her work with new gusto.

"Yes, much better. But get that arse up! Show me your pussy!"

Xiao shuddered at the coarse attitude and the derision with which she was being regarded. Nevertheless, the flogger and the woman's brutal tones were not to be denied and so even though it savaged her with derogation to do so, she brought her legs inward and elevated her rear.

She felt a boot step onto her buttock and then jab the heel into her.

"Leg's apart! Nice and wide!"

Scrubbing and weeping, Xiao drew her knees apart and arched her front down towards the ground to comply. It made scrubbing even harder, but she persevered as best she could.

"Yes, much better. Maybe I should fuck this tight little hole," murmured Uzume.

The rounded toe of her boot reached up and nuzzled between Xiao's rear. She wriggled the end against her sphincter, digging into it and churning it around.

"Would you like that? Hmmm?"

Xiao's eyes widened with humiliation as she was abused. She could not believe that another being could be so disgustingly depraved. The Kami were like nothing she could have expected. They gained intense satisfaction from the most bizarre and unseemly behaviour and acts, as though all composure and conscious had been stripped from them. Truly they were devils incarnate and if she did not accept their obloquy, they would brutalise her instead.

"Would it be fun for you, slave? To feel me rape your arse. Maybe I should have you beg for it first."

Xiao tried to ignore the animus coming from the woman and focus instead on her task. It became harder when her captor shifted her foot up and started to prod at her rear with her heel. When she acquired no response, she put the sole back into place and gave a vituperative shove that threw Xiao forward and dropped her onto her front. She landed into the puddle of water and onto her chains. The uneven links afflicted her front and she rolled and struggled to get back up off them. Pressing hands and knees into the coils was a further trial and then Uzume started to apply the flogger again. The leather dropped down onto her back and rear, spanking her with venom until she was again scrubbing the floor.

Uzume paced around the demeaned form of Xiao and continued to offer insult and crass comments that she dispersed with a bilious application of the flogger.

Xiao was made to scrub every inch of the floor, often being called upon to repeat an area that was deemed unsuitable. These areas were the hardest to finish because Uzume beat her with alacrity while she rectified her mistake.

Eventually though, the room was finished and Xiao sagged from fatigue. Uzume hung her flogger on a hook on the wall and took down a bamboo cane with a curved handle and a wickedly lithe length.

"You're not done yet, slave. There's more!"

Xiao gave a resigned sigh as she anticipated being ushered to another storey and made to repeat her entire ordeal over again. Instead the elegant leather-clad leg of her oppressor stamped down between her chained wrists.

Xiao let go of the brush with one hand and drew backwards. Uzume swung her foot back and kicked the utensil from her grasp. Xiao gave a brief squeak and clutched the battered fingers to her breast as she looked up Uzume. The tyrant leaned down and grabbed the back of her plait before yanking up. The harsh pull made Xiao drop her face back down whereupon the rear of the gag was set free. The buckle was drawn up, twisting her head around and dragging the bloated orb from her lips.

Uzume placed the handle of the cane under her armpit and then held it there so the same hand could grab the tip and then hoist the weapon high into the air. She hooked the handle into a ringlet in the ceiling above them and with the freed hand she grabbed Xiao. She sank fingers and thumb into her cheeks to purse her lips together. She snarled and applied more pressure, digging in and making her jiggle in her kneeling pose.

"Mmmm. This makes your mouth look like your bottom. Maybe I should fuck this hole first."

Uzume tossed the ball gag aside and started to trace her forefinger around the puckered orifice.

"Maybe that would be preferable for you though. You seem virginal, but maybe the men of your village have already made use of this opening," she mused cruelly.

The finger started to push into her mouth and then ride back and forth. The woman pushed in and squeezed her other hand to ensure Xiao's lips were kept pressed to the intruder. The thought of having a male use her in such a way had never occurred to Xiao. Her life had been kept away from such things and to be taken in such a manner was outlandish and absurd, yet through Uzume's actions she could now see how it could be done and it horrified her.

The woman giggled as she saw the confusion written in Xiao's eyes. The finger slipped out and tapped her nose.

"Tongue. Out. Now."

Xiao pushed and managed to strain the organ through the tight hole.

"Now use your tongue, slave."

Uzume used the hold to her slave's face and threw her back down at her feet before straightening up and folding her arms across her chest. Xiao started to rise but Uzume merely lifted her other leg and placed her boot between her shoulder blades. The heel gathered fresh weight and demanded that she lower while guiding her towards the other boot.

"Lick it," ordered Uzume and took the cane back down from its lofty anchor.

Fearful of the consequences of disobedience, Xiao swallowed her pride and started to lap at the red leather. She spread saliva on the hide and traced around the toe and instep before hoisting the tip up and down the dagger heel. When she reached the woman's ankles, Uzume took the subjugating boot from her back and stood with legs apart to let Xiao curl round and round, rising higher with every lap.

"Veeeery good, slave. It's so pleasing to watch that impudent rear swinging in the air as you work and worship my legs."

There was a hum of displaced air, and the tip of the cane sank into Xiao's left buttock. She jerked into a ball and quaked. The assailed area seemed to bloat with a thumping havoc that refused to fade.

"No slacking!" snapped Uzume and applied another swipe to Xiao's other cheek. The second detonation of lucid pain made her throw her head down and embrace the toe of the boot in her mouth. She sucked on it for comfort and security as she flashed her tongue to the hide and quaked from the awful effects of the cane. As the scorching pulse started to ebb, she let her jaws widen so she could start to lick easier.

When she reached Uzume's heel, another stinging swipe landed on the side of her thigh. The stroke made her rear tumble aside and slap to the floor. She clutched her arms to her chest and her shins tangled upon themselves as she jolted and fought to endure the withering amerce. Sprawled on her side, it was easier to swing her head left and right and lick the heel, but another stroke to her hip again corrupted her efforts.

Uzume turned around and stamped her heels down to gain Xiao's attention.

"From ankle to hem in single laps, slave. Do it! Do it, now!"

Xiao rolled onto her front and gasped for breath before she set free her tongue and laid it the warm leather. Shivering, she trailed the organ all the way up the long, elegant legs and stopped just before she trespassed onto skin. The leather rippled with sultry motions as the woman clearly savoured both Xiao's plight and the feel of a subservient tongue upon her footwear.

When she had attended the rear of the boot, Uzume turned around and had her attend the front. After she had made her eighth voyage from floor to upper thigh, Uzume grabbed her by the plait.

"Suck."

The dildo prodded her lips and caused Xiao to give a re-pelled spasm.

"I said suck it, slave!"

"I ca-" she began, and the woman exploited the protesta-tion to throw her hips forward and sink the toy into Xiao's mouth. Her eyes bulged as it breached the back of her throat and made her retch. Uzume let go at the same moment and this caused Xiao to catapult herself away and collapse onto her flank where she continued to cough and gurgle.

A moment later, her reactions became far more drastic as the cane started to rain down upon her. The bilious rod hissed through the air and laid itself to her thighs and rear, and when she flipped over to defend the regions, it filled the fronts of them with equal servings of harrowing.

The intensity of the caning was more than Xiao could stand and she became a mindless creature of response. There was no ability to fight or try and escape, all she could do was throw herself around on the floor. She was even ignorant of the times when she travelled across her chains and pained her body.

Screaming for mercy and wailing in despair, Xiao con-vulsed and wrenched at her restraints while trying in vain to defend her abused body.

The withering blizzard of swipes stopped, and Xiao was left in a tight bundle, sobbing and quaking as every searing line continued to pound with a steady and remorseless pulse of its own. Slick with sweat and with tears streaking her face, she wept freely and became dizzy from the strange intoxicat-ing surge that ran through her mind. The pain had been more than she dared believe possible and the stark contrast to an unpunished state was enough of a decline to bring a creepy form of rapture.

Uzume used the toe of her boot to kick Xiao's thighs apart and then she leant her toe to her prisoner's groin. The sole of the boot started to stroke with small and precise movements. Still phased by the caning, Xiao only registered a sultry pleasure and not the manner in which it was being delivered. She gave a groan and trembled as the toe continued to tease her loins and the sound of moisture cackling against the leather suddenly snapped her from her torpor.

"Oh God! No! Stop! No!" she cried and threw her thighs together against the boot while trying to scuttle away.

"Goddess!" corrected Uzume and made Xiao shriek as she laid her most brutal stroke yet. Employing all of her considerable strength, the weapon dropped with meteoric intent and caused her breast to ripple from the impact. The single stroke dropped her back to the floor and her chest arched into the air as her jaws stretched wide and a long and soul-torn howl raged in her throat.

Xiao clamped her hands to the site of woe and dropped back to the floor. She entered a sobbing fit of despair and her oppressor's foot exploited her quiescent state and again started to tease her. Appraised of the penalty for resisting, Xiao laid where she was and just accepted this dissolute attack. As demeaning as it was, the pleasure of being played with was at least mitigating the throbbing angst lurking in the countless rosy stripes that were crossing her body. Some were already darkening into crimson streaks, and these were the ones that were throbbing the most distinctly.

"Yeeesss, you like that, don't you. You can offer this virginal façade, but I know there's a wanton little whore in there somewhere, and I intend to find her!" said Uzume with a sibilant and libidinous purr.

Xiao bit her tongue and declined to retort. The foot started to find its work easier as it conjured fresh moisture from its subject and Xiao started to lose herself to the play. She hated everything this woman did to her, but the skill with which she was being manipulated could not be resisted. All she knew here was pain, so what could be the harm in embracing this vague moment of pleasure?

The toe started to work harder and Xiao's breathing deepened as her belly rolled and her knees swayed in the air. Her hips began to roll her loins and she pushed up to grind herself against the toe with every increasing enthusiasm.

"Yes, there we are. Look at you on the floor. Fucking my toe like a horny little slut. That's it, slave. I want to see you come against the boot of your Goddess!"

The words were an insult that snapped her from her trance and Xiao thrust her hindquarters back to the ground to try and escape. If she allowed herself to give in and climax, she would have given in to the desires of this vile devil. Was Uzume trying to seduce her, defile her, make her willingly subject herself to these twisted pleasures and heinous pains? Sorcery was clearly afoot, and Xiao had to fight it lest she lose her soul.

"If that's what you want, then so be it."

The cane shot forth on an underarm swing that caused its hissing tip to land in the very area that had been so full of rhapsody just seconds ago. The effect was catastrophic. Xiao's world vanished amidst a sheet of effulgent misery, and she shot out from under the cane. Rolling across the floor like a leaf in the wind, she eventually crashed into the wall. Xiao dropped down and shrivelled into a ball, her breath jumping in and out as she screamed and howled for deliverance from the unbelievable level of pain.

Finally she heard the sound of Uzume walking over to her and through blurred and tear filled eyes she saw the tip of the cane. Xiao whimpered and quavered under its shadow. She was utterly defeated by its impossible potency.

"You want another caning, slave?" asked the woman.

Xiao's tardy response resulted in the bamboo tip prodding at a particularly vivid intersection of welts. The assaulted flesh responded poorly to the bullying and the fresh influx of pain forced words from Xiao's listless mouth.

"No, Goddess. Please, I'll do whatever you want. Just no more of the cane. I . . . I can't survive it."

"Nonsense. You can take much more, and you will. But for now, I want to see this cringing bitch suck this cock and masturbate as she does it."

The defamation of such a deed struck her like a slap, but it was nothing compared to the kisses of the cane. With a resigned push, Xiao managed to pull herself back up onto her knees whereupon her eyes greeted the jutting erect replica.

"Weeeeell," hummed Uzume.

Xiao opened her mouth and slotted it onto the toy. Closing her lips, she mimicked the motions that Uzume had shown with her finger.

Uzume stood to attention and watched her efforts with stark amusement.

"That's it. Take it nice and deep," she murmured.

Xiao pushed further and recoiled as it made her gag. Uzume just laughed.

"And don't forget to play with yourself, slut," she hissed and grabbed the back of Xiao's head before offering a small pelvic thrust to repeat the trauma. Xiao gurgled and retched before dropping her manacled hands into position. Masturbation was a rare indulgence for Xiao. Due to the dangers of slavers, raiders, rapists, and kidnappers she was always being watched, even at night. The opportunity rarely came and when it did, it was usually in the halcyon splendour of her secret lake. Now she was being forced to do something she dearly loved, but could hardly ever embrace because of publicity. This made performing for another person a potent taboo and Xiao found trouble in complying. Even the fake fellatio was easier on her.

Xiao tightened her oral hold and started to stroke her

humid loins.

"No teeth!" snarled Uzume and offered some light slaps to Xiao's cheeks by way of correction.

Xiao hastened her autoerotic activity to compensate for the minor fury that was now saturating her cheeks. She hollowed her cheeks with suction and tried to keep her jaws apart to a degree where the toy would not scrape against her teeth as she hauled on it with her mouth.

Attending the toy started to become easier as she continued to dance her digits to her sex, stroking her lips and pawing at her clit with faster and more drastic movements. Soon, the pleasure was weaving its magic on her and her hips began to sway as she started to suck with greater devotion and murmur with delight.

Suddenly, Uzume revealed that she was now aroused beyond tolerance. After placing a hand to Xiao's cheek she simply shoved her to one side. The dildo stretched her mouth as she slithered from it and then dropped to the floor, collapsing down onto her moistened hands before her body struck the ground.

Before she could react, Uzume jumped behind her, grabbed her plait, and hauled up. She slapped the other hand under her chin to apply another grapple and then thrust. The dildo rushed into Xiao and opened her for the first time.

Uzume's holds were tested to their limit as Xiao jerked with a monstrous pulse of reaction. The pain of penetration immediately swirled around the rapture of having the saliva sodden length glide into her already wet tracts. Xiao screamed even more potently than when she was being caned and this wail rose in octaves when Uzume drew back and then thrust into her again.

Xiao tried to leap away and escape the penetration but Uzume held tight and continued to jolt back and plough the toy into her captive. Xiao's hands jumped back to try and fend the woman off but the chain brought her efforts to an abrupt halt.

Screeching for mercy against this excruciating bliss, Xiao was ravished with cold-blooded fury until she swore that she would be torn apart by another thrust. The pleasure of being ravished was unlike anything she had experienced, it had a deep, potent quality that she found terrifying and exhilarating.

Uzume again flung her aside and off the toy before she got up, leaving her captive to quake on the ground and recover from the pleasure in the same way she permitted her moments to recuperate from the pain of chastisement.

"I'm going to give you a choice, slave. I can jump on you and fuck you until you come. Or you can go free. I can give you sexual release, or physical release. Your choice."

Xiao spun her head around and regarded the woman.

"Y . . . you're serious. I can leave?" she burbled, not able to believe that an offer of freedom was being made. Was it true or just some cruel trick designed to further batter her psyche?

"If you want to. Do you?"

The savagery of the molestation was still haunting her pussy and Xiao knew that if she felt that succulent device in her a moment longer, she would not be able to defy and would beg for the chance to orgasm. Penetration had shown her a form of pleasure that she had never felt before, and she was intrigued to see how much further it would take her. She had to get out. Now.

"I want to leave. I want my freedom."

"As you wish. First you'll need the key to those cuffs," she said and began to unbuckle the harness. The toy came away and she flung it aside before standing with legs astride and hands on hips.

"Well, come and get it then."

"B . . . but it's . . . I . . . I mean . . ."

"Your feeble gibberish won't get it out, slave. Only your tongue will."

"Oh please, don't make me do that. Just let me take it out with my hands. Isn't that bad enough.?"

"If I'm to let you go free, I believe I can lay down the parameters. So, if you want the key to uncuff yourself, you'll have to take it by force, from my pussy. Understand?"

"Y . . . yes, Goddess."

Xiao crawled forward on hands and knees with chains dragging and rattling beneath her. She stopped at the woman's feet and rose up. With a final resigned glance upward she looked at the red leather thong and swallowed.

"Take down my underwear first."

Xiao took the sides and drew down to pull them out from under the corset and then she dragged them down to Uzume's ankles. The smooth-shaven sex of the woman appeared, and Xiao filled her mind with the recall of what she had endured here, and the possibility of escaping it if she could just perform this one final act of derogation.

With a sudden mental bluster of commitment she leaned in, closed her eyes, and stretched her tongue into the wet sex of her tormentor. Uzume stiffened and groaned aloud as she felt the entry and instantly clenched her tracts.

Xiao squeezed her hands into fists and pushed her tongue against the internal muscles of the woman. The organ burned from strain as she tried to get deep enough to find the key, but Uzume was not making it easy. Xiao started to push with steady motions, trying to wear down the internal defences but this just seemed to excite the woman and bolster her resistance. Xiao pushed her lips to those of the woman and swirled her tongue around to try and locate the elusive key. Uzume shuddered against her.

"Oh yes, slave. Almost there. All . . . most . . . I . . ." panted Uzume and in an uncharacteristic act she placed her hands about the back of Xiao's head and neck and pulled her in. Even so, she still held her pussy tight, so Xiao had to fight harder to slither around and find her means of redemption. Uzume's words gave Xiao heart for they meant that she was close to getting the key. When she increased her efforts, Uzume jerked and cried out. With a long howl she convulsed and held forcefully to Xiao.

A metal taste spread on Xiao's tongue as the key slithered free and dropped onto her tongue. Uzume staggered back, seemingly exhausted by her fight and now drained in defeat.

Xiao seized the chance and started to uncuff herself. The wet key slipped against the metal as her hands trembled and the taste of the woman continued to hang on her tongue. The cuffs sprang open and fell from her extremities before she fumbled for the one on her neck. When she found the hole and opened the collar, she scampered onto her feet.

"I can go now?"

"Pardon?" said Uzume with a sultry purr while she leaned against the wall.

"You said I could go free!"

"So I did. Come this way."

Uzume pulled up her thong, strolled past her, and walked onto the stairs. Xiao could not believe her luck. By resisting Uzume had she proved herself immune to seduction? Could the Kami only keep an innocent for a certain duration and if they failed to corrupt them, then they had to set them free?

Xiao followed the woman down to another chamber that was clearly some sort of lounge or reception hall. The floor had several deep fur rugs and on the other side of the room was a dense double door. Uzume walked over to it and turned round. A wicked glower was now on her lips.

"All you have to do is get by me," she growled.

"Bu . . . but you . . . you said I . . ."

"I said that if you got the key, you could go free. You have freed yourself. You are free. You wanted to leave. We left the chamber in which I was holding you. I mentioned nothing of total freedom, but am willing to let you try and grab it."

"Monster!" screamed Xiao, her tolerance finally gone.

She ran at the woman with hands outstretched and fingers twisted into claws to gouge at her. If she could quickly disable the woman, she could open the door and run away.

Uzume side stepped, and a knee jumped up and sank into Xiao's stomach, doubling her over with a startled croak. With her breath stolen and a ghastly throb in her belly, Xiao was momentarily crippled.

Uzume chuckled and grabbed her sides to spin her about and then place her foot to Xiao's bottom. A disdainful shove sent her careening across the room to drop at the bottom of the steps.

"If that's the best you've got, you may as well put the cuffs back on and march yourself back upstairs, slut. Then I'll fuck you so hard, you'll faint."

Xiao coughed and straightened up. With another ferocious charge she ran at her enemy and desperately tried to grab her. Uzume moved almost faster than Xiao could keep track of and suddenly a pair of slim hands clamped about her outstretched wrists. The strength in them and in Uzume's stance stopped Xiao dead in her tracks and as her arms folded on the last of her momentum, a swift knee between her legs lifted her feet from the floor. When she landed and her legs folded under her, Uzume threw aside and sent Xiao into a clumsy sprawl.

Mewling and holding her aching pussy, she gave a shriek and struggled as hands grabbed her left ankle and turned it. The rending sorrow in the joint caused her to roll over onto her front. The instep of a thigh boot nudged into the back of her neck and pushed her face into the floor. A moment later she wailed as her ankle was turned further, twisting her leg and making her squirm and flounder. She tried to reach back and move the pinning foot but she had no leverage and nowhere near the strength.

"Say you want to be my slave!" ordered Uzume.

"Never! I hate you!" she shrieked.

"Hate me all you want, but you'll still be my slave, and I want you to ask for it!" hissed Uzume. She hoisted the ankle higher and turned it to make Xiao shriek even louder.

"Noooooo!" she roared defiantly.

Uzume let go and backed up towards the door. She stood poised on her heels as Xiao awkwardly got back to her feet and limped to the wall to catch her breath.

"The only way out of here is either back upstairs to be my slave, or through me to freedom. Come on, you weak little tramp. Let's see if you have any backbone, or have you been pampered all your life and don't have any fight in you."

Xiao gave a cry of indignation and rushed back at the woman with all the venom she could muster. Uzume ducked and let the attacking arms sail overhead. She sprang up, grabbed shoulders, deviated Xiao's impetus, and delivered her into the door she so desperately sought.

A flash of white signalled the connection and Xiao bounced from the timbers with a jarring thud. Just as her senses cleared, she saw red stretch before her eyes, and the back of Uzume's leg suddenly hooked around the front of her throat and jerked back and down. Xiao was folded backward until the woman's other thigh met the small of her back. Xiao screamed from the pose as she was contorted over Uzume's thigh, the back of her head now on the ground. Arched into an incredible bow over the woman's leg, her arms rushed out to claw at her, only to be grabbed at the wrist and then turned to lock them into position and make every joint thunder with distress.

"Say you want to be my slave!" she ordered. The tyrant

turned her holds before pushing and arching Xiao even further.

"No! No! No!" she bellowed and threw her legs up to try and cast her knees into Uzume's head. The woman stretched back, and the incoming limbs flashed past and sailed over Xiao's body, causing her to perform a backwards roll that devolved into a disorganised tumble when her wrists were released.

Uzume returned to the door and stood with arms folded across her breasts.

"Is that it. Are we done?" she asked coolly and then examined her nails to check for any damage caused by Xiao's trivial offensives.

"Let me go!" howled Xiao and again charged, employing all her lingering strength.

Uzume performed a sudden pirouette and Xiao caught a brief glimpse of red and black before a scathing slap dodged her arms and crossed her cheek. The ferocity threw her head aside and the pirouette continued and dropped so that a shin could swing out and take her feet from under her.

Xiao landed on her back, and the wind was thrown from her lungs. Uzume skipped forward, dropped a foot on either side of the prostrate girl, nudged her arms in against her sides and then dropped down onto her. The woman's legs clenched in and squeezed Xiao's arms to her sides, leaving her hands pawing impotently at the boots and heels.

She squirmed, and Uzume let her discover just how helpless she was.

"Ready to be mine, slave?"

"No!" barked Xiao and a slap stung her cheek before striking the other.

"How about now?"

"Get off me, you demon!"

Uzume clapped a hand across Xiao's mouth and the other

pinched her nose shut to stop her breath. Xiao jerked and fought to get away but there was nothing she could do.

"Admit you want to be my slave."

The hand on her mouth lifted a little. Xiao tried to think of something to say, but was lost for words. The woman slapped her cheeks a few more times, and each swipe stole away more of Xiao's ability to defy.

"Well? Do you? Answer me!"

Uzume curled an arm back across her body and held the back of the hand towards Xiao. Readying to slam it down onto her face, the vile creature grinned malignantly.

"Okay, okay . . . I . . . I . . ."

"Yes?" purred Uzume, and the muscles of the limb visibly flexed as she readied to deliver a hearty smack.

"Please, Goddess, let me be your slave," she uttered miserably. There was no point fighting any more. She was vanquished, and she knew it.

"Good. Now pick up your cuffs, go back upstairs, and lock yourself back in them," she said lightly while climbing off of the defeated form.

Xiao rolled over and started to crawl towards her restraints. She picked them up and trudged drearily upstairs, readying to once again surrender to their control and become the property of this sadistic monster.

Lady Uzume heard the drawbridge being operated and with a huff of irritation wandered upstairs after her slave. She padlocked the middle of her chains to a ring in the wall and told her to kiss each of her nipples in gratitude. The slave complied with sombre reverence, and each peck made Uzume quiver with glee at having so effectively subjugated her property. After complimenting her slaves act of obeisance, she hurried back downstairs.

Uzume's heart was still racing from the fight and she tried to calm herself while waiting for the portcullis to rise.

When the knock came, she opened the doors and stepped out onto the drawbridge as two officers of the Mitama laid the body of Masuda down on the ground and then remained on their knees. The warriors armour was cracked in places and every inch of surface was riddled with dozens of impact craters from arrow and bullet. Finally, the integrity of his protective shell had failed under this withering abuse and then eaten through the woven discs of dense material beneath. Dried lines of red emerged from six holes across his chest.

"Tell me what happened," she uttered sombrely.

"Masuda was planning to circumvent the mountains and commence an attack on the Provincial towns along Calolloom Lake. He was sure that the army would retreat to tackle the threat, but they emerged from the mountains and began a march towards our position here. The Wani battalions intercepted them and held firm. Masuda led the cavalry against the flank of the enemy as they emerged, but even so, their numbers were too vast and although we managed to break their lines, they have fled into the peaks and are regrouping. The Wani have dug in to defend our retreat so we might inform you, Lady Uzume, but they are unlikely to hold for long."

"Masuda was a great man and a loyal servant of the Kami. This will not be the last chapter in his career. Ready all forces. I will not leave our Wani to stand alone while we crawl back to the Empire in disgrace. Ready my mount. We go to finish what my second in command started."

"Bu . . . I . . . Lady Uzume, we are outnumbered at least fifty to one. A Kami of your status cannot be-"

"Do not presume to tell a Kami what they can or cannot do," she said sternly.

"My absolute apologies, Lady Uzume. It is just . . . well . . .

they are so many . . . we are so few. We must not let you be put in jeopardy, th-"

"I am Kami in the Great Houses of Fire. I ride with those who worship me, and I will lead us to victory. Then we will return to the Empire and give Masuda a fitting burial, one that is proudly cloaked in victory, not stained with defeat."

"I conquer!" roared the officers.

"*We* conquer," corrected Uzume and both men jerked as though struck. Their deity was riding with them into war. All trace of doubt was now gone.

Uzume turned to go and gather her armour. The supply force would be despatched to begin the return voyage and take Xiao out of harm's way. Lady Uzume would ride with her forces and engage the enemy. Defeat was certain, and she would have to retreat, but by reinforcing the Wani she was sending a powerful message. To the Empire, the Wani were expendable and would accept catastrophic losses on the whim of the Kami, by siding with them, and fighting to save them, she would astound Toyotama-hiko and make him believe that she cared a great deal about these loyal foot soldiers. His seduction would come even more swiftly because of it. If she perished in the fight, her replacement would be propositioned instead, just as she had anticipated and, in some ways, hoped for.

Destiny would now decide the fate of Uzume, her slave, and that of the Empire.

The fates of Kami and slave entwine and are revealed in Dragon Candy 3: Bondage Plaything.

# Glossary for the Kami Empire

*Izanagi* and *Izanami*: The creator deities, the names of the two forces whose interplay create and move the Vortex between Earth and Pangaea.

*The Kami*: the various deities of earth and heaven. The lords and manifestations of thought, deed, and substance.

*Mitama*: The essence or emanation of god or spirit. The name given to the Imperial Army that enforces the will of the Kami and marches under the banner of *A-Katsu* (I conquer).

*Shintai*: The God body, the earth form, or symbol of a deity.

The Primary Powers of the Kami Empire

*Yatakagami*: The Sun Goddess. Supreme Ruler of the land who is always accompanied by her sacred crow — *Yatagarusa*.

*Musubi*: Lord of growth. He is the tactician, the planner, and chief advisor to the Sun Goddess.

*Tsuki-yomi*: The Moon God. The lord of darkness. He is the keeper of time, and his House plots the path of the Vortex on Earth. His House alone is not subject to the rule of the Sun Goddess.

*Amatsu mika hoshi* (Dread star of heaven): He knows all, but cannot leave his shrine. He controls a vast and highly secretive spy network that watches the Empire, the lands about them, and trains the operatives that go across to Earth to send ships and planes into the Vortex. He is the chief advisor to the Moon God.

## The Kami of Water

*Toyo-tama-hiko* (Rich jewel prince): Supreme Warlord of the Water.

*Naka-tsu-wata-dzu-mi* (Middle sea body): His House conducts submerged patrols in the ocean waters. His troops ride aquatic Dinosaurs such as the seventeen-metre long Kronosaurus.

*Uha-tsu-wata-dzu-mi* (Upper sea body): His House provides surface vessels and reptilian steeds to protect and patrol the ocean traffic.

*Soko-tsu-wata-dzu-mi* (Bottom sea body): Warlord of the deep. His House oversees seabed construction and harvesting, along with ocean bed mining for valuable minerals.

*Midzu-chi* (Water-father): Warlord of the Rivers. His House conducts river patrols to maintain security and order either by boat, or on trained fifteen-metre-long Phobosuchus (Horror crocodile).

*Midzuha no me* (Water-female): The concubines of the Great Houses of Water.

*Idzu no Midzuha no me* (Sacred-Water-female): Concubines that have been elevated through exemplary conduct, like Kamube.

## The Kami of Air

*Ame no minaka-nushi*: Supreme Warlord of the air

*Shinatsu-hiko*: Lord of the Wind. His House is responsible for the sending of all radio communication.

*Shinatobe*: Lady of the Wind. Her House is responsible for the receiving of all radio communication.

*Hayachi* (Swift father): The Messenger. His House handles all overland messages and items of import, and sees to their safe delivery.

## The Kami of Fire

*Take-mika-dzuchi* (Brave-dread-father): The master of thunder, Warlord of the artillery regiments.

*Hachiman*: the Warlord who commands the Mitama.

*Ame-waka-hiko* (heaven-young-prince): His Mikado and highest-ranking general.

*Uzume* (Dread female): His most feared and ruthless agent.

*Ashua*: Guardian Warlord of the courtyard, protector of the inner lands. His House is the police force of the Empire.

*Toyotama-hiko*: the Dragon Warlord. He is part Wani and second in command to Warlord Hachiman.

*Wani* (Dragon): Eggs of the Dinosaur tribes were taken centuries ago, and the offspring raised as Wani. From the best of these warriors were bred more until an army was created. They are now fanatically loyal warriors. They are fierce, fearless, and serve as the backbone of the Mitama.

## The Kami of Earth

*Kagu-tsuchi* (Radiant father): The fire god. Lord of power and energy, his House runs the nuclear plants.

*Kamado no Kami*: The furnace deity. Lord of the furnaces of wood, oil, coal, and hydroelectricity.

*Inari*: The Lord of the rice fields. His House sees to the feeding of the general population.

*Susa no wo*: The Lord of rain. His House oversees all plumbing and irrigation.

*Oho-toshi* (Great harvest): The lord of gathering. His House sees to the harvest and the safe storing of all food.

*Uka no mitama*: Lord of the food spirit. His House ensures good crops and plentiful harvests. They provide knowledge, equipment, and expertise to guarantee growth. They breed and raise the best herds for slaughter. They also train humans to fulfil the role of beasts.

*Ho no Susori*: Lord of the fishermen. His House builds boats, provides equipment, and sees to the smooth running of the fishing fleet.

*Hohodemi*: Lord of the hunt. His House hunts Dinosaurs to replenish the stock. They also see to the breeding and training of new steeds and herd animals for domestic use. They also train human ponies.

*Sukuna-bikona*: (Little prince): A House of dwarves that see to the brewing of wines and other drink. They also produce many medicinal remedies and maintain a large medicinal thermal springs. It is in his underground palace that the sacred spring of longevity is located.

*Temmangu*: The Lord of learning and calligraphy. They are the teachers of the young and old, and indoctrinate and educate new slaves.

*Ishikoridome*: The stonecutter Lord. His House is one of architecture and building.

*Toyo-tama*: (Rich jewel): His House are jewellers, and makers of finery.

*Ohonamochi*: Lord of physicians. His House tends the injured, the sick, and the many slaves of the Empire to ensure their health and survival.

*Yama tsu mi* (Mountain-body): Lord of the trees. His House is responsible for tree-cutting, lumber, timber, and the maintaining of forests.

## The ranks of the Kami Priesthood

*Mikado*: Chief Priests of a Kami. They see to the running of the House and its affairs and responsibilities.

*Nakatomi*: Mediators between the priests and the Kami. They regulate and assign the slaves of a House as the Kami or Mikado decree.

*Imbe*: The preparers. They ensure that the lower ranks see to the preparation, cleanliness, and order of slaves, equipment, and chambers.

*Hafuri*: Inferior grade priests that see to the basic tasks of the House and its responsibilities.

*Negi*: The lowest priestly rank that is responsible for the most mundane functions of the House.

*Kamube*: A slave who has earned freedom through exemplary conduct and service and now tends the House as the priest's dictate while still holding authority over other *Kami-tsu-ko*.

*Kami-tsu-ko*: A slave dedicated to a House.

## The Underworld of the Kami Empire

*Yomi*: The land of darkness where slaves and criminals are banished. Once sent to Yomi, one may never return unless via personal pardon from both Sun Goddess and Moon God.

*Bimbo-gami*: The Lord of poverty. The Kami of sexual frustration, teasing, and enforced chastity.

*Naki-sahame*: The Lady of weeping. The feared sadistic dominatrix of Yomi.

*Ashiki kami*: The rulers of Yomi.

*Oni*: The inhabitants of Yomi. Many are former *Hafuri-tsu-mono* and have been elevated from that caste to assist in the running of the realm.

*Hafuri-tsu-mono* (flung away things): Those sent to Yomi.

# About the Author

Born and raised in San Francisco, Talia Skye spent part of her early career living and working in Japan where she discovered her passion for writing, scifi, and BDSM. She currently lives in London, and continues to explore those worlds.

www.ingramcontent.com/pod-product-compliance
Lightning Source LLC
Chambersburg PA
CBHW061550170626
46811CB00001B/155